DRAGON AND JUDGE

A TOM DOHERTY ASSOCIATES BOOK | NEW YORK

DRAGON AND JUDGE

THE FIFTH DRAGONBACK ADVENTURE

TIMOTHY ZAHN

DRAGON AND JUDGE

Copyright © 2007 by Timothy Zahn

Edited by James Frenkel

A Starscape Book
Published by Tom Doherty Associates, LLC
175 Fifth Avenue
New York, NY 10010

www.tor.com

Library of Congress Cataloging-in-Publication Data

Zahn, Timothy.
    Dragon and judge / Timothy Zahn.—1st ed.
        p. cm.
    "A Starscape book."
    Summary: Just when fourteen-year-old Jack Morgan thinks he and his symbiont, the dragon warrior Draycos, are on the brink of finding information about the destruction of Draycos's race, he is kidnapped by aliens who ask him to serve as a judge, as his parents did before him.
    ISBN-13: 978-0-7653-1418-5 (alk. paper)
    ISBN-10: 0-7653-1418-5 (alk. paper)
    [1. Adventure and adventurers—Fiction. 2. Mercenary troops—Fiction. 3. Dragons—Fiction.
4. Soldiers—Fiction. 5. Kidnapping—Fiction. 6. Orphans—Fiction. 7. Science fiction.] I. Title.
    PZ7.Z2515Dj 2007
    [Fic]—dc22

                                                                                2007007448

First Edition: June 2007

For all those who work for justice

DRAGON AND JUDGE

" 'The quick red fox jumps over the—' " Taneem paused, her glowing silver eyes narrowing in concentration, her whiplike K'da tail making little circles in the air behind her long, gray-scaled body. " 'Lassie dog'?" she suggested.

" '*Lazy* dog,' " Draycos corrected, keeping his own tail motionless. Having grown up among the Phookas instead of proper K'da, Taneem's body language was very different from his. He didn't want to make any gestures that she might interpret as impatience. "The 'y' at the end of the word makes the 'a' long."

" 'The *lazy* dog.' " Taneem gave her tail another flick. "There are so many rules to this language," she said ruefully.

"And so many exceptions to those rules," Draycos agreed, his mind going back to his own introduction to written English. He and the others of the K'da/Shontine advance team had learned a fair amount of the spoken language from their peoples' earlier contacts with the Chitac Nomads. But it wasn't until the advance team had been ambushed and destroyed, and Draycos had linked up with Jack Morgan, that he'd been introduced to the written form. "But you'll make it through," he assured Taneem. "I know you will."

"Then I will," she said firmly, turning back to the display. " 'When the tall cliff is lit by the sunlight . . .' "

Draycos listened with half an ear, his eyes tracing down the smooth lines of her neck and across the sleek scales along her flank. She did so much remind him of the other Taneem, the friend he'd lost so many years ago to the Valahgua and their horrible Death weapon.

Which made it even more of a shock sometimes when he remembered that only a couple of weeks ago this Taneem had been little more than an animal. A Phooka, rooting around in the forest of Rho Scorvi for grubs, with no knowledge of starships or computers or written English.

Or of war or hatred or enemies. Enemies who had launched a war of conquest against the K'da and Shontine in their distant homelands, ultimately driving them out and into a fleet of refugee ships that was still making its long journey here to the Orion Arm part of the galaxy.

Enemies who had now made that same long trip across space in order to intercept and destroy those K'da and Shontine refugees. Bringing his gaze back to Taneem's silver eyes, Draycos wondered if he'd really done her a favor by taking her away from that simpler, safer life.

Taneem finished the page, and Draycos keyed for the next one. Nothing happened. Feeling his tail curve in a frown, he tried again. This time the next page came up.

But that second's delay meant that the ship's computer was busy. Very busy.

Had Jack made it in?

"Please continue with your exercises," Draycos told Taneem as he headed for the dayroom door. "I'll be back soon."

He found Jack in the *Essenay*'s cockpit, sitting in the pilot's seat and glowering at the displays. Alison Kayna was standing behind him, leaning an elbow on the back of his seat as she gazed thoughtfully at something on a handheld computer. "Anything?" Draycos asked as he padded up behind Alison.

"No," Jack growled. "For a minute there I thought we were in. But then it locked back up on me."

"I told you it wouldn't work," Alison said. "Malison Ring computers aren't easy to get into without the proper passkeys and protocols."

"I suppose you want to give it a try?" Jack suggested acidly.

"Well, not *now* I don't," Alison said. "The whole system's been alerted."

"What do you suggest?" Draycos asked.

"We pull up stakes and try a different base." Alison cocked her head. "Only next time *I* get to try first."

"Forget it," Jack said. "*My* ship. *My* mission."

"Your ship, *Draycos's* mission," Alison corrected calmly. "It's *his* people at risk out there, not yours."

"Maybe his people happened to be the first ones on the field," Jack countered, "but that doesn't mean the rest of us are sitting on the sidelines. Once the Valahgua finish them off, what's to keep them from turning that Death weapon of theirs on everyone else in the Orion Arm?"

"Numbers, for a start," Alison said, shutting off her computer. "If and when you're ready to give up on that, I've got something to show you."

"Fine," Jack said, keying a handful of switches. "I'm done."

"Thank you," Alison said. "Uncle Virge? Pull up your record of the Iota Klestis battle, will you?"

"Jack, lad?" Uncle Virge asked.

"Sure, go ahead," Jack said in a tone of strained patience.

"While you're at it, go ahead and call the port tower for clearance. We might as well get off this rock."

"Preferably before the Malison Ring traces your intrusion attempt," Alison said.

"Alison—"

"Okay, here we go," Alison interrupted him smoothly as the main display lit up with a set of slightly fuzzy spaceship images. "Four Malison Ring attack ships, four K'da/Shontine advance team defenders. Note how the Malison Ring ships open up with that whatch-ya-call-it—"

"It's called the Death," Draycos said, his tail lashing the air as the memory of that horrible day came rushing back. "The weapon that kills right through bulkheads and walls and even the heaviest metal or ceramic shielding."

"And I still don't understand how that can work," Alison said. "But I'll take your word that it does. Anyway, note how the Malison Ring ships all open up with the Death in perfect unison?"

"Yes, we see," Draycos said.

"And we've been through it a hundred times," Jack added.

"Maybe you should have gone through it a hundred and one times," Alison countered. "Remember your theory that Neverlin and the Valahgua must be really good allies because the Valahgua gave him their precious Death weapon to play with?"

Jack's back visibly stiffened. "*Look*—"

"We're listening," Draycos cut him off, his eyes on the display. Arthur Neverlin was the brains behind this plot. He'd been the second most powerful man in the megacorporation Braxton Universis until he'd tried to kill Cornelius Braxton and take over the company. Jack and Draycos had foiled that attempt, driving Neverlin underground in the process.

But even on the run, the man had plenty of resources to draw on. One of his allies was the Chookoock family of Brum-a-dum, with their collection of slaves and big Brummgan soldiers. Another ally was Colonel Maximus Frost and his team of Malison Ring mercenaries.

All of them with just one goal: to assist the Valahgua in their attempt to utterly destroy the K'da and Shontine.

"Okay," Alison said. "Let me fast-forward a bit . . . *there*. See how all four Death weapons also cut off in perfect unison?"

"Because all the K'da and Shontine were dead," Jack said with exaggerated patience.

"No, they weren't," Alison said. "That's the point. The *Havenseeker*'s little twitch maneuver had slipped it out of the beam for a few seconds, which is why Draycos and the rest of the bridge crew were still alive at this point. So why did the mercenaries quit firing?"

"We were already on the path to a crash landing," Draycos said grimly. "They had no need to continue."

"No, what they didn't have was the capability," Alison corrected.

Jack frowned over his shoulder at Draycos. "Is she making any sense to *you*?"

"Yes," Draycos said, the pain of memory fading into cautious excitement as he suddenly saw where Alison was going with this. "The Malison Ring ships didn't shut off the Death weapons. The weapons shut off by themselves."

"Bingo," Alison said. "Probably with their innards burned to slag. The Valahgua didn't trust their new allies not to double-cross them and fly away with their wonderful little Death weapons. So they put a timed self-destruct into each of them, giving the mercenaries exactly three minutes forty-seven seconds' worth of juice they could use to take out your advance force ships."

"Which is two *birs* of Valahguan time measurement," Draycos said.

"Even a nice round number." Alison looked at Jack. "You see now what I meant about them not being ready to take on the whole Orion Arm? They don't even have enough people here to secure and operate the weapons aboard four ships."

"Which also makes sense," Draycos said. "In order to have arrived before our advance team, they would have had to travel faster, with more fuel and fewer passengers."

"It also means they don't trust their new allies any farther than they can spit them," Alison said.

"Not really surprising, I guess," Jack said. "Not with what we know about Neverlin and Frost. Though that doesn't mean they don't have a few more Death weapons stashed away to use against the main refugee fleet."

"Oh, I'm sure they do," Alison agreed. "But at least this means we'll mostly be tangling with Neverlin and his buddies. At least those are known quantities."

"Known quantities who want to kill us," Jack muttered.

"Well, they want to kill Draycos, anyway," Alison said coolly. "Possibly me, too. *You* they just want to capture."

"That's so encouraging," Jack said, stroking his cheek thoughtfully. "I wonder what their plan is."

"That's easy enough," Alison said. "Neverlin wanted to kill Cornelius Braxton so that he could take over his company."

"For the money," Jack said.

"Sure, that was part of it," Alison said. "More importantly, though, controlling Braxton Universis would give him access to the corporation's security force. Including a *lot* of armed ships."

"Would the Braxton security men really have cooperated in this kind of venture?" Draycos asked.

"I doubt it," Alison said. "But he didn't need them. That was where the Chookoock family came in—they were going to supply Brummgan mercenaries to crew the security ships. Frost and his renegade Malison Ring buddies would provide leadership and also form the core of the attack force."

"And while they engaged the K'da/Shontine ships, the Valahgua would be moving in and out of the fleet using the Death weapon on everyone," Draycos said, a shiver running along his crest.

"At which point they would be free to loot the fleet for new technology, which they'd probably market through Braxton Universis," Alison concluded. "Very simple, actually. And very, *very* profitable."

"That's what their plan *was*," Jack said patiently. "*My* question was, what's their plan *now*?"

"Oh," Alison said in a slightly more subdued tone. "Good point. Neverlin can't get those Braxton ships now, can he? They'll have to go with some other plan."

"Which I believe is what I just said," Jack reminded her. "The question is what that plan might be."

"Jack, lad?" Uncle Virge spoke up. "We've got clearance to lift."

"Take us up," Jack instructed him. "And give me the two next closest Malison Ring bases."

"Montenegro and Vers'tekim," the computer said. The record of the Iota Klestis battle disappeared from the display and was replaced by a star map. "Montenegro is about twenty hours away, Vers'tekim about thirty-two—"

"We'll take Vers'tekim," Jack said, his voice suddenly odd.

"Montenegro's closer," Alison pointed out.

"I said we're going to Vers'tekim," Jack said in a voice that left no room for argument.

He looked over at the computer camera/speaker/microphone module. "And on the way," he said, "we're going to stop off at Semaline."

"Semaline?" Alison echoed. "What in space is on Semaline?"

Jack didn't answer, but continued to stare at the computer camera. "Jack?" Alison said. "Yo. Jack?"

"Uncle Virge, what's on Semaline?" Draycos asked.

"Go ahead, Uncle Virge," Jack invited. "Tell them."

"Nothing much," Uncle Virge said. His voice was calm enough, but Draycos could hear the stress beneath it. "There's a lockbox in one of the banks at the NorthCentral Spaceport. We used to drop by sometimes when our cash supply was low."

"No, *we* didn't," Jack corrected darkly. "Uncle Virgil did. He never even let me out of the ship there, let alone let me go to the bank with him."

"It's nothing you need to worry about, Jack lad," Uncle Virge said, his voice low and earnest. "Maybe some other day."

"Some other day is now, Uncle Virge," Jack said firmly. "We're stopping at Semaline, and I'm checking out that lockbox."

"The lives of Draycos's people are at stake," Uncle Virge objected. "Go ahead—ask *him* if this is the time for unnecessary side trips."

"Actually, I have no objection," Draycos said.

Alison frowned at Draycos over her shoulder. "You don't?"

"We have nearly two months until the refugee fleet arrives," Draycos reminded her. "This will only take a few hours."

"A few hours can make all the difference between victory and defeat," Uncle Virge countered. "Shall I cite you a few historical examples?"

"No need," Draycos said, hearing his voice darken. "I have more than enough of my own."

There was a moment of awkward silence. Even Uncle Virge apparently couldn't think of anything to say. "So; Semaline it is," Jack said, climbing out of the seat. Alison and Draycos moved aside, and he brushed past without looking at either of them. "Give it your best speed," he added as he left the cockpit.

"Whatever you want, Jack lad," Uncle Virge muttered.

Jack was lying on his bunk in his cabin, staring at the ceiling with his arms tucked behind his head, when Draycos arrived. "Are you all right?" the K'da asked, padding across the room.

"Sure," Jack said. His voice sounded oddly distant. "I just wanted to be alone for a while, that's all."

"Shall I leave?"

"No, that's all right," Jack said. "I was just thinking about Semaline."

"You remember it well?"

"That's just it—I hardly remember it at all," Jack told him. "Just a few scattered images." He shook his head. "You'd think I'd have clearer memories of the place where my parents died."

Draycos felt his tail arch. "I didn't know that."

Jack shrugged. "That's what Uncle Virge told me, anyway. Like I said, I don't really remember."

"You *were* only three at the time," Draycos reminded him.

For a moment Jack was silent. "You think it's wrong for me to want to go there?" he asked at last.

Draycos hesitated. "In general, no," he said, choosing his words carefully. "The past is important to all of us."

"But you don't think this is the right time?"

"We do seem to have troubles and concerns enough just now," Draycos reminded him. "Still, as long as you don't intend to launch a complete examination of your life there, I see no problem with stopping by."

"I just want to see what Uncle Virgil has stashed in that lockbox," Jack promised. "Then we're out of there and off to Vers'tekim."

"Where you'll let Alison try to break into the Malison Ring computer?"

Jack made a face. "Don't *you* start with me, too. Anyway, what makes you think she's any better at computer hacking than I am?"

"Nothing in particular," Draycos said. "But your techniques just now didn't succeed. There seems little point in refusing to allow Alison to try her methods."

"I suppose not," Jack conceded. "Fine. It can be her turn next."

"I'm sure she'll appreciate that."

"As much as she appreciates anything we do," Jack growled. "I just can't figure her out. She picks at me about twice an hour—"

"More often if you've actually done something to annoy her," Draycos murmured.

"Yeah, well—yeah," Jack said. "But every time we try to drop-kick her off the ship, she refuses to go."

"She has Taneem to think about now," Draycos reminded

him. "They're beginning to share the same symbiotic bond that you and I do."

"And, what, Alison thinks the two of them will be safer from Neverlin and the Valahgua if they hang around us?" Jack shrugged. "Maybe. I don't know, though. I still think she's working some angle."

"Perhaps," Draycos said. "Only time will tell."

Jack snorted gently. "Or else time will slap us flat across the head," he muttered. "I guess we'll find out which."

CHAPTER 2

Jack couldn't remember ever having walked the soil of Semaline. But the soil itself, or at least the aromatic variety around the NorthCentral Spaceport, had most certainly found its way into the ship during their brief visits.

Now, as he walked down the *Essenay*'s ramp, the half-remembered smells flooded across his face like a softly smothering blanket. For a moment his feet seemed to tangle against each other, as if unwilling to move him deeper into the aroma.

"Are you all right?" Draycos asked quietly from his right shoulder.

"I'm fine," Jack assured him, working on getting his stride going again. "I just . . . there's a smell here that really gets to me."

The K'da's head, flattened into its two-dimensional form across Jack's shoulder, rose slightly against his shirt, his tongue flicking out briefly as he tasted the air. "I don't detect anything dangerous," he said.

"I didn't say it was dangerous," Jack countered tartly. "I just said it got to me."

Draycos didn't answer, and Jack grimaced. *That* had been rude. "Sorry," he apologized. "I guess I'm a little on edge."

"Maybe you should reconsider letting Alison go with you," Uncle Virge suggested from the comm clip on his left shirt collar.

"I could be out there in two minutes," Alison's voice seconded.

Jack squared his shoulders. Whatever was on this world, he could handle it. He and Draycos. *Not* he and Alison Kayna. "Thanks, but I can do this," he said. "You just take care of Taneem. Help her with her English lessons if you get bored."

"Jack, lad—" Uncle Virge began.

"And *you* just take care of *them*, okay?" Jack cut him off. "I can *do* this."

Uncle Virge sighed. "Whatever you say."

The spaceport was laid out in a series of concentric rings, with the ground and air transport pickup point in the center. "Odd design," Draycos commented as the trickles of passengers and crews from the docking slots on the outer edges began to form themselves into a more densely packed inward-moving crowd. "Why would anyone deliberately build a spaceport that actually *creates* congestion?"

"You got me, buddy symbiont," Jack said, dodging out of the way as a couple of Compfrins pushed past him. "Maybe they don't *want* big crowds coming through here. It's only a small regional spaceport, you know, on a small out-of-the-way world."

"Not a very wealthy one, either," Draycos commented.

"No, but it *could* have been," Jack said as he ducked past a group of chattering Jantris through the doorway into the next ring inward. "There are supposed to be some really nice beryllium and iridium deposits in the Golvin territories east of here."

"Why weren't they developed?"

Jack shrugged. "Uncle Virgil told me that some mining

corporation had managed to get the whole area tangled up in red tape and paperwork."

Something brushed his back, pulling at the light jacket he'd put on to help conceal the tangler belted at his waist. Jack twitched himself free and kept moving. The brush came again, more insistent this time. Again, Jack pulled away, then turned to see what the problem was.

He found himself gazing half a head down at a Golvin. The alien's long face was gazing up at him, his thin, wiry body visibly trembling. He wore nothing but a knee-length tan-colored vest covered with bulging pockets. "Is there a problem?" Jack asked.

"It is he," the Golvin said, his voice sounding like sandpaper rubbing across slate. "It is the Jupa."

"The Jupas are gone," another Golvin voice objected from behind Jack. Jack turned to find that two more of the wiry creatures had come up behind him. They joined the first in pawing at his jacket, their wide noses snuffling like bloodhounds on a fresh scent.

"Then perhaps this is a third Jupa they have sent to us," the first Golvin said firmly. "He smells much as they did."

"But the Jupas are gone," the second Golvin repeated.

"But there is so much that needs to be done," the first countered. "He smells like the Jupa Stuart and the Jupa Ariel. He must therefore *be* a Jupa."

"Or I'm just a human," Jack interjected, wondering what in space a *Jupa* was. "Maybe what you're smelling is just normal human scent."

"I have smelled other humans," the first Golvin insisted. "You are a Jupa."

"The One will know the truth," the third Golvin spoke up. "We should take him to the One."

"Yes, indeed," the first Golvin said, brightening. "You must come with us, Jupa."

"Wait a minute," Jack protested, trying to pull away. But their hands had some sort of odd stickiness to them, and the more he pulled the more he seemed permanently attached. "I can't go with you. I have to get to the bank."

"You are the Jupa," the first Golvin said firmly. "We have awaited your arrival for a long time."

"I have to go to the bank," Jack insisted, twisting his arms free of his jacket. But the three sets of sticky hands merely transferred themselves to his shirt and jeans. "Look, you're confusing me with someone else. I'm not who you think I am. Really."

"Jack?" Draycos murmured urgently from his shoulder.

"No—stay down," Jack warned quietly, eyeing the crowd around them. The last thing he and Draycos needed right now was for the K'da's existence to burst into public knowledge. He and Alison needed a certain freedom of movement if they were going to stop Neverlin and the Valahgua.

The Golvins were moving Jack along now, herding him like a prize sheep as they headed for one of the exits into the inner transportation area. Maybe out in the open, Jack thought, he would have a better chance of escaping.

He was still waiting for that chance when the Golvins ushered him into the backseat of a cramped, beat-up old air shuttle and piled in around him. The driver produced a starter from one of his vest's pockets, and ten seconds later they were in the air and heading east.

It was only then that Jack noticed that both his comm clip and his tangler were missing.

. . .

"Where was he when you lost him?" Alison asked, checking the clip in her compact Corvine 4mm pistol as she raced toward the airlock.

"Third ring toward the middle," Uncle Virge said, his voice as agitated as Alison had ever heard it. "He was talking to someone—at least two people, maybe more—and then the transmission cut off."

So whoever they were, they'd made sure to shut off Jack's comm clip when they grabbed him. That was a bad sign. "He's got the spare in his shoe, right?"

"If he can get to it," Uncle Virge said grimly. "There's a comm clip for you on the shelf in the airlock."

"I've got my own," Alison reminded him.

"This one's already tuned to my frequency and pattern specs."

"Fine," Alison growled. "Whatever."

Taneem was waiting in the airlock, her gray scales shimmering in the light as she paced restlessly around the room. "There is danger?" she asked anxiously as Alison picked up the comm clip Uncle Virge had mentioned and fastened it to her collar.

"Don't know yet," Alison said, trying to put the best possible light on the situation. Despite her adult K'da body, Taneem was still not much more than a child intellectually, and scaring her wouldn't do either of them any good. "Come on—get aboard."

She held out her hand. Taneem lifted a paw and set it on her palm, and a second later had gone two-dimensional and slithered up Alison's arm onto her back.

Alison hunched her shoulders, her skin tingling as the K'da slid across her back to the wraparound position she'd found to be the most comfortable for her. Even after two weeks of doing this a couple times a day she still wasn't used to it. "Uncle Virge?" she called, tapping the comm clip.

"Signal's clear," the computer personality confirmed tightly. "Watch yourself."

"I will," Alison promised as the hatch popped open and the gangway ramp slid down to the stained concrete of the landing pad.

From the air, the spaceport had looked rather poorly designed. Now, as Alison fought her way through the crowds streaming toward the central bottleneck, she realized just how badly designed it really was. She kept her eyes open as she walked and shoved and was shoved in turn. But if Jack was still here, she wasn't spotting him. "Still nothing from his comm clip?" she asked Uncle Virge.

"No," the answer came, just audible over the background noise. "But you're about the same place he was when the transmission cut off."

Alison worked her way to the nearest wall, pausing there to crane her neck over the crowd. No Jack, but also no one who looked like they might be a Malison Ring mercenary. Unless they'd just grabbed Jack and run.

No. For some reason, they still seemed to want Virgil Morgan. They wouldn't just run off with Jack without at least hanging around long enough to leave a ransom demand.

"It sounded to me like there was something there at the end about going to the bank," she said.

"Jack said he needed to go to the bank," Uncle Virge corrected. "No one said they were actually going there."

"Maybe not, but it's as good a place to start as any," Alison said. Rejoining the crowd, she continued inward.

She reached the center to find an entire half circle dedicated to ground and air taxis. Working her way to the first vehicle in line, she got in.

"To?" a long-faced Golvin asked, his flat nose snuffling at the air between them like a piece of paper flapping in a stiff breeze.

"Bank of Lloffle," she told him.

His nose snuffled another moment, and then he turned back to the wheel and pulled out into the drive. Alison leaned back, trying to look all directions.

Ten minutes later the driver pulled up in front of the bank. Jack, unfortunately, was nowhere in sight. "Now what?" Uncle Virge asked as Alison climbed the steep steps toward the front door.

"I'm going in," she told him. "They could easily have gotten here ahead of me. If not—" She shrugged. "I might as well at least clear out the box."

"With Jack holding the only key?" Uncle Virge retorted. "That'll be a neat trick."

"Not really," Alison said, smiling despite the seriousness of the situation. If he only knew. "It's Box 433, right?"

"Right," Uncle Virge said suspiciously. "What are you—?"

"I'm shutting down," Alison said. "Stay cool, okay?"

"Alison—"

She tapped the comm clip, cutting off his protest, and went inside.

The bank interior was small and modestly decorated, as befit a small operation on a world most of the Orion Arm's society and culture had long since left behind. Two Compfrins were working the counter, and a bulky Trin-trang was seated at a desk by the doorway leading into the back room. "May we assist?" one of the Compfrins asked.

"I need to get into Box 433," Alison said, walking toward the Trin-trang at the desk. "The name of record is Virgil Morgan."

The Trin-trang typed for a moment on his keyboard, then peered at his display. "Yes," he confirmed, opening a drawer and pulling out a shiny gold-metal electronic key. "You have the key?"

"Of course," Alison said, digging her right hand into her pocket for her collection of small keys. Picking by touch the one she knew looked the most like the Trin-trang's, she pulled it out and held it up. "Right here," she said, keeping her hand moving so that he couldn't quite get a clear look at the key. "I'm in rather a hurry," she added, lowering her hand to her side.

The Trin-trang's shoulders hunched in the equivalent of a frown, but without a word he stood up and gestured toward the doorway. "Come."

He led the way into the back room and the vault beyond it. Keeping her left hand out of his view, Alison squeezed her thumb against the base of her left forefinger.

And the plastic lockpick surgically implanted beneath the fingernail silently slid out into ready position.

Recessed into the side of the vault were three rows of private lockboxes. "Four thirty-three," the Trin-trang said, pointing a thick finger at one of them as he went to the far end of the row and inserted his key into the master lock at the end. "At your convenience."

Alison stepped to the indicated box, turning a little to put her shoulder between the Trin-trang and the lockbox. Using both hands as if she was having trouble inserting the key, she slid the lockpick into the keyhole. The semifluid plastic did its magic, flowing up against the markpins and triggering the proper transponder connections, and with a twist of her wrist the lock came open. Sliding the lockpick back into conceal-ment, she pulled the drawer open.

The only thing inside was a small shoulder bag, flattened and compressed to fit into the narrow space. She picked it up, noting that it seemed surprisingly light, and looped the strap over her shoulder. "Thank you," she told the Trin-trang as she returned the empty box to its place.

"You are welcome," the Trin-trang said, turning his key in the master lock again. "We live to serve."

Alison headed for the door, the bag bouncing gently against her side. So much, she thought sourly, for the lockbox being full of cash, the way Jack had implied.

A minute later, she was back outside, heading briskly down the steps and wondering what to try next. Obviously, Jack hadn't gotten to the bank ahead of her. Should she wait around and see if he might still turn up? Or should she assume that he and Dray-cos would get free and call Uncle Virge on their spare comm clip?

Maybe Uncle Virge would have an idea. She reached to her collar to turn her comm clip back on—

"I don't think so," a deep voice murmured in her ear as a large hand curled solidly around her wrist. "Just keep walking."

Alison twisted her head around. The man holding her arm was large and muscular, with short hair, a bushy mustache, and the bent nose of a man who'd been in more than his share of fights. "What do you think you're doing?" she demanded.

"So Virgil Morgan finally sent someone to open his lock-box," the man said. "You'd better hope he's willing to come out and play."

He smiled a grim smile. "Because if he's not," he added, "you're dead."

CHAPTER 3

They'd been flying for nearly an hour, and Jack was developing a serious crick in his neck from the shuttle's low ceiling, when they finally started down.

Their destination seemed to be a wide canyon cutting through the buttes and rock pillars and sand of the desert around them. As they flew closer, he could see that there were more rock pillars dotting the floor of the canyon, some of them reaching all the way up to the level of the surrounding desert surface. The canyon's pillars also had slender stone archways and guy wires linking them, creating a spiderweb of connections between them and the canyon's steep walls on either side.

Near the center of the canyon was a long, flat structure that seemed to straddle the river itself. From the air, it looked like a cross between a meeting hall and a covered bridge. At a dozen places north and south of the structure, the river had been spanned by narrow bridges.

The canyon floor, in contrast to the light brown sand of the desert around them, was a patchwork of vibrant green. Plants of some sort, probably crops. Along both sides of the canyon floor, the areas farthest from the river, were numerous clusters of trees.

I need to see more to the right.

Jack winced. Draco should know better than to talk to him in such close confines.

But if the Golvins pressed against him on either side had heard the K'da's murmur, they gave no sign. Carefully, Jack turned his torso a little to the right.

He felt the subtle movement as Draco eased along his skin to where he could look through the open shirt collar. Jack looked that direction, too, wondering what exactly the dragon was looking at. Aside from the canyon, all of the desert looked pretty much the same.

"We have returned," the driver said, pointing at the canyon below. "You will be ready to begin at once?"

"Let's first see what kind of accommodations you have for me," Jack improvised.

"We will provide the best," the Golvin seated beside the driver assured him. "Low down by the river, near to the Great Assembly Hall and the Seat of Decision."

"Ah," Jack said, a sinking sensation in his stomach. *Low down* in the canyon and surrounded by all that rock would severely limit the range of the spare comm clip in his shoe. Alison and Uncle Virge would pretty much have to fly directly over the place in order to pick up his signal.

And flying over it was the best they were going to manage, too. With all the archways and guy wires connecting the rock pillars, there was no way a ship the size of the *Essenay* would be putting down inside the canyon itself anytime soon.

In fact, the shuttle driver himself nearly didn't manage it. With the shifting wind currents along the canyon's edges buffeting the shuttle, Jack had a few very bad moments as they worked their way through the guy wires toward the landing pit by the river a couple hundred yards south of the big building.

But they made it, the engines sending ripples through the tall plants surrounding the landing pit as the pilot shut them down. More Golvins were starting to gather, Jack saw, all of them wearing the same long, pocketed vests as his kidnappers. Some of the outfits were differently cut, though, while others had colorful bits of decoration sewn onto them. By the time Jack maneuvered his way out of the shuttle there were at least fifty of the creatures standing silently watching him.

"I don't suppose it would do any good to tell *them* I'm not this Jupa you're looking for, would it?" Jack suggested as the driver and the other front-seat passenger joined him.

"You are the Jupa," the driver said firmly. "As indeed they can now tell for themselves."

Jack looked back at his audience. Sure enough, the entire crowd had that fluttering-nose thing going. Something about him apparently smelled really tasty.

He just hoped it wasn't going to be in the culinary sense.

"You wished to see your accommodations," the driver continued. "Come. I will show you."

"And I need to talk to your leaders, too," Jack added as the Golvin started along a path leading from the landing pit toward one of the taller stone pillars a hundred yards away. Aside from the various paths and the landing pit itself, Jack noted, the entire canyon floor seemed devoted to cropland. The trees along both sides, he suspected, probably produced fruit or nuts as well as wood.

"The One will see you shortly," the Golvin assured him. "Come."

Jack followed, the other Golvins from the shuttle coming behind him like an honor guard. There was a doorway in the base of the pillar, he could see, leading into a shadowy room or series of rooms. The doorway itself was decorated with multicolored streamers on both sides and a long colored fringe hanging from the top most of the way to the ground. Twenty feet above the opening, offset a little to the right, was another doorway, a little less lavishly decorated. Above it were more doorways, extending nearly to the pillar's top, most of these with only a sheet of plain cloth covering them. The other pillars were similarly honeycombed with doorways. Apparently, the Golvins liked to live up off the ground.

He was still looking around when his guide reached their destination. Without pausing, the alien spread his hands out onto the stone and started to climb.

"Whoa," Jack said. "Excuse me?"

The Golvin paused five feet up and looked quizzically back over his shoulder. "Yes?"

"I can't do that," Jack told him. "I'll need another way to get up."

"Strange," one of the other Golvins said. "The other Jupas had no problem climbing the grasses."

The grasses? "I already told you I wasn't a Jupa," Jack reminded him, looking more closely at the pillar. Sure enough, there was a crisscrossed mesh of ivylike plants growing out of the rock. Was that what the Golvins' sticky hands were holding onto? "How about giving me the ground-level room instead?" he suggested.

"Impossible," the Golvin beside him said, the skin of his face suddenly wrinkling all over. "That is the dwelling of the One."

"Then you'll need to find me a ladder," Jack said. "I can't climb the way you can."

"Who is this you have brought?" a new voice demanded from behind him.

Jack turned to find an older Golvin striding toward him. His vest was the most elaborately decorated yet, with streamers like those of the ground-floor doorway attached to both shoulders and a matching fringe along the vest's bottom. The implication was obvious. "I gather you're the One?" Jack hazarded.

A ripple of excited murmuring ran through the crowd at Jack's deduction. The leader himself, however, didn't join in. Silently, he continued forward until he was only a couple of feet away from Jack. Then, with a double flick of his wrist, he gestured to the three Golvins still standing beside Jack. Hastily, they backed up a half-dozen paces. "I am the One Among Many," the leader said, his voice stiff and formal as he studied Jack's face. "You claim to be the Jupa?"

Jack looked over the One's shoulder at the crowd. They'd gone silent again, their faces intent as they watched the confrontation. "To be honest, I have no idea what they're talking about," Jack admitted, lowering his voice. "But I can't seem to convince them of that."

For a moment the One eyed him. Then, leaning forward a little, he gave Jack a gingerly sniff. "You *do* smell like the Jupa Stuart," he admitted with clear reluctance as he leaned back again. "But he is dead."

"As is the other Jupa, I hear," Jack agreed. "Look, I know you're not crazy about me being here. Me, neither. So let's see if we can find a way to make me quietly go away."

The One's face wrinkled. "Go away?" he repeated, his voice suddenly sounding strange.

"I mean leave and go home," Jack said, frowning at the other's reaction. "So how about you give me another sniff, tell them that I'm close but no holiday prize, and they can take me back to the spaceport."

"But you are here," the One said thoughtfully. "And they are right, you *do* smell like Jupa Stuart. And there is much work to be done."

"You wouldn't like the quality of my work," Jack warned, a sinking feeling in his stomach.

"You are a Jupa," the One said, all the hesitation gone from his voice. "You are *the* Jupa."

And before Jack could say anything, the One turned toward the crowd and lifted his arms. "The Jupa Stuart will not return," he called, his voice echoing across the canyon. "But he has sent another Jupa. The Jupa—" He turned a quizzical look toward Jack.

Jack sighed. "I'm Jack," he said.

"The Jupa Jack," the One intoned, turning back to the crowd. "Welcome him to your lives and his duty."

The entire crowd exploded into a cacophony of whistles, shrieks, and birdcalls. "Look, there's been a mistake," Jack called, trying one last time. "I'm not—"

"Let a bridge be constructed to the Jupa's new home," the One ordered.

The crowd surged forward, the whistles and birdcalls louder than ever. Jack took an involuntary step backward, half expecting to be trampled.

Fortunately, the flow split apart before it reached him. Some of the Golvins headed for the pillar, while the rest swarmed toward a pile of large flagstones stacked at the base of one of the other pillars. Grabbing stones half as big as they were, they staggered their way back to the pillar.

And as Jack watched in amazement, they proceeded to build a bridge.

Not just a stack of stone, but a real bridge. They started the project some twenty feet out from the pillar, manhandling the stones together into an arch curving upward. Jack wondered how they were holding the stones together, and gradually realized that they were using nothing but their own spit.

Within minutes the arch was high and curved enough that it was threatening to tip over. But other Golvins were standing ready, putting in vertical supports beneath the far end as the rest continued working on the bridge itself.

Fifteen minutes later, it was finished: a climbable archway leading from the ground to the second-floor doorway the Golvins had indicated was to be Jack's new home.

"It is complete," the One said with clear satisfaction as a pair of aliens at the top spit-glued the whole thing to the pillar wall. "Unless you will require handrails?"

"No, this will do fine," Jack assured him, wondering what their spit would do to human flesh if it happened to get on him. Best to make sure he never found out. "Thank you. I'd like to rest a bit, and then you can explain my duties."

The One's face wrinkled. "You do not—? But of course. You wish to see the lists of sides and uprights."

"That would be a good start," Jack agreed. "I'll be out presently." Stepping to the archway, he got a grip on the edges and started climbing.

At first he went carefully, not quite ready to believe the thing was as solid as it looked. But there was no give or jostle at all to the structure, and by the time he reached the top he was convinced. Pushing aside the hanging fringe, he went inside.

The apartment turned out to be brighter than it had looked from outside. Though there were no actual windows, there were a half-dozen waist-high openings in the inner walls where slabs of white rock angled against the outer walls sent a soft glow into the room. Between that and the light filtering in through the doorway fringe, there was enough for him to see that the room was furnished with a couch, two chairs, a small table, a battery-powered light, and a small self-contained galley setup that looked like it had been pulled straight out of an old cargo hauler. Through another pair of doorways in the back he could see what looked like a bedroom and a bathroom. The bathroom's inner workings also seemed to have been scavenged from a spaceship.

"The light must be streaming down onto the stones from above," Draycos murmured from his shoulder.

"Keep it down, buddy," Jack warned quietly, walking around the room and making a quick check of the walls and furnishings. He couldn't imagine a simpleminded people like the Golvins bugging the room of their great and glorious Jupa, whatever the blazes that was. But surrounded by unknown aliens in a canyon three hundred feet deep was no place to take chances.

As it turned out, his first gut feeling was right. The living area wasn't bugged, nor were the bedroom or bathroom. "And so here we are," Jack said, dropping tiredly onto the bed. The mattress felt a little stiff, but not too bad. "Wherever in the name of vacuum sealant *here* is."

With a brief pressure of paws against Jack's shoulders, Draycos leaped out of the boy's shirt and landed with his usual silent grace on the stone floor. "We are approximately four hundred miles east of the NorthCentral Spaceport," the K'da said, stepping over to one of the white-stone openings and twisting his neck to peer upward into the gap between inner and outer walls. "The western edge of the desert is approximately seventy miles away."

Jack winced as he lay back onto the mattress and closed his eyes. Seventy miles. So much for any chance they could simply walk out of here. "Any other helpful tidbits?" he asked, more sarcastically than he'd really intended.

"Possibly," Draycos said calmly. "There are the remains of a mining operation less than a mile to the southeast."

"I already told you there was some mining out here."

"Yes, you did," Draycos acknowledged. "You also told me your parents had been killed in a mine accident."

Jack opened his eyes, frowning at the K'da. "What exactly are you suggesting?"

"And," Draycos added, "the people here seem to recognize your scent."

For a long moment the room was silent. Jack listened to the sudden thudding of his heart, the vague and half-formed memories of his parents flooding back through his mind. "Are you saying," he said at last, "that *this* is where they died?"

"I don't know for certain," Draycos said, padding to the bed and resting his upper body on the mattress beside Jack. "But the facts seem to point that direction."

Jack's gaze darted around the room, a sudden inexplicable panic flooding into him. *Get away!* was his first reflexive reaction. *Run, before they get you, too.*

He took a careful breath, forcing down the panic. He wasn't

three years old anymore, after all. "Let's assume you're right," he said. "What do they want from *me*?"

"That may depend on how they remember your parents," Draycos said. "Fortunately, they seem to hold Jupas in great esteem."

"Only *I'm* not a Jupa," Jack reminded him.

"Perhaps there is some task your parents were attempting when they died," Draycos suggested. "They may hope you'll complete it."

"I hope they don't want me to reopen the mine," Jack muttered, a sudden lump rising into his throat. "I don't know the first thing about mining."

"Yet you learn quickly," Draycos pointed out.

Jack snorted. "I hate to tell you, symby, but a hundred feet underground is no place to start learning a trade. Mining is a lot trickier than it looks."

"We'll take it slow and easy," Draycos assured him. "And we'll do it together."

"Terrific," Jack countered. "How much do *you* know about mining?"

The whiplike tail arched thoughtfully. "It involves digging," he said helpfully.

"Thanks," Jack said dryly. "*That* much I knew." Sitting up, he twisted his left shoe around and prodded at the molded rubber of the sole. The secret compartment popped open, and he dug out his spare comm clip. "First things first. Let's see if the cavalry was paying attention back there." He clicked on the device. "Uncle Virge?" he called. "Uncle Virge? Alison? Anyone home?"

There was no reply. "We'll have only limited range surrounded by this much rock," Draycos pointed out.

"I know," Jack said. Getting up, he went out of the bedroom and crossed the living room to the exit door. The crowd had dispersed, the Golvins having apparently gone back to tending various parts of the cropland. Looking more closely, Jack could now see that there was an intricate and efficient-looking irrigation system leading off from the river. Maybe these people weren't as simpleminded as he'd first thought. "Uncle Virge?" he called again quietly.

Still no response. With a sigh, Jack shut off the comm clip and went back to the bedroom.

Draycos was by one of the white stones, peering up between the walls. "The gap is quite spacious," he said. "It would be easily passable."

"And it probably conducts sound like crazy," Jack warned, crossing to his side.

"Perhaps, but not between apartments," Draycos said. "These shafts appear to lead only to this particular set of rooms. There may be other shafts extending downward to other apartments."

Jack craned his neck and looked up. The entire shaft seemed to be made of white stone glowing in the reflected light from the sky above. The shimmer made it difficult to see more than a few dozen feet, but there were certainly no other openings within that distance. "Took a heck of a lot of digging to open these up," he commented.

"True, if they burrowed these rooms and shafts from preexisting stone columns," Draycos agreed. "But having watched them build the bridge, I suspect they constructed the pillars themselves. In that case, they simply designed the structures with these double walls."

"That's almost worse," Jack said, wrinkling his nose as an odd scent drifted down between the two walls. "There must be almost forty of these things scattered around the canyon."

"They have clearly been at this a long time," Draycos agreed.

Jack shook his head as he eased his way out of the shaft. "I don't know," he said. "If push comes to shove, I think I'd rather take my chances holding on to your tail while you climb up the outside."

"For three hundred feet?"

"You're right," Jack agreed. "I may have to tie a knot in it first."

The dragon tilted his head warningly. "What?" he rumbled.

"Kidding," Jack hastened to assure him.

"Good," Draycos said. "I find it interesting that the other Jupas seemed to have had no problem reaching this apartment."

"Probably had climbing gear or lift belts," Jack said. "Unfortunately, all that stuff's back aboard the *Essenay*."

"They'll come for us," Draycos assured him quietly. "Uncle Virge will not abandon you. He and Alison will somehow learn where we are."

"Or maybe he already knows," Jack said, frowning as a sudden thought struck him. "If this is where my parents died . . ."

He looked sharply at Draycos as some of the pieces fell together. "Why that rotten—" he bit out, a sudden anger flooding through him. "He *knew* these Golvins were looking for me. *That's* why he never let me off the ship whenever we were on Semaline."

"That does now seem likely," Draycos agreed.

"Likely, my left foot," Jack growled. "It's a dead cert. Geez. First Neverlin, and now these Golvins. Is there *anyone* out there who doesn't want a piece of me?"

Draycos flicked his tail. "You're a very popular person."

Jack glared at him. "This isn't funny, buddy."

Draycos ducked his head. "My apologies," he said. "I was trying to lighten the mood."

Jack sighed. "I know," he said, reaching over to scratch Draycos behind his ear. "I'm sorry. I'm just . . . I thought I'd buried all these memories a long time ago."

"Memories are not a bad thing," Draycos reminded him. "They anchor us to the past—"

"And give us a sense of the present, and point the way to the future," Jack finished for him. "Yes, I remember the spiel you gave Noy back in the Chookoock slave quarters."

"It was *not* a spiel," Draycos said stiffly. "The boy was ill, and I was trying to comfort him."

"I know," Jack said, his mind drifting back to that terrible time. At least these Golvins didn't seem to want him as a slave. "I wonder how he's doing."

"I'm sure he's fine," Draycos said. "He and the others had Maerlynn to look after them. Perhaps Fleck, too."

"Maybe." Jack took a deep breath. "Well, no point putting this off any longer. Climb aboard, buddy. Let's go see what the One Among Many wants with me."

CHAPTER 4

In those first crucial seconds as the man's hand closed on her wrist, Alison tried her best to break free. But the man was a good eight inches taller and a *lot* of pounds heavier than she was. He also knew all the same tricks she did, and he clearly wasn't in any mood to be trifled with. A moment later, despite her best efforts, she found herself being hauled bodily down the street.

"Who are you?" she demanded, hearing her voice crack with strain. "Let me go. Let me *go.*"

The man ignored her. Alison thought about her Corvine, tucked away out of sight beneath her jacket. But she was pretty sure he would be ready for something like that, too. Clenching her teeth, trying to keep from getting dragged off her feet, she left the gun where it was.

It was probably just as well that she did. As the man pulled her into a café with a CLOSED sign on the door, a second hard-faced man slipped out of concealment in one of the nearby doorways and followed them in.

The inside of the café was deserted. "What in Gringold's mother is going on?" Alison demanded as her captor dragged her to one of the back tables where they'd be less visible to the people passing by on the street. "Are you cops?"

"Got a news flash for you, buddy," the second man said as he frowned at Alison. He looked a lot like the first, except that instead of a bushy mustache he had wide muttonchop sideburns. "This is definitely *not* Virgil Morgan."

"No kidding," Mustache growled. He plucked the comm clip from her collar and slid the bag off her shoulder. Almost as an afterthought, he reached under her jacket and took the Corvine from its holster. Putting his palm against her chest, he shoved her backward into one of the chairs. "Morgan played it cute and sent in a stooge to pick up his goods."

"I don't know what you're talking about," Alison insisted. "That's *my* bag and *my* stuff."

"Where is he?" Mustache asked, sitting down in the chair facing her. Checking to make sure the comm clip was still off, he set it and the bag onto the table in front of him. The Corvine he tucked away inside his own jacket.

Alison had had plenty of time to get her puzzled look ready. "Where is who?" she countered. "I don't know any Morgans."

"Of course you don't," Mustache said. "You just happened to find a lockbox key lying there on the street."

"No, I went in and opened my own lockbox," Alison said.

"I don't think so," Mustache said. "I paid good money to be alerted when Virgil Morgan's box was opened. It was. You were the only one who left the bank." He picked up her comm clip. "You want to call Morgan and tell him to show or we kill you? Or would you rather I do that?"

"Okay, look," Alison said, feeling sweat breaking out on her skin. This was *not* what she'd signed up for here. "I don't know any Virgil Morgan. I'm a thief—okay? I tap into bank computers and find out which lockboxes haven't been opened for a while. Then I go in and clean them out."

"Right," Mustache said contemptuously. "And you just happened to pick Morgan's box first?"

"What first?" Alison countered. "This is the fifth box I've opened at that bank this week."

"And the manager didn't notice anything strange about that?" Sideburns put in.

"The manager's a Trin-trang," Alison said scornfully. "And the two tellers were Compfrins. They couldn't pick out a human face between them."

"So you've been here a week?" Mustache asked.

"Three weeks," Alison corrected. "I came in from Pintering on the *Missing Link*."

"You have a payment receipt, of course?"

"As a matter of fact, I do," Alison said. She did, too, since one of the first lessons her father had hammered into her was to always, *always* carry proof of having been somewhere else. "You want to see them?"

"Maybe later," Mustache said, looking at Sideburns again. "What do you think?"

"I think we should call the boss and see what he wants to do," Sideburns said, pulling out a flat, palm-sized UniLink. Punching a couple of buttons, he held it up to his ear.

Slowly, Alison looked around the room. A UniLink instead of a comm clip meant that the boss was off-planet, and that he liked the kind of privacy that a UniLink's heavy encryption provided. Whoever had accidentally sicced Mustache and Sideburns on her, it wasn't just somebody with a casual grudge against Virgil Morgan.

"Semaline, sir," Sideburns said. "We just had a ping on Morgan's lockbox . . . no, sir, it was a girl. She claims not to know Morgan, that she taps bank lockboxes for a living."

He listened a moment, then looked at Alison. "Empty your pockets," he ordered. "Everything on the table."

Alison complied, laying out her set of keys, her makeup kit, her wallet, her small multitool, and her pen and notebook. Sideburns gestured to the keys, and Mustache picked them up and sorted quickly through them. He paused a moment at the one Alison had showed the Trin-trang, then continued on. "No bank keys here," he reported when he'd reached the end.

"How'd you open the box?" Sideburns asked.

"How do you think?" Alison retorted. "I picked the lock."

"Right in front of them?"

"I'm good at what I do."

"She says she picked it," Sideburns relayed. Again he listened a moment, then gestured to the wallet. Mustache tossed it to him, and he opened to the ID. "Alison Kayna," he read aloud. "No, sir, not to me."

He looked at Alison. "He wants to know if you do anything besides simple lock picking," he said.

Alison shrugged. "Sure. Combinations, time-beats, freeze-darks—pretty much the whole range."

"Let's find out." Sideburns glanced around, pointed at a half-curtained doorway leading to the café's back room. "There'll be a safe somewhere back there. You're going to open it."

Alison didn't miss a beat. "Oh, no, you don't," she said darkly. "I know how these little games work."

"What, you think we're *cops*?" Mustache scoffed.

"I'm not doing it," Alison said firmly, folding her arms across her chest. "And you try to repeat what I just told you and I'll flat-out deny it. You cops are all alike."

Mustache gave a theatrical sigh and dropped his hand to his side.

And suddenly there was a gleaming pistol six inches from Alison's face, pointed squarely between her eyes. "Listen to me, little girl," he said quietly. "You're, what, fifteen?"

"Fourteen," Alison managed between suddenly dry lips. In that single heartbeat she was back on Rho Scorvi again, fighting for her life.

"Do you want to live to reach fifteen?" Mustache asked. "The boss wants the safe open. You're going to open it."

Alison's pulse was thudding in her throat, her arms and legs starting to tremble, her stomach wanting to be sick.

Then, like a slap across the face, something slid subtly across her skin beneath her shirt . . . and in that instant, the terrible feeling of helplessness vanished.

Because she wasn't alone. She had Taneem. And if the young K'da female wasn't nearly as well trained as Jack's own poet-warrior friend, Alison had seen enough of Taneem's abilities to know the kind of help she would be in a pinch.

She took a careful breath, rubbing her shoulder gently as if massaging a stiff muscle. Taneem took the hint and subsided. "All right," she said. "For five hundred."

She had the satisfaction of seeing Mustache's eyes widen slightly. *"What?"*

"Five hundred," Alison repeated. "I know the law. If you pay me to commit a crime, it's entrapment and you can't charge me."

"This is *not*—"

"Give her the frinking money," Sideburns snapped.

Glowering, Mustache put his gun away and pulled out his wallet. "Two hundred up front," he growled, dropping the bills on the table in front of her.

"All right," she said, forcing calmness into her voice as she stood up. She'd convinced them—maybe—that she wasn't associated with Jack or Virgil Morgan. But cracking safes wasn't really her area of expertise, not like it was Jack's. The whole thing could still blow up in her face. "I'll need my tools."

Mustache gestured to the items scattered around the table. "Help yourself."

Alison picked up her multitool and makeup kit. On the other hand, she would bet heavily that her collection of gadgetry was a lot more impressive than anything Jack had.

The safe was in a tiny office, tucked away beneath a cluttered desk to the right of the kneehole. It looked to be a typical low-end device: standard tumblers, with probably only a single-stage hazer to block audio intrusion. "Well?" Sideburns prompted.

"Patience is a virtue," Alison reminded him as she opened her makeup kit and pulled out the slender powder case.

"What's that?" Mustache asked.

"It's powder and powder applicator," Alison said, throwing him a scornful look as she snapped it open. "Don't you know any actual women?"

"What's it for?"

"It helps cover skin blemishes and imperfections—"

"I know what it's *supposed* to be for," Mustache snapped. "What are *you* going to do with it?"

"With the powder?" Alison asked, unscrewing the mirror set

into the case. "Nothing." Setting the case aside, she held the mirror by the edge and squinted through one of the pinholes in the back.

They were there, right where she'd expected: a trio of infrared lasers slicing invisibly through the space in front of the desk. "Got some pingers blocking access," she said, handing the mirror to Mustache.

He peered through the pinhole a moment, then handed it back. "Nice gadget," he said. "Must have set you back some."

"You just have to know where to shop," Alison said, setting down the mirror and pulling out her mascara tube. Unscrewing the bottom end, she wedged it into her ear. Then, being careful to avoid the lasers, she pressed the open end of the tube against the escutcheon plate beside the combination dial.

A soft hum of static issued from the earphone: the hazer she'd expected. She counted off the seconds as the tiny computer inside the tube analyzed the sound, patterned it, and phase-countered it.

Before her count reached thirty, the sound was gone. Single stage, all right. Leaning forward, again being careful not to brush the laser pattern, she got a grip on the dial and started turning.

Two minutes later, with the clicks from the tumblers as loud and solid as if the whole thing had been a basic training exercise, she had it.

"Careful," Mustache warned as Alison pulled the door open a couple of inches.

"I know," Alison assured him, stopping the door's swing before it reached the nearest of the laser beams. "I trust there's nothing in here you actually wanted?"

Mustache raised his eyebrows at Sideburns, who had been

murmuring a running commentary on Alison's progress into the UniLink. "Go ahead and close it," Sideburns said. "We'll continue the conversation in the main room."

"Okay," Alison said when the three of them were back in the café proper again. "What now?"

"The boss is impressed," Sideburns said. "He wants to offer you a job."

Alison shook her head. "Sorry. I'm kind of booked at the moment."

"Interesting choice of words," Sideburns said, gesturing to the shoulder bag. "Considering we have some stolen property here with your fingerprints and DNA all over it."

Alison glared at him. "You said you weren't cops."

"We're not, but we don't mind turning scum like you over to them," Mustache said.

"Or you can listen to the boss's offer," Sideburns suggested.

"Like I have a choice?" Alison growled, suppressing a sigh. Jack had made it clear he didn't really want her on the *Essenay*. This was his big chance to get rid of her for good. "What's the job?"

"Basically, the same thing you just did," Sideburns said. "He wants you to open a safe."

"Where?"

"You'll see when you get there."

"Where?" Alison repeated. "I need to know up front how dangerous it's going to be."

Sideburns made a face. "She wants to know where," he said into the UniLink. He listened a moment, then nodded. "It's on Brum-a-dum."

"No police, no curious bystanders, no awkward questions," Mustache added.

"That helps," Alison said. Brum-a-dum was the planet where Jack had briefly been made a slave a couple of months back. Interesting that whoever was chasing Virgil Morgan had also picked that world to—

Her throat seemed to squeeze shut. Someone currently on Brum-a-dum. Someone looking for Virgil Morgan. Someone who desperately needed a safe opened.

Arthur Neverlin.

Oh, no, she thought, her heart suddenly racing. *No no no no no.*

"You'll get twenty thousand for doing the job," Sideburns went on. "Any equipment you need will also be provided."

And if that *was* Neverlin on the other end of the conversation, that meant the safe had to be one of the ones from Draycos's advance team, containing the rendezvous data for the main fleet. The information Neverlin needed if he was going to destroy the refugees.

The same information Jack and Draycos needed if they were going to save them. "Must be a tricky safe," she managed.

"Very tricky," Sideburns agreed, his voice darkening. "I trust you weren't going to try to talk up the price?"

That had, in fact, been exactly what Alison had been planning to do. It would be expected of a professional thief.

But one look at Sideburns's face and she changed her mind. "Twenty is fine," she said. "But I also want private passage away from there when I'm done, someplace like Capstone or Glitter. Brum-a-dum isn't a place I want to get stuck on."

An actual, real smile touched Sideburns's lips. "I don't blame you," he said. "Don't worry, they'll make sure you get out of there."

Alison felt a shiver run through her. Yes, they'd get her off Brum-a-dum all right.

But not to some nice, safe, civilized world. More likely to some nice, quiet, lonely grave. "Okay, it's a deal," she said. "How do I get there?"

For a minute, Sideburns listened to the UniLink, his forehead creased with concentration. "Yes, sir," he said. "Yes, sir. Don't worry—we'll be there."

Shutting off the device, he put it away. "The boss has a ship he can divert this way," he told Mustache. "It'll be in the system in four hours—I've got the coordinates for a quiet rendezvous."

"Fine." Mustache pointed at the shoulder bag. "What about this?"

"Might as well send it along," Sideburns said. "Unless it's full of money."

Mustache opened it and peered inside. "Old newspaper and magazine clippings, copies of bills of lading and invoices, and a few fuzzy photos," he reported, sifting through the contents. "And a couple of data tubes. No money."

"In that case, send it along," Sideburns said. "The boss might like to see what Morgan's been hiding all these years."

Mustache handed the bag to Alison. Looping the strap over her shoulder, she scooped up the rest of her personal belongings from the table and stuffed them back into her various pockets. She reached for her comm clip—

Mustache's hand got there first. "I'll take this," he said. He started to put it in his pocket, then paused. "Let's check, shall we, just for the fun of it?" Clicking it on, he held it to his own collar. "Hello, Virgil?"

Alison held her breath. But from the wry pucker of Mustache's lips she could tell that Uncle Virge had anticipated this possibility. "I see you like classical music," he said. "Beethoven, isn't it?"

He handed the comm clip to her. Alison held it against her collar, to find that Uncle Virge had piped in the feed from one of Semaline's music broadcasts. "Schubert, actually," she said, starting to fasten it back on.

"Don't bother," Mustache said, taking back the clip and shutting it off again as he put it into his pocket. "There won't be any news or music broadcasts for you to listen to along the way."

"Come on, girl," Sideburns said, gesturing toward the door. "You're in the big time now. Don't want to keep them waiting."

Alison shivered. "No," she murmured. "Of course not."

CHAPTER 5

The stone bridge was just steep enough that Jack decided he didn't want to try walking down it face first. Instead, he backed his way down, wondering whether this was the sort of thing a grand exalted Jupa would do.

By the time he reached the ground, a half-dozen Golvins had gathered at the foot of the bridge. One of them, who Jack tentatively identified as the one who had first accosted him at the spaceport, was clutching a handful of small notebooks. "Jupa Jack," he said, his eyes bright. "I bring you the lists."

"Thanks," Jack said, eyeing the notebooks with a sinking feeling. Specs and records from the mine Draycos had spotted upstairs? "Just, uh, just put them in my apartment, will you?"

"As you wish, Honored Jupa," the other said, selecting one of the notebooks and handing it to him. "I thought you might wish to study the list of uprights right away."

"Good idea," Jack said, opening it to a page at random. There was nothing but lists of numbers down the left-hand side of each page, along with some sort of chicken scratchings beside them that was probably the local writing.

"We have not yet had time to translate them into Broadspeak," the Golvin said apologetically. "But rest assured that all those listed are uprights. And the lists themselves have all been done in Broadspeak, as the Jupa Stuart taught us to do."

"That's good," Jack said. He eyed the list of numbers again, a sneaking suspicion beginning to tug at him. If the head man here was called the One . . . "What's your name, by the way?"

"I am One-Four-Seven Among Many," the Golvin said proudly. "But if your wisdom shows the path, I may soon be raised to a higher—"

"Onfose!" one of the others cut him off, clearly shocked. "How *dare* you suggest such a thing?"

One-Four-Seven—Onfose?—cringed. "I meant nothing, Nionei," he said hastily. "I merely meant—"

"You will allow Jupa Jack to make his own decisions, at his own time, in his own way," Nionei said firmly. "*And* not with you and he alone, but with all present and sided."

"Of course," Onfose said. "My most abject apologies, Jupa Jack."

"He really does mean no harm," the critic said, still looking a little cross as he glared at Onfose. "But you will note *his* name does not appear among the uprights."

Jack flipped a few pages over. Sure enough, between 135 and 177 there were no entries. "I'll keep that in mind," he said. "If you'll take the rest of the notes to my apartment as I asked, I'd like to walk around a little. Get a feel for the place."

"As you desire, Honored Jupa," Onfose said. "Do you wish an escort?"

"So that you can try again to speak your side?" one of the other Golvins asked dryly.

"I don't think I'll get lost," Jack assured him. Picking a direction at random, he set off, making sure to stay on the paths and off the crop plants. The Golvins, to his quiet relief, made no move to follow.

"Interesting," Draycos murmured from his shoulder as Jack reached one of the narrow irrigation channels and took a long step over it. "Did you notice how they form their names?"

"What names?" Jack countered. "They're nothing but a bunch of numbers."

"Though the listing is apparently not simply by birth order or any such random assignment," Draycos pointed out. "Recall that Onfose appeared to think a decision by you could change his number."

Jack thought back to the conversation. "Okay, I guess I can buy that," he said. "So they're ranked by status or position or nearness to the throne. Or whatever the One sits on."

"Note too how they simplify the awkwardness of long numbers," Draycos went on. "They take the first two letters of each number and form a name from them."

"The two-letter abbreviation thing is actually pretty common across the Orion Arm," Jack said, thinking back again. The critic who'd jumped all over One-Four-Seven had called him Onfose. So that made Nionei—"So Nionei is Nine-One-Eight?"

"That would appear to be the pattern," Draycos agreed.

On a hunch, Jack flipped open his notebook again. "Looks like our friend Nionei is an upright," he said. "I wonder what they are."

"I don't know," Draycos said. "But the direction I was going with this—"

"Jupa," Jack said as it suddenly hit him.

"Exactly," Draycos said. "If they're following their usual pattern, Jupa is likely a contraction of two words: Ju something and Pa something."

Jack ran the two syllables through his mind. But nothing leaped out at him. "Sorry," he said. "But I already told you I don't know the first thing about mining."

"Jupa Jack?" a voice called.

Jack turned to see another Golvin hurrying toward him, a paper-wrapped bundle clutched in his hands. "I have brought you your attire," he said, panting a little as he trotted to a halt. "I do not know if it will fit—Jupa Stuart was somewhat taller than you. I will adjust it later if it does not."

"Thank you," Jack said, frowning as he unwrapped the paper and pulled out the items one by one. On top was a light gray robe with vertical pleats equipped with a wide black sash fastened with a brushed silver clasp. Next came a black sleeveless duster with angled royal blue stripes on the shoulders and sleeves. Tall gray boots of some soft material were wrapped in a package of their own; and between them, also in its own paper wrapping—

Jack's breath froze in his lungs as he stared down at the black-and-royal-blue hat folded neatly in its packaging. Part tricorne and part biretta, the old description ran through his numbed mind. Part tricorne and part biretta . . .

"Jupa Jack?" the Golvin asked into his thoughts.

"Yes," Jack managed, forcing his mind back to the present. "Yes. Go ahead and take the—take everything back to my apartment. Except this," he added, snatching the hat as the Golvin started to close up the paper.

"As you wish, Jupa Jack," the Golvin said. "There will be a dinner in your honor at the twelfth hour, two hours from now, at the Great Assembly Hall."

Jack forced moisture into his suddenly dry mouth. "Fine."

The Golvin made as if to say something else, apparently thought better of it, and headed back toward the pillars.

"Jack?" Draycos asked quietly, his voice anxious.

"I'm all right," Jack said, gazing down at the hat cupped in his hands. "I just . . ." He took a deep breath. "This is it, Draycos. This is the hat I remember my parents wearing."

The K'da shifted on his skin, and Jack felt a slight pressure against his shirt as the gold-scaled head pressed against the material for a better look. "Are you certain?"

"Absolutely," Jack said, memories flashing once again across his mind. "I actually had one of them for a year or so until Uncle Virgil found it and took it away."

"And he told you it was a miner's helmet?"

"Yes," Jack said, frowning. "But it can't be, can it?"

"Unlikely," Draycos said. "The material is too soft for protection against dangerous impacts."

"Unless it's a topside boss's hat," Jack suggested.

"It does indeed look like a symbol of authority," Draycos said. "But you said Uncle Virgil had told you specifically that your parents were miners."

"Right, he did," Jack admitted. "Anyway, how could they have been killed in a mine explosion if they were topside bosses? So Uncle Virgil lied. Wouldn't be the first time. But if it's not a miner's helmet, what is it?"

"We know that the job of Jupa involves decisions of some sort," Draycos said. "As well as Golvins in a group speaking their sides. Could it be some sort of mediator or arbitrator?"

"That would fit with Onfose's ham-handed attempt to cozy up to me," Jack agreed. "And if your Golvin naming theory is right, it starts with Ju and Pa."

And for the second time in two minutes Jack felt his breath catch. He held the hat up, staring at it as if seeing it for the first time. Which, in a sense, he was. "*Ju Pa,* Draycos. *Judge-Paladin.*

"My parents were members of the highest-ranking judicial group in the entire Orion Arm."

Draycos stared out through the opening in Jack's shirt, gazing at the hat with new respect. He had always thought Jack's character was out of balance with that of the thief who had raised him. The logical solution was that his parents had instilled their values in him before their deaths.

But for Jack to have come from *this* kind of heritage was a twist he'd never expected. "That's incredible," he murmured. "How could Uncle Virgil have kept such a secret from you all these years?"

"Easily," Jack said, still sounding a little dazed. "All my book learning came from the *Essenay*'s computer." Beneath his flattened body, Draycos felt the boy's muscles tighten again. "*Essenay.* 'S and A.' Stuart and Ariel."

"Exactly as Alison suggested back on Rho Scorvi," Draycos reminded him.

"I'm sure she'll love hearing she was right about that," Jack said. "I wonder what my real last name is. Anyway, like I was saying, everything I ever learned about the Judge-Paladins came from the *Essenay*'s computer. It would have been easy enough for Uncle Virgil to delete any pictures from the ship's encyclopedias."

"Yes," Draycos murmured. "I know you've mentioned Judge-Paladins before, I believe in conjunction with the ongoing slave trade. But you've never told me exactly who and what they are."

"It's not a secret," Jack said, turning the hat over in his hands. "They were the Internos answer to the lack of courts and proper judges in some of the less populated worlds. Kind of like the old circuit riders they used to have back on Earth. They'd travel from planet to planet, region to region, dealing with whatever cases had accumulated since the last time they'd been there."

"What went wrong?"

Jack shrugged. "Nothing, as far as I know, except that there aren't nearly enough of them to go around. It started as just a human thing, like I said, on just the Internos worlds. But a lot of the alien governments in the rest of the Trade Association decided they liked the idea, and the Judge-Paladin project was extended to pretty much the whole Orion Arm. They fly around in these—"

He broke off with a snort. "In these really high-class ships with InterWorld transmitters and high-level P/S personality simulator computers," he went on. "Blast it all—Alison was right again. The *Essenay* really *is* way out of Uncle Virgil's class."

"Which leads to the question of how he acquired it," Draycos said.

And immediately wished he'd kept his jaws shut. There was one obvious answer as to how a thief and con man like Virgil Morgan might have done that, and at the moment it wasn't a possibility Draycos really wanted to burden Jack with.

Fortunately, Jack's own thoughts were already headed off in an entirely different direction. "Which leads *me* to the question of how come Alison's so smart," he growled. "*Way* too smart for someone who claims she's just running cons on mercenary groups."

"Perhaps there is more to her than we know," Draycos murmured.

"Bet on that, buddy." Jack looked up at the sky above them. "*I* just wonder what she's doing back there all alone with my ship."

"Uncle Virge answers to you, not her," Draycos reminded him. "What I don't understand is why your parents were not missed."

"I don't know," Jack said. "Maybe their schedule was random enough that no one could pin down where they'd been when they disappeared." He hissed between his teeth. "Or maybe no one tried very hard."

"You said the alien governments all approve of the program."

"The central governments do, yes," Jack said grimly. "But not all the local top hats like the idea of outsiders poking around their territories."

"Hence the *Essenay*'s built-in weaponry?"

Jack shrugged. "I assumed that was part of the stuff Uncle Virgil added afterward, like the chameleon hull-wrap," he said. "But now, who knows?" He hunched his shoulders. "For that matter, I don't even know why *I'm* still alive."

The sky was growing noticeably darker, Draycos noted as he peered up through the opening in Jack's shirt. They should be heading back soon. "That poem your mother used to sing to you," he said. "The one that contained the unknown word?"

"You mean *drue*?" Jack asked. " 'We stand before, we stand behind, we seek the *drue* with heart and mind'?"

"Yes, that one," Draycos said. "I wonder if perhaps you simply remembered the word wrong."

"And you think it should be . . . ?"

"Truth."

Jack looked at the hat in his hands. "We stand before," he began hesitantly. "We stand behind,

"We seek the truth with heart and mind.
From sun to sun the dross refined,
Lest any soul be cast adrift.

"We are the few who stand between
The darkness and the noontime sheen.
Our eyes and vision clear and keen:
To find the truth, we seek and sift.

"We toil alone, we bear the cost,
To soothe all those in turmoil tossed,
And give back hope, where hope was lost:
Our lives, for them, shall be our gift."

For a long moment they stood together in silence, and Draycos felt the subtle movement of Jack's shirt as a pair of teardrops hit it. "Jack?" he asked quietly. "Are you all right?"

"I hate this place, Draycos," the boy said, swiping a hand across his eyes.

"I understand," Draycos said quietly, the images of his own places of great sorrow drifting like ghosts across his memory. "After the dinner tonight, once everyone's asleep, we'll take the shuttle and go back to the spaceport."

"Good." Abruptly Jack spun around on the path. "Let's get it over with."

CHAPTER 6

The long-range shuttle Alison was taken aboard had average engines, purely functional interior design, and standard if reasonably comfortable seats.

The starship the shuttle rendezvoused with flipped every one of those descriptives on its head. It was large and long and sleek, fast and powerful and elegant, with all the proper trim of a top-class corporate star yacht.

And long before the gold nameplate beside the docking station came into view, she knew what ship it had to be.

The *Advocatus Diaboli.*

Memories flickered back to her as Sideburns brought the ship to dock. Jack had been aboard this ship four months ago, when Arthur Neverlin tried to blackmail him into helping in Neverlin's scheme to murder Cornelius Braxton, founder and head of Braxton Universis. Jack and Draycos had managed to turn the tables on his plan and expose his treachery.

At the time, of course, everyone had assumed that it was just a particularly nasty attempt at a corporate takeover. Now that Alison knew the full story, though, she could see how much nastier the big picture really was.

And as far as she knew, the only thing standing in the way of

Neverlin's plan was the fact that he didn't know where the refugee fleet was supposed to meet Draycos's advance team. That information had been carefully locked away aboard the four advance team ships.

They were apparently counting on Alison to get it for them.

The past four hours of contemplation on such matters had led her to the inevitable conclusion as to who she would find aboard this ship. But though her face was properly prepared for the encounter, she still couldn't quite suppress a shiver as the shuttle's docking hatch opened into the *Advocatus Diaboli*.

And she came face-to-face with Colonel Maximus Frost.

Fresh from the trouble on Rho Scorvi, too. Though he had long since cleaned off the grime of that world, there was still something of that encounter's fatigue around his eyes. It was a fatigue Alison knew all too well: the weariness of having pushed and schemed and fought, only to have victory snatched away at the last second.

But there was more than just tiredness in his eyes. There was also a deep, simmering anger.

"This is her?" Frost demanded, looking Alison up and down.

"This is her," Mustache confirmed. "Alison Kayna."

For another moment Frost studied Alison's face, and she found herself holding her breath. But the colonel merely grunted. "Fine," he said. "You two can go."

"Right," Mustache said. "A word of advice: don't let her near your locker." He stepped back into the shuttle, and with a thud both ships' hatches closed and sealed.

"I hope you're as good as they say you are," Frost warned. "For your sake."

"I'm good at what I do," Alison said, hoping that wasn't just bluster.

"We'll find out," Frost said. "It's going to take nine days to reach Brum-a-dum in this tub. Your meals will be delivered to your stateroom, and you'll be allowed out at my convenience and pleasure. Questions?"

"Not right now," Alison said. "If I do, I'm sure the room has an intercom."

"And feel free to use it," Frost said with an edge of sarcasm. His eyes narrowed slightly. "I've seen you before, Kayna. I know I have."

"I've just got that sort of face," Alison said, feeling her heartbeat speeding up. There had been no pictures taken of her for the past five years—her father had seen to that. And there were precious few pictures from previous years out where anyone could get hold of them.

But there was nothing that could be done about personal memories . . . and if Frost tracked down this particular memory, she was going to be in very serious trouble indeed. "I don't think I've seen *you* before," she went on. "You have a name?"

He took a moment to consider his answer. "Frost," he said.

"Nice to meet you, Frost," Alison said. "Or would you prefer I call you by your rank?"

"What makes you think I have one?"

"The way you stand." Alison nodded back at a group of humans and aliens loitering a little ways down the corridor. "Them, too. You guys are military of some kind."

"Military of the *best* kind," Frost said. "You can address me as 'Colonel.'" He gestured to the loitering mercenaries. "Dumbarton?"

One of the men came to full attention. "Sir?"

"You and Mrishpaw escort our guest to her quarters," Frost ordered. "Make sure she's comfortable."

"Yes, sir." Dumbarton and a typically ugly Brummga stepped forward. "This way."

The stateroom they took her to was an easy match for the rest of the ship. It had a raised platform for the surprisingly large bed, with matching nightstands and a complete wraparound music system. To one side of the sleeping area was a fair-sized conversation/ entertainment area with two couches, several small tables, three soft-looking armchairs, and a complete entertainment center. The whole thing was separated from the sleeping area by a waist-high wall with a built-in soothe-scent and the glossy raised edge of a holographic light show system.

In one corner of the conversation area was an ornate wooden computer desk, facing outward into the room, with polished brass trim and a high-backed wooden chair. The part of the chair she could see over the desktop looked at first glance to be something stiff and old-fashioned, but beneath the desk's shin-high modesty panel she could see the chair's modern rollers and the control bars of a fully adjustable pneuma system. The front of the desk included another light show system setup.

Off the conversation area, convenient to both it and the sleeping section, was a bathroom with separate shower and swirl tub enclosures.

Alison spent the first half hour wandering around the suite, the bug detector from her lip liner pencil humming in one hand, the other hand resting casually on her shoulder in silent warning for Taneem to stay put. The *Advocatus Diaboli*'s original builders would hardly have included surveillance equipment, but she thought Frost might have tried to throw something together in the four hours he'd had to play with.

He had. He'd installed two microphones, though so amateurishly that she hardly even needed her detector to find them. One was behind the desk's privacy panel, the other by the bed behind the intercom speaker. She got rid of both, then swept the suite again just to make sure.

And when she was finished, she kicked off her shoes and socks and climbed into the squishy-soft bed. Pulling the comforter all the way up to her chin, she settled down for a quiet conversation. "Taneem?" she murmured. "How you doing, girl?"

"I'm frightened," Taneem murmured back. Her voice was shaking, her two-dimensional body sliding restlessly along Alison's skin. "I'm sorry."

"That's okay," Alison said, trying to hide her own growing fears about this whole thing. "You've been very brave."

"This is the same human who tried to kill us on Rho Scorvi, isn't it?"

"Yes, it is," Alison confirmed. "But that's all right, because he doesn't know who we are. Or rather, who *I* am. We absolutely have to make sure that he never finds out about *you* at all."

"Because he wants to kill Draycos and all others of our kind?"

"*Wants* is the key word," Alison agreed. "But he's not going to, because you and I and Jack and Draycos aren't going to let him. That's why we're here."

"Is it?" Taneem asked. "Or is it the money he promised you?"

"No reason I can't have both, is there?" Alison asked, keeping her voice light.

For a moment Taneem didn't answer, but there was a definite sense of discomfort to her silence. Alison waited her out, wondering if all K'da were like this or whether Draycos had been pounding his warriors' ethic into her during their language lessons. "Perhaps we should have run," Taneem said at last.

"Unfortunately, there was never any safe time when we could have done that," Alison said. "From the moment Mustache grabbed my arm, we were stuck."

"I could have helped you," Taneem said, a bit hesitantly.

Alison's mind flashed back to Taneem's reaction the first time she'd been forced to kill. "Even with your help, it would have been dangerous," she told the K'da. "The two men on Semaline were never close enough together that we could have been sure of taking both out before they could fight back."

"What then is our plan?" Taneem asked. "Or do we even *have* a plan?"

"Of course we do," Alison assured her, trying to sound more confident than she felt. "We do what Frost wants and open his safe for him."

"Because of the money?"

Alison pursed her lips, mindful of Taneem's still limited intelligence and understanding. "Taneem, do you remember Jack and Draycos talking about the upcoming meeting that's supposed to take place between the K'da advance team and the full refugee fleet?"

"Yes, of course," Taneem said, sounding a little insulted by the question.

"And you also remember that we don't know where that meeting's supposed to take place?"

"Of course," Taneem said again. "That's why we went to Nikrapapo, to see if we could learn the location from the Malison Ring computer there."

"Right," Alison said. "Only it's starting to look like Frost and his friends don't actually have that information. Not yet. I think it's in this safe they want me to open."

"Why haven't they opened it themselves?"

"Maybe they tried and couldn't," Alison said. "I think that's why they've been chasing so hard after Jack these past couple of months. His Uncle Virgil used to be one of the very best at this sort of thing."

"Then you also must fail in your attempt," Taneem said. Some weight came onto Alison's shoulder as the K'da lifted her head partially from the skin. "If the location is in the safe, you must not open it."

"I wish it was that easy," Alison said. "But it's not. They've got four safes—maybe only three if the one on Draycos's *Havenseeker* was too badly wrecked in the crash—and the whole Orion Arm to choose safecrackers from. Sooner or later, somebody will get one of them open."

"Then perhaps we can destroy it?" Taneem suggested hesitantly. "Perhaps we can destroy all of them?"

"We can't do that," Alison said. "There are just too many things we don't know."

"What do you mean?"

"Well, for instance, what happens if none of the advance team shows up at the meeting point?" Alison asked. "Do the refugees just wait there until someone does? Do they go home? Do they continue on to Iota Klestis, which Neverlin and Frost already know about?"

Taneem's glowing eyes seemed to dim a bit. "I don't know," she admitted.

"Neither do I," Alison said. "Besides, this is way too good an opportunity to pass up. Ever since Draycos's team was attacked, he and Jack have been playing catch-up."

"What does that mean?"

"Neverlin and his buddies have always had the initiative," Alison explained. "That means they were always deciding what to do, and Jack and Draycos were always having to react to their action and try to block it. But if we can get to the refugee fleet information first, we'll finally be ahead of the game."

"The game?" Taneem echoed. "Is that what this is to you, Alison? A game?"

Alison was still trying to come up with a good answer for that when, behind her, there was a soft click and the stateroom door slid open.

"What do you want?" she demanded, sitting bolt upright as Dumbarton and Mrishpaw strode into the room. On her shoulder, she felt Taneem's weight vanish as the K'da again flattened herself and moved out of sight. "How *dare* you just waltz in here?"

"Can it, kid," Dumbarton said. "Colonel wants your clothes."

"My *what?*"

"Gotta scan 'em," he said.

Alison clenched her teeth. With Taneem riding her skin . . . "Fine," she said. "Go on out. I'll toss everything out to you."

"Just do it," Dumbarton growled, not making the slightest move toward the door. "We haven't got all day."

"I'll tell Colonel Frost," Alison threatened.

Striding over to the intercom on the nightstand, Dumbarton jabbed one of the buttons. "Colonel?" he said. "Dumbarton. She's being uncooperative."

"I just want a little privacy," Alison called toward the intercom.

"You think you've got something we haven't all seen before?" Frost countered.

"Colonel—"

"You got two choices, kid," Frost cut her off. "Take 'em off yourself, or Dumbarton and Mrishpaw will do it for you." There was a click, and he was gone.

"Well?" Dumbarton asked.

Alison glared at him. "Fine," she gritted. Rolling to the opposite side of the bed, she put her hand on the edge of the mattress as she threw off the comforter and swung her legs over the side.

And to her horror felt a surge of weight on the back of her hand as Taneem dropped off onto the floor.

Alison clamped down hard on her tongue, potential disaster flashing in front of her eyes. Taneem clearly had it in mind to hide under the bed. Only it was a pedestal bed, fastened to the deck, with barely a three-inch overhang.

For the moment, the K'da was out of the mercenaries' view. But Dumbarton was already headed back around the side of the bed, clearly intent on catching up with Alison and making sure she didn't waste any more of his time. As for the Brummga, all he had to do was unglue his big feet from the floor and take three paces to his left and he would likewise get the shock of his life.

"Come on, come on," Dumbarton growled.

"I'm coming," Alison snapped back, pretending her foot was tangled in the comforter as she lowered her hand toward the crouching K'da and tapped her fingertips vigorously on the side of the bed.

To her relief, Taneem got the hint. A dragon paw grabbed on to Alison's wrist, and a moment later the K'da was back on her skin. "No room," Taneem whispered.

"I know," Alison whispered back. "Off my left foot, when I signal." Making a show of freeing herself, she stood up. "Can I at least change in the bathroom?" she asked aloud.

Silently, Dumbarton planted himself directly between her and the bathroom door and folded his arms across his chest. "Fine," Alison growled, coming around the bed toward them. "Would you at least get me one of the robes from the bathroom?"

"Sure." Dumbarton looked at the Brummga, jerked his head.

The big alien turned and lumbered off. "Thanks," Alison said, unfastening her belt, her eyes darting around the room. With the Brummga's back toward her, and Dumbarton's attention about to be elsewhere, getting Taneem off her body without being seen ought to be easy enough.

But that was only the first problem. In an open room like this, there were precious few places something the size of a small tiger could hide.

And then Alison's eyes fell on the computer desk in the corner. It would be a tight fit, she knew, but it should work.

Provided she could make Taneem understand what she wanted.

"Don't think I'm not going to go straight over to that computer and log a complaint when this is over," she warned Dumbarton, walking up to him and looking him straight in his eye.

"I'm sure the colonel's real scared," Dumbarton said dryly.

"He should be." Out of the corner of her eye, Alison saw the Brummga disappear through the bathroom door. Lifting her left foot past Dumbarton's legs, she wiggled her ankle furiously.

She nearly lost her balance as Taneem shot out the leg of her jeans. The K'da hit the deck silently, her neck turning back and forth as she looked around. Alison held her breath . . .

Then the long neck straightened, and Taneem headed off in a fast lope toward the desk. Ducking under the modesty panel, she rolled over onto her back and reached all four legs up toward the underside of the desktop itself. Because Alison was listening for it, she heard the faint scrunch of claws digging into wood.

And the gray-scaled K'da body pulled upward and disappeared behind the panel.

"I'm going to need more clothes, too," she told Dumbarton as the Brummga emerged with the robe and tossed it on the end of the bed. "At least one more outfit, plus a nightshirt or something to sleep in."

"Check the closet," Dumbarton said shortly. "There's probably something in there you can use."

"Oh," Alison said as she turned and snatched up the robe. "I never thought of that."

Dumbarton snorted under his breath. "Some criminal mastermind," he muttered.

Alison smiled to herself. Being underestimated, her father had often said, was nearly as good as not being noticed at all.

Half an hour later, when they brought back her clothes, Alison was sitting at the desk, her knees helping to support Taneem's weight, pounding out the indignant entry she'd promised into the ship's log.

Dinner was served at seven o'clock that evening, ship's time. By then Alison had found and disabled the two microphones that had been sewn into her clothing while Frost was having them scanned.

The colonel was apparently not the type to give up easily.

She and Taneem ate together in silence, finishing off the entire selection of food that had been provided. Alison wondered if her seemingly vast appetite was going to raise any red flags among Frost's men. Still, she was fourteen, and fourteen-year-olds' appetites were the stuff of legend. Hopefully, that would be the conclusion Frost would draw from the next nine days' worth of cleaned plates.

Later, with Taneem again riding her skin, she pulled out her array of gadgets and began double-checking all of them. Her life was riding on this job, not to mention the lives of all those K'da and Shontine out there. Whatever it took, she was going to succeed.

If only to see the look on Jack's face afterward.

CHAPTER 7

The Great Assembly Hall turned out to be the long structure straddling the river that Draycos had noticed on their flight into the canyon earlier that day. A good two hundred feet long and thirty wide, with open sides and a wood-and-weave roof, it was supported by a set of wide, ten-foot-high stone pylons sunk deep into the edges of the river.

The positioning of the Hall puzzled him for a while until he remembered that with the high canyon walls, the crops spread out along the floor would receive only limited sunlight each day. Whatever land lay beneath the Hall would receive none at all. The Golvins had therefore built the structure over the river, which couldn't be farmed anyway.

Dinner was a crowded and noisy affair, with at least two hundred of the aliens present. Jack was seated at the One's table, laid out just beneath a tall thronelike chair at the northern end of the Hall. From the flurry of one- and two-syllable names being tossed around the table, Draycos concluded that the boy had been seated among the very top crust of the canyon's social structure.

But while the Golvins chattered and laughed through the meal, Jack himself was uncharacteristically quiet. He was polite enough, answering any questions put to him, and smiled and nodded when appropriate. But his heart clearly wasn't in any of it.

Draycos's chance came late in the meal, when local custom apparently required the diners to get up and mingle with those of different rank. Jack left his seat as well, but instead of milling around he went to the side of the Hall. Leaning his elbows on the waist-high wall, he gazed out at the moonlit canyon around them. "Jack?" Draycos called tentatively from his shoulder.

"Right here," the boy said, his voice sounding as distant as the rest of him.

"I need to check out the shuttle," Draycos told him, trying without success to read the boy's face. "Is the area clear?"

Jack took a deep breath, as if forcing himself out of distant thoughts, and glanced around. "Looks okay," he said. Turning a little, he stretched his right arm over the wall and let it dangle downward.

Draycos slithered down the boy's arm and popped out of his sleeve. A quick snap of his front legs, and he had caught the outside of the wall with his claws. For a moment he hung there, confirming for himself that the area was clear of observers. Then, with a last look at Jack's troubled face, he let go and dropped onto the edge of the cropland below.

There were at least eight different plant species being cultivated in the canyon, Draycos had noted during Jack's walk that afternoon. Generally, there were two to four different types in each of the plots marked off by the narrow irrigation channels.

The farmers probably saw the arrangement as an efficient way of using the different needs of the different plants. A poet-warrior like Draycos saw instead the possibilities of having differently sized plants to move through. Flicking out his tongue every couple of breaths to sample the subtle odors of the area, he headed downstream toward the landing pit and the shuttle.

He was halfway there when he spotted a lone Golvin on the far side of the river moving along the walkways between the crop plots, heading the same direction Draycos was.

Draycos froze, crouching down beside a wide stand of wheat-like plants, frowning to himself. The alien wasn't carrying any tools, so he probably wasn't going out to work in the fields. He probably wasn't simply going for a stroll, either—he was behaving far too furtively for that.

And aside from the crops and a couple of the apartment pillars, the only thing in this direction was the shuttle.

Draycos lashed his tail thoughtfully. Unfortunately for him, the Golvin didn't have to worry about being seen out here. Draycos did, which meant that in a straight head-to-head skulking race through the cropland, the alien would almost certainly reach the shuttle first.

But there was nothing that said Draycos had to keep to the cropland.

The river water was cool, but not nearly as cold as he'd thought it might be. He slipped beneath the surface, leaving only the top of his head above water, and paddled quickly and quietly toward the landing pit.

He reached it well before the Golvin and eased up out of the river. Crouching in the shuttle's shadow with the water dripping off his scales, he gave the vehicle a quick look.

As he'd seen on their earlier trip, the passenger compartment contained front and rear bench seats, each capable of seating three Golvins. There was also a wide hatchway in the rear of the vehicle, he could see now, probably leading to a storage area.

But there was no connection between it and the passenger compartment. If Draycos wanted to be able to see anything, the storage area was out.

The Golvin was only about seventy feet away now. Scooping up a small stone from the riverbed, Draycos wrapped the tip of his tail around it and flipped it, sling style, over the alien's head.

It landed with a soft rustle in the plants behind him. Startled, the Golvin spun around, his head wagging back and forth as he searched for the source of the noise.

And with the other's back turned, Draycos popped the shuttle's rear door and slipped inside.

Pulling the door closed again, he lay on his side on the rear seat floor and looked around. The back of the front bench seat was upholstered with a thick dark blue cloth, he saw, as were the rear seats. Extending a claw, he cut the cloth away from both the bottom and the side edges of the front seat, creating a wide flap.

Rolling onto his other side, he did the same with the cloth extending down from the front of the rear seat. Then, flipping both flaps up, he lay down on the floor and arranged the flaps on top of himself.

It was an absurdly simple deception, and in the full light of day it wouldn't hold up for a second. But the night was dark, and the Golvin out there was in a hurry. Chances were good he wouldn't give the rear seat even a first look, let alone a second.

The front driver's side door opened, and Draycos braced himself. But from the quick and shifting pressures on the seat cushions in front of him, it appeared the Golvin was intent on just getting in and getting away.

A few seconds later, the shuttle lifted off into the night. Cutting hard away from the center of the canyon and the party still going on in the Great Hall, they headed up. Draycos eased the corners of the flaps away from his eyes and settled in to wait.

They'd been flying for nearly an hour when Draycos's sense of balance told him they were starting down. The starlight was joined now by a diffuse glow reflected from the shuttle ceiling, indicating the lights of civilization below. Draycos arranged the camouflaging flaps over himself again, and a few minutes later they were down.

The door opened, there was another quick shifting of the Golvin's weight on the seat, and then he was gone, closing the door behind him.

Draycos gave it a twenty-count. Then, pushing aside the flaps, he eased up to the level of the window and looked out.

They had landed in a large parking area, apparently not far from the spaceport where the *Essenay* had arrived a few hours earlier. Surrounding the landing area on three sides were squat buildings housing various small shops.

And on the fourth side was a single, large building. Above the door, in glowing letters, were the words *InterWorld Corporation, NorthCentral Semaline.*

Draycos felt his claws scratch gently against the shuttle floor. So that was the reason the Golvin had sneaked away from the big celebration. He'd had an urgent offworld message to send.

Right after Jack's arrival at the canyon.

Fifteen minutes later, the Golvin emerged from the InterWorld building and headed toward the shuttle at a fast jog. Draycos was back under his camouflage flaps before the door was pulled open. Once again, the Golvin didn't bother to check his rear seat before taking off.

This time, that inattention was going to cost him.

The flight back to the canyon was uneventful. Draycos waited patiently . . . and as the Golvin eased the shuttle into the landing pit, the K'da silently brushed aside the flaps and rose up behind the other. "Don't turn around," he growled.

The Golvin jerked as if he'd been hit by a bolt of lightning. Reflexively, he started to turn his head.

He brought the movement up short as his cheek came up against a waiting K'da claw. "Who are you?" he gasped.

"I ask the questions," Draycos said. "You sent an InterWorld message. What was the message, and to whom did you send it?"

"I sent no—"

He cut off in a strangled gasp as Draycos pressed the claw firmly into his skin. "What was the message, and to whom did you send it?"

"I have no name," the Golvin said, his voice starting to take on an edge of panic. "Only a number."

"Give me the number."

The Golvin did so. It was a long number, and Draycos could only hope he would be able to remember all the digits. "Now the message," he said.

The Golvin didn't answer. Draycos prodded him again—"I was just to let them know if another Jupa came to the canyon," he said, the words practically tumbling over themselves in his effort to get them out. Apparently, no one had told him there might be danger involved in this little errand.

"And then what?"

"That's all," the Golvin said. "I was just to tell them. That is all I know."

It probably was, too, Draycos knew. No one would be foolish enough to trust a pathetic creature like this with any genuine secrets. "You will tell no one about this conversation," he said. "And you will make no further trips outside this canyon."

"I will do as you say," the Golvin said. "You may trust my word in—"

The rest of the promise was lost as Draycos slapped him firmly across his neck below his ear.

He slumped down in his seat, unconscious. Draycos waited a moment to be sure, then opened the rear door and slipped outside.

The Great Hall was quiet and dark, he noticed, the party apparently over. Still, there might still be stragglers wandering around the cropland. Lowering himself once again into the river, he headed upstream.

He reached Jack's pillar without incident. The bridge the Golvins had constructed was the obvious way up, but it might be interesting to see if he could climb the ivy plants the way the Golvins did. Setting his front claws into the mesh, he started up.

It was a mixed success. The ivy was strong enough to support his weight and was solidly rooted into the stone. But Draycos's claws were sharper than whatever small barbs or hooks the Golvins had in their hands that allowed them to climb. He had to be constantly on the alert lest he slice through the plants and dump himself onto the ground.

If worst came to worst, he decided, it would probably be faster to ignore the plants and dig his claws directly into the small cracks in the stone, the way he'd done on his way out of the Great Hall.

The apartment, when he reached it, was dark and quiet. But a quick tasting of the air confirmed that Jack was there, and that the boy was alone. Padding silently across the main room, he slipped into the bedroom.

"About time," Jack said quietly from the bed. "I was starting to wonder if you'd gotten lost."

"My apologies," Draycos said, coming up to him. "I ended up taking a small side trip."

"Sounds interesting," Jack said. "By the way, if you're hungry there's bread, meat, and fruit in the refrigerator."

"Thank you," Draycos said, suddenly realizing just how hungry he was.

"Don't thank *me*," Jack said with the first touch of humor Draycos had heard from him all day. "The One caught me slipping some food into my pocket from the serving platter and told me that wasn't necessary, that they would supply whatever I wanted for breakfasts and midnight snacking."

"Very kind of him," Draycos said, changing direction back to the door. "If you don't mind . . . ?"

"No, help yourself," Jack said. "I can't vouch for what kind of meat it is, though."

"There are many species of animals who live in deserts," Draycos reminded him.

"Maybe," Jack said doubtfully. "But in a farming area like this, I'm guessing most of what they get is some sort of rodent."

"Or fish."

"Oh, right," Jack said, his voice brightening. "Yeah, that sounds a *lot* better. Good. Go have some fish."

The platter in the refrigerator was a welcome sight, piled high with thin strips of dried and seasoned meat. Draycos ate his fill, not actually caring what kind of creature it had come from.

And when he was finished, he returned to the bedroom and told Jack all about his unplanned trip to the city.

Jack listened in silence until the K'da had finished. "What do you think it means?" he asked.

"I think it's fairly obvious," Draycos told him grimly. "Someone out there doesn't want a Judge-Paladin visiting this canyon."

"Or maybe they don't want him visiting the mining area you spotted outside the canyon?" Jack suggested.

"Possibly," Draycos said. "However, at this point the specifics aren't important. There was no one outside as I came in, and the shuttle's controls seem straightforward enough. We can be back at the spaceport within an hour and—"

"We're not leaving."

Draycos broke off in midsentence. "What do you mean?" he asked carefully.

"Uncle Virgil told me my parents were killed by an explosion," Jack said, his voice going dark. "That made sense when I thought they were miners. But I can only think of one situation where a Judge-Paladin would die that way." In the darkness Draycos sensed the boy brace himself. "I think they were murdered."

Draycos twitched his tail in a grimace. He'd come to that same conclusion the moment Jack had learned their true professions. "All the more reason for us to leave."

"All the more reason for us to stay," Jack countered. "Judge-Paladins aren't just roaming benchwarmers, you know. They have the authority to investigate and to even pass summary judgment in some cases. I'm apparently a Judge-Paladin now. Let's investigate."

Draycos sighed. "Jack, we don't even know what we're looking for," he said. "Not to mention the fact that all your detection and sensor equipment is aboard the *Essenay*."

"That just means we'll have to make do with our eyes and your nose and tongue," Jack said. "Hey, you're the one who told *me* that K'da warriors had the right and the duty to pass judgment on murderers."

"That was under K'da and Shontine law," Draycos reminded him. "At any rate, my prime duty is to protect my host."

"You will be," Jack assured him. "You'll be right here with me the whole time. Look, Draycos, it'll be a week or two at least before anyone can get here. Maybe even longer—that number your buddy called was a Barcarole exchange, and that system's nearly all the way across the Orion Arm."

"Unless they choose to spend extra fuel to obtain extra speed."

"Which assumes whoever it is even bothers to send anyone," Jack went on doggedly. "It's been eleven years, after all. I doubt anyone even cares anymore."

Except you, the thought flicked through Draycos's mind. "We should at least go back to the spaceport and try to contact Uncle Virge," he urged. "Let him know what we're doing, and have him standing by in case of trouble."

For a long moment Jack was silent. "Actually, I don't think the *Essenay*'s here anymore," he said at last.

Draycos felt his neck arch. "That's impossible," he said. "Uncle Virgil programmed the ship to stay with you and protect you."

"Then where is it?" Jack demanded hotly. "Uncle Virge knew about all this, remember? He should have been buzzing around overhead before we even landed."

"But where would he have gone?"

Jack shook his head. "I don't know," he said, his brief flash of anger fading away. "Maybe Frost or Neverlin tracked us here and was able to nail him. Or maybe they didn't actually get him, but he's had to go to ground like he did on Rho Scorvi."

He inhaled deeply, then let the air out in a long sigh. "Or else Alison's taken control and flown off on her own."

Draycos hesitated, the automatic denial sticking in his throat. Ever since Alison and Jack had met, back at the Whinyard's Edge training camp, he'd somehow felt that the girl was trustworthy. That trust had only deepened during their time together on Rho Scorvi. It was hard to believe she would betray them.

But then, Draycos had been wrong before. "I don't think Uncle Virge would permit himself to be blocked or neutralized for long," he said instead. "He was programmed by Virgil Morgan, and we both know how clever and devious he was."

"Yeah, well, I get the feeling Alison's a lot more clever and devious than she lets on," Jack said. "But never mind that. The point is that whatever's happened to the *Essenay,* we've still got access to that shuttle out there. We can leave pretty much anytime we want to."

Draycos flicked his tail. There were some serious flaws in that argument, of course. But it was clear Jack didn't want to hear them. "And until we so decide, you wish to investigate your parents' deaths?"

Rolling half over in bed, Jack reached over to the nightstand and picked up the Judge-Paladin hat. "I can't just walk away, Draycos," he said quietly, fingering the hat. "I just can't."

"I understand," Draycos said, conceding defeat. It was still a terrible idea to stay here—every thread of warrior instinct in his heart was screaming at him to get them out of this place.

But he was a poet-warrior of the K'da, and his first responsibility was to his host. Jack wanted to stay, so stay they would.

And he really *did* understand Jack's need to do so.

"Hey, don't look at me that way," Jack admonished him, some of the darkness in his mood lifting. "It'll be all right." In the dim light from outside, Draycos saw the boy smile tightly. "Trust me."

CHAPTER 8

"Jupa Jack?"

Behind his closed eyelids, Jack frowned. What in the *world*—?

"Jupa Jack?" the call came again.

With an effort, Jack pried open one eyelid. There was a faint glow coming from the other room, but nothing any reasonable person would consider actual daylight. "I'm here," he called back. "What is it?"

"It is sunrise, Jupa Jack," the Golvin said. "Time to awaken and prepare for your duties."

Jack frowned. "What, already?"

"Most others are already awake and refreshed and going about their own duties," the voice replied reprovingly.

"Terrific," Jack muttered under his breath. "All right, I'll be right there."

"I will wait outside to escort you to the Great Assembly Hall," the other said, and Jack heard the subtle rustling of the fringe as the visitor exited.

"The Great Hall?" Draycos murmured from Jack's shoulder.

"The One said they'd be setting up a judgment chair for me next to his Seat of Decision," Jack told him. "Blast. The way

Onfose was talking yesterday, I was hoping they'd take a few days first to translate all those case files into English."

"Or Broadspeak, as I believe they called it," Draycos said.

"Whatever," Jack said. "Maybe give us a chance to check out the mining area up there. But I guess we're kicking off the schedule today. I hope they're not expecting me to read that chicken scratching of theirs."

"I'm sure they've considered that."

"Maybe." Steeling himself, Jack threw off the covers and landed his feet on the floor. The stone was every bit as cold as he'd expected it to be. "Either way, I sure don't remember anything in the *Essenay*'s encyclopedias about Judge-Paladins starting work before the birds are even up."

"Perhaps it's a local custom," Draycos said, peeling himself off Jack's back and leaping onto the floor. He stretched, cat-style, a quick shiver running through his scales. "I hope the clothing they gave you is warmer than it looks."

"I imagine the canyon will warm up once the sun is actually up," Jack said, heading for the bathroom. "*I* just hope this shower comes equipped with hot water."

"Is that likely?"

"It's possible," Jack said. "A lot of spaceship galleys and bathrooms are designed to be mostly self-contained—"

"Stop," Draycos said suddenly, his ears stiffening.

Jack froze in midstep, holding his breath. He didn't hear anything. "What is it?" he whispered.

Slowly, the K'da's ears went back to their usual angle. "I thought I heard a noise," he said. "Like someone scratching at the stone."

Jack looked toward the door. No one was visible. "Hello?" he called. "Is someone there?"

There was no answer. "I don't think it came from outside," Draycos murmured. "There was a faint echo to it."

Jack's skin tingled as he looked over at one of the white stones in its between-walls alcove. "One of the shafts?" he asked.

"Possibly," Draycos said. "At any rate, it's stopped now."

Jack took a deep breath. "Well, keep an ear out," he warned. He started again for the shower—"By the way, did I tell you I think I've figured out what sides and uprights are?"

"The sides are most likely the political or social groupings which tend to face off on issues concerning the administration of the canyon," Draycos said. "The uprights are possibly those Golvins who have generally proven honest and trustworthy in their testimonies in the past."

Jack made a face. "I don't know sometimes why I even bother to talk to you," he growled. "Go eat your breakfast mouse meat. I'll be out in a minute."

The shower turned out to be gratifyingly hot. The soap the Golvins had provided didn't seem very effective, but the towel was thick and strangely spongy. Jack washed up, threw on his shirt and jeans, and had a quick breakfast.

And now that he was thinking about it, the meat *did* taste much more like fish than rodent.

After breakfast, he went back into the bedroom, took off his other clothes, and dressed in the robe, sash, duster, and boots of his new office.

Despite the Golvin's concerns, the clothes seemed to fit reasonably well. The boots were a shade too big, but not enough to be a problem. "How do I look?" he asked, holding his arms out to his sides.

"Very noble," Draycos said.

Jack looked sharply at him. But if there had been any sarcasm in the comment, it wasn't visible in the K'da's face or posture.

In fact, the odd thought crossed Jack's mind that it was just the opposite. It was almost as if Draycos was seeing him for the first time.

Jack looked down his front at the strange clothing, a flurry of not entirely pleasant emotions chasing across his mind. Maybe he was seeing himself for the first time, too.

Or maybe not. "Kind of hard to move, though," he commented, swinging his arms experimentally from the shoulders. He could play all the dress-up he wanted, he reminded himself firmly, but underneath it all he was still only Jack Morgan, fourteen-year-old former thief.

"You look fine," Draycos assured him. "Shall I get your hat?"

"I'll do it." Crossing to the nightstand, Jack picked up the hat and set it carefully on his head. He took a deep breath, again forcing back the swirl of emotions, and held his hand out to Draycos. "Okay," he said. "Let's you and me go dispense some justice."

Two male Golvins and a female were waiting on the ground as he emerged from the apartment and made his way down the bridge. "Good morning to you, Jupa Jack," the female said gravely, touching the fingertips of both hands to her forehead, the gesture briefly covering her eyes. "I am Three-One-Six-Five Among Many. I will be your assistant and reader-of-records."

"I will be pleased to have your service, Thonsifi," Jack said. Briefly, he wondered if he should repeat her gesture, decided against it.

"I am honored to be of such service." Thonsifi waved a hand toward the Great Hall. "Your Seat of Judgment is prepared. Shall we go?"

She headed off along the narrow path that led to the Great Hall. One of the males walked behind her, with Jack and the other male bringing up the rear.

Many of the canyon's residents were already hard at work, Jack saw. Most were tending the cropland, while others arranged cloth and leather and metal goods on small tables around the bases of some of the pillars. From somewhere in the distance came the rhythmical clank of metal on metal.

About thirty Golvins were waiting inside the north end of the Great Hall. As promised, a chair had been set up for Jack in front of and to the right of the One's own Seat of Decision. "Jupa Jack," the One greeted him gravely from his chair as Jack stepped in front of him. "You are ready to begin?"

"I am," Jack said, eyeing the chair with fresh trepidation as he walked over to it. What in the world did he know about judging other people? For that matter, what gave him the right to even try?

But he was here, and there was nothing for it but do his best. Bracing himself, he gathered the skirts of his robe and duster around him and sat down.

Thonsifi stepped to the right side of the chair. "The first dispute lies between Three-Seven-Seven and Six-Nine-Naught," she said. "It is a question of irrigation and water rights."

Two older Golvins stepped forward out of the group, one of

them glowering, the other practically radiating pride and self-righteousness. "Describe the situation," Jack said, studying them.

"The wall of the irrigation channel that separates their crop-lands has become chipped on Thsese's side," Thonsifi explained. "Some of the water that might otherwise go to Sinina's land is thus going instead to Thsese's land."

Jack frowned. This was a legal problem? "Why can't the chipped area simply be fixed?" he asked.

"It can," Thonsifi said. "But as I said, it is on Thsese's side."

"And?"

"It is on Thsese's side," Thonsifi repeated, starting to sound a little flustered.

Jack nodded as he finally got it. A Golvin whose name started with Three clearly outranked a simple Six, which probably meant no one could come onto his property to fix the channel wall without his permission.

And since he was getting more than his fair share of water as a result, he had no reason to fix the channel himself. "What about the people downstream?" he asked.

"They are all lesser numbers," Thonsifi said.

Which meant that although they were probably getting cheated as well, none of them had the rank to go fix the channel either. "And this damage occurred when?"

"Six seasons ago," Thonsifi said.

Jack blinked at her. "Six *seasons?*" he echoed, turning to look up at the One.

The One held his gaze steadily. "I rendered a decision," he said. "Thsese appealed to the higher authority of the Jupas."

"And the last time a Jupa was here . . . ?"

"The last were Jupa Stuart and Jupa Ariel," the One said.

Jack grimaced. Eleven years with no Judge-Paladins in sight. No wonder Thsese had felt safe appealing his case.

Well, at least the game was over now. He'd simply order Thsese to let Sinina come over and fix the channel, and that would be the end of it.

But even as he opened his mouth to say so, he took another look at Thsese's expression. *Radiating pride . . .*

And suddenly he saw the trap he'd nearly walked into. These people had built their whole society on status and position, and on who could do what and with whom. Throw in their dependence on their limited crop area, and there was the potential here for long-term trouble. If he casually brushed their cultural legs out from under them, it would leave scars and resentment that would linger long after he was gone.

Still, even in places where status was king, greed was always queen. And if there was one thing Uncle Virgil had taught him, it was how to deal with both of those.

"Very well," he said, turning back to the complainants. "It's clear that through the extra water obtained for his crops, Thsese has been taking unfair profit from his neighbors."

"Yet I did not cause the rupture," Thsese put in stiffly.

"I understand that," Jack agreed. "Nevertheless, you did profit from it. I therefore decree that until the channel wall has been returned to its proper condition, twenty percent of your crops will be forfeit, to be divided between Sinina and the—"

"What?" Thsese all but screeched. He started forward, stopping only when one of the two silent males who had accompanied Jack stepped into his path. "This is outrageous!"

"To be divided between Sinina and the other landowners downstream," Jack continued. He gestured to his right. "The choosing and distribution of that twenty percent will be handled by my assistant, Thonsifi."

Out of the corner of his eye, Jack saw Thonsifi stiffen with surprise. Apparently, she wasn't looking forward to invading Thsese's territory any more than Sinina was.

But most of Jack's attention was on Thsese, and the resulting show was well worth it. The older Golvin's eyes widened, his skin wrinkling violently at this casual piling of insult onto injury. For a Three to have to allow a Thirty-One onto his land for the purpose of confiscating some of his crops—

"The channel will be fixed," he ground out.

"By sundown today?" Jack suggested.

Thsese sent a glare at the One. But he was stuck, and he knew it. "By sundown today," he agreed blackly.

"Good," Jack said. "Then I declare this case settled. Next?"

He spent the rest of the morning handling more water cases, a few land disputes, and one involving crops that had migrated from one plot to another. Most of them were quickly and more or less easily handled. A couple of them took a little more thought, and one was tricky enough that he decided to postpone it to the next day.

As the group in the Great Hall thinned, runners quietly left and rounded up the next batch of complainants.

There didn't seem to be any particular pattern to the cases. Jack wasn't being given the oldest complaints first, or those involving the highest-ranking Golvins. Certainly they weren't dealing with the most urgently pressing. His only guess was that Thonsifi had put some of the easier ones up front so that she and the One could see whether their kidnapped Jupa actually knew what he was doing.

Finally, thankfully, they broke for the midday meal.

"You're doing well," Draycos murmured from Jack's shoulder as the boy wandered along the edge of the Great Hall munching on a stalk of something sweet and crunchy he'd snared from the buffet table Thonsifi's people had set up.

"Thanks," Jack murmured back, glancing down at his shoulder before he remembered that the Judge-Paladin robe ran right up to his neck. "I hope you'll still be saying that when they start throwing the tricky stuff at me."

"Some of this morning's cases have been tricky enough," Draycos said. "You've had to deal not only with legal questions, but social and political ones as well."

"Actually, I don't think I'm doing much legal work at all," Jack said. "Mostly I'm just getting everyone to do what they should have done months or years ago on their own."

"Perhaps you're not so much a judge as a mediator," Draycos offered. "Your success here has been in bringing opposing sides together in a compromise."

"What I'm doing is finding the right levers to use on them," Jack corrected. "It's not a lot different from con work."

Draycos was silent a moment. "Some of the techniques may be similar," he said. "But the intent is far different. Under Uncle Virgil's direction, you used these methods to steal from people. Here, you use them to bring justice and harmony."

"Maybe," Jack said reluctantly. Draycos might be right, but he wasn't quite ready to agree that what he was doing was nearly so noble. It still felt way too much like what he'd been doing for Uncle Virgil all those years.

"I am concerned, though, by the fact that apparently no other

Judge-Paladins have been here in all this time," Draycos went on. "You said they traveled in circuits through the less populated areas."

"I also said there weren't enough of them," Jack reminded him. "Actually, this whole planet probably qualifies as a less populated area. My guess is that any Judge-Paladin who's touched down on Semaline has stuck to the cities and towns. I doubt most of them even know this canyon is out here."

"I wonder how your parents found it."

"I don't know," Jack said. "Maybe we'll find out when we get a chance to go up to that mining area. I wonder if there are any cases that'll give us an excuse to do that."

"You believe that's where your parents died?"

"Look around," Jack said, turning around and leaning his back against the wall. "Well, no, I guess you can't. But this seems to be where Jupas judge, and there's no sign anywhere of any kind of explosion."

"It *has* been eleven years," Draycos reminded him. "They would surely have repaired any damage."

"If they did, they did a really good job of it," Jack said. "Don't forget, I've had a pretty good look at the building. It's all the same type of stone, and all the stone shows the same wear pattern. The floor stones in particular fit perfectly together."

"I'll accept your analysis," Draycos said, though Jack thought he could hear an unspoken *for now*. "But that brings up another possibility. If they were visiting the mine, could the explosion that killed them have been an accident after all?"

Jack chewed the inside of his cheek. That was a good point. Maybe there *was* no real mystery here, no hidden crime to be uncovered and avenged. "We won't know until we get up there," he decided. "Let's put our heads together and come up with some reason to go topside."

Finishing off the sweet stalk, he turned back toward his Seat of Judgment. "In the meantime, I've got more justice to dispense."

The afternoon's cases were pretty much a repeat of the morning's stack. Most of them involved water and crop problems, with a few apartment and neighbor troubles thrown in.

Most of the cases struck Jack as rather feeble, with the appeal to a higher authority in each case probably having been made by whichever side had been the loser under the One's original decision. Close to half the canyon, he reflected, had probably been rather annoyed when a new Judge-Paladin had actually shown up.

It was on the last case of the day, as the sky was beginning to darken overhead, that the pattern suddenly changed.

"This is Four-Eight-Naught-Two," Thonsifi said as a slightly bedraggled Golvin was brought forward. "He was discovered this morning sleeping in the flying transport of the Many."

"Really," Jack said, noting the bruising along the right side of Foeinatw's neck where Draycos had knocked him out. "Why didn't you simply sleep in your apartment, Foeinatw?"

The other didn't answer, his eyes focused on the floor in front of Jack's feet. "He claims to have been set upon by others," Thonsifi said. "At least one, possibly more. He further claims that these others damaged the flying transport's interior."

"I see," Jack said. Thonsifi's voice was steady and professional enough, but he could sense contempt lurking beneath the words. From some of the other neighbor-conflict cases he'd heard that afternoon he gathered that accusing someone of assault was a very serious charge among the Golvins. Doing so without proof was apparently even more so. "Can you name these assailants?" he asked.

"I cannot," Foeinatw said, his voice low.

Jack pursed his lips. Without proof of the assault, his logical legal course would be to assume Foeinatw was lying and come up with some punishment for sleeping in the shuttle and some compensation for damaging it.

But on the other hand, maybe this was exactly the right time for a little creativity. "Step forward," he ordered the Golvin.

Foeinatw hesitated, then shuffled a few steps closer. Jack leaned forward, peering closely at him. "Did these assailants strike you or merely lock your arms?" he asked.

"They struck me." Gingerly, Foeinatw touched his neck. "Here."

"Yes, I see." Jack leaned back again in his chair. "I will make inquiries among the Many," he said. "You are released for the moment without punishment."

Thonsifi turned to Jack, her skin wrinkling in surprise. "Jupa?"

"Clearly, he's been hit," Jack said, pointing out the bruise. "If he was assaulted and others did the damage to the flying transport, he cannot be held accountable."

"No, of course not," Thonsifi murmured. "Foeinatw, you may go."

"I thank the Jupa," Foeinatw said, his face as wrinkled with surprise as Thonsifi's. But along with the surprise, Jack could see a hint of puzzlement as well.

Small wonder. The Golvin had probably concluded that his attacker was Jack himself, or someone in league with him, and that his trial would thus be a complete sham.

Except that the Jupa had not only accepted his explanation, but had even let him off.

He would, Jack suspected, be doing a lot of rethinking tonight.

"That is the last case for the day," Thonsifi said, closing down her notebook as Foeinatw headed for the door. "It has been an honor to serve with you, Jupa Jack. I look forward to doing so again tomorrow."

"As do I," Jack said, standing up and stretching his shoulders. "How badly was the flying transport damaged, by the way?"

"Not badly," Thonsifi assured him. "Merely some torn cloth. It has been taken to the Fabric-Makers' shop for repair."

"Ah," Jack said. And as long as it was there, presumably, it wouldn't be available for Foeinatw to borrow again, which was good.

Unfortunately, it also wouldn't be available for Jack and Draycos to borrow should the need arise. That wasn't so good. "I trust it will be repaired soon," he added.

"Sooner than we will find Foeinatw's assailants, I expect," Thonsifi said, a hint of her earlier disapproval coloring her voice.

"I take it you don't think much of him?" Jack suggested.

Thonsifi's ears stretched out briefly. A shrug? "He is not one of the uprights," she said. "Far from it. I will say no more."

"I suppose every place has a few scoundrels," Jack said, a part of him noting the irony. A few months earlier, he would have qualified as one of the scoundrels himself. "If they didn't, we wouldn't need Judge-Paladins."

Thonsifi bowed her head to him. "And we are most grateful for your service and wisdom."

"You're welcome," Jack said, suppressing his automatic impulse to downplay his so-called wisdom. "Speaking of service, how many cases did we serve today?"

"Forty-one," Thonsifi said. "An excellent start."

"How many cases are left?"

She consulted her notebook. "Seven hundred ninety-two."

Jack suppressed a groan. Great. "I guess we won't be running out of work anytime soon, then," he said as cheerfully as he could manage. "Good night, Thonsifi. Good night, One Among Many," he added, looking at the One.

"Good evening to you, Jupa Jack," the One said gravely. "Your evening food is waiting in your apartment."

"Thank you," Jack said. He was, he suddenly realized, ravenously hungry. And he would bet that Draycos was even more so.

"Sleep well and peacefully," the One added. "I will see you tomorrow."

CHAPTER 9

Taneem had changed a great deal in the past couple of weeks, in many ways, as if having awakened from a long dream. Her former life on Rho Scorvi was like a vague and distant memory. There had been little to do back there beneath the edges of the great forest except hunt for berries and grubs and small animals, or to perform the little dances the Erassvas had taught them, or to sleep against her host's large, soft body.

Sometimes there had been a little more excitement. A small predator might arrive and need to be driven off, or a low-flying bird could be snatched from midair and eaten. But for the most part, life there had been slow and lazy, comfortable and rather boring.

Still, she was quite sure it hadn't been nearly as boring as *this*.

Alison wouldn't let her get very far away, for one thing. That was reasonable, Taneem supposed, since they didn't know when any of the bad people aboard might decide to come into their room. But it meant she had to either rest on Alison's skin or else follow the girl around like a baby linzling.

Alison didn't talk to her very much either. Partly, again, that was because she didn't want anyone suddenly opening the door to hear her talking to a room that was supposed to be empty. Taneem could understand that, too. But mostly it was because Alison was spending most of her time with her pack of tools and with the pieces of paper from the bag she'd brought from the safe on Semaline.

Sometimes Taneem tried looking over Alison's shoulder as she studied the papers. But most of the written ones were in a type of writing Draycos hadn't yet taught her, while the pictures were of places and people of which she had no knowledge.

It didn't seem as if Alison understood much of it, either. All she ever did was scowl at the notes and pictures or lay them out on different parts of the room's low table. Sometimes she gathered them all together again and sorted them out into a different order.

It was on the fifth night of their journey when the routine suddenly changed.

Alison had been asleep for nearly two hours, and Taneem was dozing lightly against her skin, when across the room the door quietly slid open.

Instantly Taneem went still, as Draycos and Jack and Alison had all warned her to do whenever others were around. The blankets were pulled up around Alison's chin, blocking any chance for Taneem to see what was happening.

But she could hear just fine . . . and as Alison's slow breathing continued unchanged she heard two of the bad people go across the room to the table. There was a soft shuffling of papers, and then they went back to the door again. It closed behind them, and they were gone.

Taneem counted slowly to twenty the way Draycos had taught her. Then, she eased herself off Alison's skin and slid out from beneath the blankets onto the floor at the side of the bed.

The bad people were gone. So were all the papers Alison had been studying.

Taneem's first impulse was to wake the girl and tell her the bad news. But she knew that wouldn't do any good. Early on in the trip Alison had discovered that the room's door was locked from the outside, and now that the bad people were gone there was no way for her to chase after them.

She should have awakened Alison as soon as they had come in, she realized glumly. Now, the papers were gone, with no way to get them back.

At least, no way for Alison to do it.

Taneem tilted her long neck to look up. Along the wall just below the ceiling was a rectangular grille covering an opening through which cool, fresh air flowed into the room. Alison had said the opening was part of a whole series of passages called ducts. Once, a couple of days ago, Taneem had jumped up and hooked her front claws in the grille, hanging there looking in until Alison had noticed and told her to get off.

The duct had been dark, but Taneem was positive she could fit in there just fine. If she could find where the men had taken the papers, maybe she could get them back.

And best of all, inside all those ducts no one would see her. She could do this without breaking any of Alison's rules.

The first task was to remove the grille. Fortunately, she had noticed while she was hanging there that time that the plate was held by four connecting devices called bolts, one in each corner.

An easy leap upward, and she had deftly sheared off the heads of two of the bolts with her front claws. On the second leap, she took off the heads of the other two, catching the grille between her jaws as it fell.

She dropped back to the deck, making sure the grille didn't bump against the floor. It was heavier than she'd expected, and now that she had it off she could see the flat panels fastened to its back. Devices to heat or cool the incoming air, she guessed, remembering now how Alison had used a wall control to adjust the temperature of the room that first night.

Leaning the grille against the wall out of the way, she took one final look at the sleeping Alison. Then, backing up a few steps, she leaped upward and slipped neatly through the opening into the duct.

It was a tighter fit than it had looked. But as long as she kept her head low and her legs tucked in close to her sides it would be easy enough to get through. The first turn was a little tricky, too, where her duct ran into another one and she had to go either left or right. For some reason turning right seemed easier, so she picked that direction. She made it around the turn and kept going.

The system was indeed complicated, more so than anything else Taneem had ever encountered. The ducts went all directions, with turns and occasional dips or raises, and with other grilles leading off into other rooms at regular intervals.

For a while she stopped at each opening and peered into the room beyond. But most of the rooms were unoccupied, and after a while she stopped even bothering to look.

A few of the rooms had voices or sounds or smells coming from them. In those cases she stopped before passing, easing one eye around the edge of the grille to make sure no one was looking in her direction before continuing silently past.

But so far there was no sign of Alison's papers.

Taneem continued on. It was getting warmer now, and there were new noises drifting through the grilles. The rooms she passed were larger, too, full of machines and people tending them. Once she had to wait a full minute before a man at a desk covered with lights turned away long enough for her to sneak past.

After a few minutes, the heat faded and the noises quieted. The machinery rooms were replaced again by rooms like hers and Alison's, with even nicer furniture.

And then, finally, from one of the grilles ahead she heard the murmuring of a familiar voice.

She crept forward, listening hard. "—know what all the fuss is about," Colonel Frost was saying. "Near as I can tell there's nothing here worth spit."

"Morgan isn't the sort of person to hold on to useless junk," a different voice answered. It was softer and strangely vague, as if coming from a great distance.

And there was something in the voice that sent a shiver along Taneem's back.

"Maybe they're personal mementos," Frost said. "Even master criminals can get sentimental."

Taneem reached the grille and looked in. The room was reasonably large, with a number of carved wooden desks and work areas, plus several comfortable-looking chairs. Frost was sitting in one of the chairs in front of a desk covered with glowing lights and symbols she couldn't make out. Alison's bag was on the table, and Frost was holding her sheaf of papers in his hand.

There was no one else in the room.

"Virgil Morgan hasn't got a sentimental synapse in his entire body," the other voice said firmly from the room's emptiness. Or rather, from the glowing-light desk, the same way Uncle Virge's voice came out of the walls aboard the *Essenay*. "I'll want to see these papers when you get here."

"Four more days," Frost reminded him. "Unless you want me to transmit you some copies."

"No, I can wait for the originals," the other said. "Right now, I'm more concerned about this girl you've picked up."

"What about her?" Frost asked. "Your stakeouts on Semaline seemed to think she knew what she was doing."

"They'd better be right," the other warned. "We're starting to run low on time here."

"You want me to test her myself?" Frost offered. "By my count, you've got four separate safes aboard this ship."

"Very amusing," the other said, his voice suddenly stiff. "Don't worry, I'll test her myself."

"I thought we were running low on time," Frost reminded him. "Besides, it might be interesting to see what you have stashed away in there."

"Don't push your luck, Colonel," the other warned, his voice turning even darker. "Not with me."

"Warfare *is* luck, Mr. Neverlin," Frost countered in the same tone. "And ours, I think, has just improved a little."

Taneem felt another shiver run up her back. Mr. Neverlin, the man Jack and Draycos had told her about. No wonder his voice had chilled her the way it had.

"We'll see, Colonel," Mr. Neverlin said softly. "Just remember that it's *our* luck, not just yours."

"You just make sure Patri Chookoock understands that," Frost retorted. "I'll see you in four days." He leaned over to the desk and touched a switch.

Some of the desk's lights went out. For a moment Frost just sat there, glaring at the far wall. Then, with a snort, he gathered Alison's papers together from the desktop and put them back in the bag. With the bag dangling from his hand, he stood up and strode from the room.

Taneem lay where she was, trying to decide what to do. She could continue on through the ducts and try to track Frost back to his own room. Maybe she would have an opportunity there to get the bag back.

But Frost had talked about giving Alison more safes to open. If he went straight there, she would have no warning of this new test. No, Taneem had better return at once.

Turning around in the narrow space proved harder than she'd expected. After a few failed attempts she hit on the plan of going to the next duct, turning into it, backing up, then turning again into her original duct. Taking care to move silently, she headed back.

She had gone perhaps half of the distance when she suddenly realized that the scents coming from the grille directly ahead weren't ones she'd smelled before.

She moved up to the grille and peered through. Beyond was some kind of food preparation room, with neat rows of cookware and large and gleaming rectangular boxes. From two of the boxes were wafting aromas similar to those of their morning breakfast bread.

Backing up a step, she turned her neck around to look behind her. The last intersection she could see looked familiar, but it clearly wasn't. Somehow, amid all the ducts and cross-ducts and grilles and risers, she had taken a wrong turn.

She was lost. Completely and thoroughly lost.

CHAPTER 10

With a start, Alison came awake.

For a moment she lay still, trying to figure out what had disturbed her. Beyond her closed eyelids the room was still dark, so it wasn't the false dawn Frost had programmed into the ship's mood lighting system to mark the beginning of ship's day. There were no sounds of movement, either, so Taneem wasn't off on one of her midnight wanderings around the room.

Taneem.

Alison reached into the neck of her nightshirt and touched her skin. A K'da in two-dimensional form didn't have much of a feel about her. But there was some, and that feel was very definitely not there.

She opened her mouth to call, then changed her mind. Hunching her way instead to the nightstand, she switched on the bedside light.

The lamp was set on low, though to darkness-adapted eyes it still was uncomfortably bright. She squinted away from it a moment until her pupils had adjusted, then gave the room a quick scan.

Taneem was nowhere to be seen. Swinging back the blankets, Alison got out of bed. Maybe the K'da was in the bathroom.

And then her eyes fell on the air system grille. Not fastened to the duct like it was supposed to be, but casually propped up against the wall.

Apparently, Taneem had decided to go off exploring.

One of the room's chairs had an especially high back. Dragging it over, Alison leaned it against the wall beneath the opening and climbed up. Carefully, she eased her head into the duct.

Nothing was visible. "Taneem?" she called as loudly as she dared.

There was no answer. Hopping down from the chair, she went to the desk and picked up her pocket flashlight.

And paused. All her tools and disguised burglar equipment were there, right where she'd left them. But the bag she'd taken from Virgil Morgan's Semaline lockbox was gone.

She turned back to the chair, stifling a curse. So that was what had happened. Frost had sent one of his goons in to steal Morgan's papers, and Taneem had woken up and decided to give chase.

The flashlight didn't show much more than Alison's unaided eyes had seen. The duct was still empty, as far as she could see in both directions.

And with that, she had no choice but to conclude that Taneem was on her own. The ducts were too small for Alison to get through, at least not without making a lot of noise. She was actually rather surprised that Taneem had managed it, though she'd noticed that K'da seemed as compressible in some ways as Earth cats.

She would just have to sit here and wait for Taneem to come back. And pray that the K'da wouldn't get spotted along the way.

In the meantime, there was the matter of the detached grille to deal with.

An examination of the corners showed that Taneem had removed the plate by the simple method of slicing through the bolts holding it in place. The tail ends of the bolts were still there, in fact, their now headless ends poking rather forlornly from their holes.

Removing the sheared bolts would be the easy part. Alison's multitool included a small set of needle-nose pliers that would do the job quickly and easily.

The problem was going to be finding something to replace them with. Climbing off the chair again, she turned on all the lights and started a tour of her room. Somewhere, she had to find four bolts—or at least two—that would fit the grille.

Unfortunately, the sheer luxury of the room was working against her. In a freighter or even a normal passenger liner there would be exposed deck or bulkhead plates with plenty of bolts to choose from. Here, all that had been discreetly tucked away beneath softwall and thick carpets.

Fortunately, the bed had been bolted to its pedestal with exposed screws of the right size. Picking four that wouldn't affect the bed's stability, she unfastened them and got them positioned in the corners of the grille.

And with that, there really *was* nothing she could do but wait. Ship's morning was nearly seven hours away, with Frost probably not stirring for another half hour after that.

But Taneem didn't have nearly that long. She had just six hours from whenever she'd left Alison's skin to return.

Because if she didn't, she would go two-dimensional anyway, and vanish into nothingness, and die.

Putting her flashlight up into the duct to give the wayward K'da something to aim for, Alison turned out the rest of the room's lights and got back into bed. She would not, she suspected grimly, get much more sleep tonight.

Don't panic.

Draycos had told her that himself, Taneem remembered, amid the terror and confusion of that last mad rush through the Rho Scorvi forest. Disobeying her instructions to stay in the rear with Jack, she'd run ahead to the front of the pack, mindlessly trying to get as far away from the danger as she could.

She would have gone even farther, probably, all the way to the river and certain death. But Draycos had seen her, and come over to try to soothe her fears. *Don't panic,* he'd said. *Panic freezes the will and darkens the mind and weakens the muscles. Remember this song.*

She frowned suddenly. A song?

Yes. There *had* been a song, now that she thought about it. A simple little song he'd sung to her as they ran. How had that gone?

> *The fear of night, of black and gray,*
> *Must never steal your heart away.*
> *When you must face your fears just say,*
> *"My heart is mine; it will not stray."*
>
> *When danger lifts its evil head*
> *And fills your heart with chills and dread,*
> *Just say, before all strength has fled,*
> *"My heart will go where I have led."*

For fear is not a thing of shame,
It comes upon each person's frame
And lights the heart with strength and flame,
If you its power can but tame.

So hold your heart, stand fast and tall
And answer to your duty's call
And you can proudly say to all,
"I passed the test; I did not fall."

Yes, that was how it had gone. Odd that she'd forgotten about it until now. Maybe it was this fresh panic that had brought it to mind.

Maybe that was what Draycos had intended, in fact. That it would return to comfort her when it was needed.

And to her mild surprise, it had worked. Her scales, which had been starting to turn black as fear pumped extra blood into her muscles, had already faded back to their normal gray. A nice color, the odd thought ran through her mind, though not nearly as noble and distinctive as Draycos's own golden scales.

As noble and distinctive as Draycos himself. She could only bless her good fortune to have him as a friend.

She took a deep breath, exhaling away the last of the fear. *Panic darkens the mind.* Thanks to Alison and Draycos and Jack, she now had a perfectly good mind.

It was time she started using it.

Silently, she backed away from the food preparation area, stretching out with all her senses. Sight was of limited use to her right now, but she hadn't lost her sense of touch or hearing or smell. Somewhere in this root-tangle of ducts were the clues she needed to get her back to Alison.

And suddenly she had it. The low rumble of the ship's engines had been behind her as she left their room. She could sense that same rumble now, much softer than it had been then.

But instead of being in front of her, as it should be, it was coming from her left. Somehow, on her way back, she must have made a wrong turn to her right.

She also hadn't yet passed through the extra-warm area she'd noticed on her way out. She needed to find a left-hand turn, then possibly backtrack a little until she found that spot.

It was still a little scary. But at least now she had a plan. Easing past the food preparation room, she headed toward the next turning spot.

The plan worked. Three turns and four ducts later she was back on track. She knew she was back, because now that she was concentrating she found she could smell Alison's scent on the breeze moving across her snout.

Five minutes later, she turned one final corner to see a small flashlight illuminating the duct and the open space where a grille should be.

Thirty seconds later, she was home.

She had expected Alison to be furious with her, especially after spending so much time being lost. To her relief, her host turned out to be mostly just glad she was back safely.

Though Taneem could tell she was a *little* angry.

"For starters, someone might have seen you," Alison told Taneem as she fastened the grille back in place. "There are also a lot of *very* unpleasant things that could have happened to you in there."

"It seemed safe enough," Taneem said.

"That's because everything was running smoothly," Alison said. "If, say, there'd been a drop in air pressure—for any reason—there are a whole set of hidden sealant doors that would have kicked in across the ducts, cutting the whole system into a bunch of small pieces. You'd have been trapped in one of them until they'd fixed whatever the problem was."

She eyed Taneem over her shoulder. "That's assuming you weren't unlucky enough to have been in the way of one of the doors when they slammed shut," she added. "In that case, you'd probably have been cut in half. You understand?"

"Yes," Taneem said. In truth, she only understood about half of what Alison had just said. But she got the idea. "I won't go off like that again. I'm sorry."

"I just don't want you getting hurt," Alison said in a gentler tone. Finishing with the last bolt, she hopped down from the chair and ran her hand along the side of Taneem's neck. "If for no other reason than that Draycos would kill me if you did."

"He wouldn't do such a thing," Taneem insisted. A shiver ran through her. "Though even if he wished to, he might never have the chance," she added quietly. "What I heard just now—"

"Hold that thought," Alison interrupted. Picking up the chair, she lugged it back to its usual place and then put her tools away. "Let's get back under the blankets," she said, holding out her hand toward Taneem as she headed back to the bed. "Then you can tell me all about it."

Alison listened in silence as Taneem described the conversation she'd overheard between Frost and Neverlin. "Okay," she said when Taneem had finished. "So they're going to test me. No big deal."

"Yet it worries me," Taneem said. "They have had over four months to open the safes, yet they're still searching for someone to do the job. Are you truly better than all the others who do this sort of thing?"

Alison grimaced. "Not even close," she admitted. "Even Jack's better at it than I am."

"What will they do if you fail?"

Alison had been trying hard not to think about that possibility. "I won't fail," she said firmly. "For one thing, my father trained me himself, and he *is* one of the best in the business."

"The business of theft."

"Everyone has to make a living," Alison said. "Besides, none of the people he targets will even miss what he takes." Which was not, of course, strictly true. In fact, even non-strictly it wasn't true. But there was no reason to burden Taneem with any more truth than she was already stuck with. "Besides, I have a secret weapon," she said instead. "You."

"Me?"

"Exactly," Alison said. "You and that K'da trick where you lean off your host's back and look through a wall."

"*Over* a wall," Taneem murmured.

"Whatever," Alison said. "The point is that you'll be able to get a look at the actual lock mechanism, which is something none of the other safecrackers will have had."

"But I know nothing of such mechanisms."

"That won't matter," Alison said, frowning in the darkness. "Well, no, actually you're right. You'll be able to draw me a better picture if you know at least the basics."

"We have only four days," Taneem reminded her.

"No problem," Alison assured her, trying to hide her own misgivings. It had taken her two whole years to learn these skills.

But then, Taneem wasn't going to have to actually open the safe. "First thing tomorrow, we start your lessons," she told the K'da. "In the meantime—" She yawned wide enough to hear her jaw crack. "I'm going back to sleep. Pleasant dreams."

"Yes," Taneem murmured. "And to you."

CHAPTER 11

The days under the desert sun quickly fell into a rhythm. At sunrise Jack would be awakened by Thonsifi, he would shower and eat, and then it was off to the Great Hall for the morning judging session. At noon there would be a break for lunch, at which time the boy sometimes quietly discussed the thornier cases with his hidden K'da companion. After lunch would be the afternoon session, and then Jack would return to his apartment for dinner, a quiet evening of talking and perhaps a little exercise to help him keep in shape.

It was in the evenings that the white stones and light shafts finally came into their own. The reflectors on top of the pillar were obviously angled to catch the rays of the sun as it dropped across the western sky, sending light down the shafts to set the white stone aglow. The effect lingered on for nearly two hours before the sun finally vanished below the horizon, giving a welcome bit of additional light where the canyon floor had already grown dark.

Once the glow faded from the white stones, it was usually bedtime. Sunrise and Jack's Judge-Paladin duties came early.

And when Jack and the rest of the canyon populace were asleep, Draycos set off on his night's patrolling.

He'd been doing this since their second night in the canyon, though he hadn't yet told Jack about it. His original goal, after the first night's shuttle incident, had been to watch for further activity by Foeinatw or other possible informants.

But Foeinatw stayed out of trouble from that point on. Or at least he stayed out of Draycos's sight.

Nor, apparently, did any of the other Golvins stir once they'd retired to their homes at sundown. Not really surprising, given the long climb most of them had to reach those homes in the first place.

And so, with the canyon floor apparently deserted, after the first three nights Draycos switched from watching for trouble to looking for a way out of the canyon.

Only to find that there wasn't one.

Certainly the steep canyon walls were climbable, at least for Draycos himself. The vine mesh that covered the stone pillars didn't grow on most of the cliff faces, but there were enough cracks and claw openings in the stone itself to provide a patient K'da with a path to the surface.

But without his climbing equipment, Jack didn't have a hope of doing the same. Draycos could carry him for short distances, but as he and Jack had already concluded, there was no way he was going to climb three hundred feet of cliff with the boy on his shoulders. There was a line of small caves about fifty feet up along the eastern cliff, but they were too low to make a convenient halfway resting point. Draycos didn't climb up to examine them, but from the pathways of ivy mesh that had been set up between them and the ground, it was clear they were being used for something by the Golvins.

The ends of the canyon were no better. At the upstream end

the river rose sharply into a series of impassable waterfalls, while the downstream end cut through a narrows that would be as tricky to climb as the cliffs themselves.

On the first night of his scouting Draycos spent so much time traveling back and forth across the canyon that he nearly got caught out in the open when the sky began to lighten. The second night, he made sure to watch his time, returning to Jack's apartment well before dawn.

He arrived to find the apartment brighter than when he'd left, the white stones in the wall giving off a soft glow as the reflectors above sent down the light from the larger of Semaline's two moons. Draycos slipped through the doorway fringe, and he was padding his way to the bedroom when the light subtly changed.

He spun around, expecting to see someone behind him in the doorway. But there was nothing there.

And then he saw it. One of the glowing stones in the wall had gone dark.

Someone, or something, was in the shaft.

Silently, he crossed to the opening. Narrowing his eyes to slits to hide most of their own telltale glow, he looked up.

The shaft was pitch-black, with not even the sky visible. The usual airflow, too, was greatly diminished. Something, clearly, was blocking most or all of the opening.

Draycos flicked out his tongue. He hadn't had much experience yet picking out individual Golvin scents, but if whoever was coming down the shaft was someone he'd met, odds were he could identify him.

But to his surprise, it wasn't a Golvin scent he found tingling across his tongue.

It was the scent of a human.

Draycos felt his neck crest stiffen as he tasted the air again and again. But there was no mistake. Somewhere above him was a human.

A human, moreover, whom the Golvins had been careful not to mention to Jack.

From high above him came a faint sound, softer than the scratching he'd heard their first morning in the apartment. A moment later, as the shaft's normal airflow resumed, a single star appeared high overhead.

The blockage had disappeared. So had the human scent.

The question was, where had they gone?

Draycos didn't know. But he was going to find out.

He waited until Jack had showered and was eating breakfast before telling the boy about his night's discoveries. His discoveries, and his plans.

"I don't like it," Jack said when the K'da had finished. "What if they won't let me come back to the apartment at lunchtime?"

"Who would stop you?" Draycos asked reasonably. "The One hasn't been there to observe since the second day. I can't imagine any of the others having the authority to refuse a simple request from their Judge-Paladin."

"Just because you can't imagine it doesn't mean it can't happen," Jack countered. "These alien cultures can take a sudden hard right-angle turn on you, usually when you think everything's going great."

He waved toward the fringed doorway. "Especially since no one's even hinted I'm not the only human in the canyon," he added. "That's grade-one suspicious all by itself."

"Though perhaps that's because you've never asked," Draycos pointed out. "Some cultures also seldom volunteer information."

Jack made a face, but nodded. "I suppose," he said. "Maybe I should ask Thonsifi some specific questions before you go charging off on this search-and-discover thing."

"It would be wiser to have information of our own before we approach the Golvins," Draycos said. "Especially if they intend to lie to you."

"I thought you just said they just didn't volunteer information."

"I said some cultures were like that," Draycos corrected him. "I didn't say this was necessarily one of them."

Jack turned his head away, glowering across the room at the suspect light shaft. "I get stuck in the Great Hall and I might not make it back in time," he warned. "You get stuck up there and *you* may not make it back in time."

"I understand the risks," Draycos said. "But we need to find the truth."

Jack took a deep breath. "I'll be back at lunchtime," he said, standing up abruptly from the table. "You just make sure you're ready."

Ten minutes later, he was gone. Draycos watched from the edge of the door as Thonsifi and the two guards escorted the boy toward the Great Hall and the day's work. Then, trying not to think of the clock ticking down, he got busy.

The light shaft was clear, its shimmery white stone extending unblocked toward the sky. Rolling half onto his back in the opening, Draycos stretched out his neck and studied the inner surface.

While the white facing seemed to be all the same kind of stone, it had been put together out of a large number of separate pieces, much the same way as the bridge the Golvins had built to

Jack's apartment. The technique had left plenty of crevices and gaps and cracks big enough for a K'da's claws to slip into.

Whether the white stone was strong enough to hold a K'da's weight, of course, was a different question. But there was only one way to find out. Sliding his front paws up into the shaft, Draycos found a set of clawholds and started to climb.

Fortunately, the stone was indeed strong enough. Searching out new gaps, thankful that he was doing this in daylight and not in the dead of night, he continued up.

He'd gone about a hundred and fifty feet when he came to a hole in the wall.

A good-sized hole, too, easily big enough for Draycos to get through. Even Jack would have no trouble, though there were some protrusions that might scrape against his shoulders.

But while the hole itself seemed to extend all the way though the stone of the inner wall, the far end was blocked by something that looked like stone but clearly wasn't.

Draycos examined the blockage, first with smell and then with careful touch. The material was soft and slightly flexible, rather like a thick paper or cardboard. It was wedged solidly into the hole, its edges curled inward against the stone.

Extending his tongue, he touched it lightly to one of the folds. It was mainly grain-based material, similar to Golvin bread but with traces of other vegetables mixed in. Some kind of homemade papier-mâché, perhaps. The color was already very close to that of the stone in Jack's apartment, and from the lines he could faintly see through the material he guessed that the other side had been made to blend in even more with the rock.

Someone had laboriously carved a hole in the side of his apartment, which was probably strictly against canyon rules. That same someone was concealing the fact with a homemade camouflage mask.

But who? The human he'd smelled last night?

More importantly, why?

It would be simple for him to push the mask aside. But from the faint sounds coming from the other side of the hole he could tell that the occupant was still at home. Perhaps later, if and when the other left, he would have a chance to check the place out.

And then, to Draycos's dismay, two sets of fingertips appeared from the far side of the camouflage mask, carefully squeezing through around its edges. They got a grip on the mask and began to pull.

There was no time to think. For the past four months, ever since his advance team had been slaughtered, the first rule of Draycos's life had been to keep his existence a deep, dark, black-scaled secret. Only twice in all that time had he broken that rule, and both had been life-or-death situations.

Bracing himself, he let go of the stone.

For perhaps the first half second he fell free and clear, the wind of his passage streaming past him. Then, his back slammed against the wall behind him.

Suddenly he was tumbling out of control, his body caroming off the four sides of the shaft, each bounce sending a fresh jolt of pain through him.

And meanwhile, the bottom of the shaft was rushing up at him at deadly speed. Bracing himself, he slammed all four paws outward.

They caught the sides of the shaft and began skidding down, the friction against the uneven stone sending agonizing fire through them. But at least he was slowing down. Clenching his jaws together, ignoring the pain, he pressed harder.

And a second later, with barely a bump, he landed in an undignified heap on top of the reflector stone.

He pulled his legs inward, pressing his burning paws against the scales of his belly to try to cool them. His whole body was throbbing with agony, every scale, muscle, and joint voicing its protest against his thoughtless treatment of them.

But he was alive. That was all that mattered. That, and—

He looked up. The glow around the shaft made it difficult to see, but he thought he could make out a dark shadowy shape leaning into the air. A face, perhaps, gazing down at him.

Draycos froze. The interfering glow from the shaft worked both ways, he knew. If he stayed perfectly motionless, whoever was up there would have trouble making anything out.

Nevertheless, the shadowy figure held its position for a good long minute. Perhaps he was likewise hoping Draycos hadn't spotted him and was waiting for his visitor to make some revealing movement.

But Draycos had the patience of a poet-warrior of the K'da. The other didn't. A minute later he stirred and disappeared from the shaft.

Still, Draycos didn't move until he sensed the subtle change in airflow that indicated the camouflage mask had been put back in place across the hole. Then, wincing with every movement, he dragged himself out of the shaft and headed for the bathroom.

A cool shower would have felt good against his bruised scales. But though Jack thought the shower system was probably self-contained, they really didn't have any proof of that. The last thing he wanted was for some Golvin monitoring the canyon's water usage to suddenly see activity in a supposedly empty apartment.

He settled instead for dampening a washcloth with water from the puddles on the shower floor and mopping away the worst of the black blood seeping through his new collection of cracked scales.

When he had finished, he went to the galley and forced himself to eat some of the cold meat from the refrigerator. He had no real taste for food right now, not with the pain lancing through him. But his body would need the extra nutrients during the healing process.

When he was finished with his meal he went back to the bedroom, easing himself carefully down onto the stone floor on the far side of the bed. If one of the Golvins happened to wander in, he didn't want to be instantly visible.

Jack had said he would be back at lunch. Hoping fervently the boy would decide he was hungry a little early today, Draycos settled down to wait.

CHAPTER 12

"Today we begin a new group of judgments," Thonsifi said as Jack settled into his Seat of Justice. "These will involve injuries caused by one of the Many against another."

"I see," Jack said, hiding a grimace. Just when he'd gotten used to sorting out land and water disputes, too. "Let's have the first case."

Thonsifi motioned and two Golvins from the usual group of onlookers stepped forward. "Eight-Seven-Two Among Many and Five-Six-One-Naught Among Many," she identified them. "Two and one half seasons ago Eisetw struck Fisionna's right arm and severely injured it. Fisionna claims it was deliberate. Eisetw claims it was an accident."

Jack gestured to Fisionna. "Let me see it."

The Golvin lifted his arm. "Move it around," Jack instructed. "Show me how it was damaged."

"It was harmed here," Fisionna said, pointing to the forearm.

"Move it around," Jack repeated.

The other did so. As far as Jack could tell, it had the full range of motion he'd seen in other Golvins. "It looks all right to me," he said.

"But it *was* injured," Fisionna said. "I deserve compensation for the pain. And my work suffered, as well."

"How long were you unable to work?" Jack asked.

Fisionna gave Thonsifi a sideways glance. "I was never *completely* unable to work," he hedged. "But it was difficult and most painful."

"For how long?"

Another sideways glance. "Over a month."

But not even close to two months, Jack suspected, or the Golvin would have fudged the number that direction. It was a game Jack knew well, having often played it himself against Uncle Virgil. "All right, then, let's try this," he suggested. "Who else witnessed the incident?"

Fisionna was starting to look like he was regretting having given up part of his morning for this. "No one," he admitted.

Jack shifted his attention to Eisetw. "And you claim it was an accident?"

"The shovel was muddy and slipped from my hand," Eisetw said. "And I offered to help with his work while he needed it."

"I am a craftsman," Fisionna said stiffly. "A worker of wooden goods. A mere farmer does not have the skill to truly assist me."

"Nevertheless, he *did* offer," Jack said. "More importantly, there were no witnesses and appears to be no permanent damage. I am therefore dismissing the case and the charges."

Fisionna threw a look at Eisetw, then another at Thonsifi, then looked back at Jack. Jack waited a moment, but if the other had been planning to complain about the verdict he'd apparently thought better of it. "The case is dismissed," Jack said again. "You may both return to your work."

The two Golvins bowed their heads in brief salute, then turned and headed off across the Great Hall. "Next?" Jack asked.

Thonsifi gestured two more Golvins forward, one of them walking with a definite limp. Unlike the last case, this one was apparently fresh. "Six-Seven-Nine Among Many and Two-Naught-One-Two Among Many," she said. "One month ago Twnaontw struck Siseni with a weeding tool and caused serious damage to his right leg."

"He was on my land—" Twnaontw began.

"Silence," Thonsifi snapped.

"You'll get your turn to speak," Jack promised. "Any witnesses this time?"

"There were two," Thonsifi said, motioning two more Golvins forward. "Four-Four-Three Among Many is an upright," she added, pointing to one of them.

Jack waved the latter forward another few steps. "Tell me what happened," he invited.

"Siseni was indeed on Twnaontw's land," Fofoth said. "He was speaking to Twnaontw."

"About what?"

"I was too far away to hear the words," Fofoth said. "But I could hear that both voices were becoming angry."

"Then what happened?"

"Twnaontw ordered Siseni from his land," Fofoth said. "I could tell that from his hand movements. Siseni stepped into the irrigation channel and continued talking. Twnaontw moved to the edge of his land closest to Siseni and said something. Siseni said something else, and that was when Twnaontw struck him."

"Thank you." Jack motioned him back and gestured to Twnaontw. "What was the argument about?"

"He was talking about my sister," the other said, his eyes darkening with the memory. "He was being highly insulting."

Jack looked at Siseni. "Were you?"

Siseni drew himself up to his full height. "I spoke truth," he said in a lofty tone. "One should not be attacked merely for speaking truth."

"I agree," Jack said. On the other hand, he'd seen enough fights among Uncle Virgil's old associates to know that tone and attitude could turn what was technically a truthful statement into something with lots of very sharp edges. "Why didn't you leave Twnaontw's land when he ordered you to?"

"I *did* leave," Siseni countered.

"To stand in his irrigation channel."

"The channel is not his," Siseni said stiffly. "None of this is relevant."

"You will not speak that way—" Thonsifi began.

And broke off, her head tilted to the side, her face turned toward the far end of the Great Hall.

"What is it?" Jack said, following her gaze. Across the way, fifteen or twenty Golvins were converging on the pillar containing Jack's apartment. Converging very rapidly.

And each of the Golvins was carrying a compact bow with a small quiver of arrows slung over his vest.

"What is it?" Jack demanded again, his heart suddenly pounding. Had someone spotted Draycos? "What's going on?"

"I will find out," Thonsifi said. She said something in the Golvin language to one of Jack's guards. He nodded and headed across the Great Hall at a fast trot. "Sefiseni will find out."

She gestured to Siseni and Twnaontw. "In the meantime . . . ?"

"Of course," Jack said, forcing his mind back to the case as he watched the unfolding drama out of the corner of his eye. The running Golvins had reached the base of the pillar now, and five of them handed their weapons to others and began climbing the stone. "We clearly and definitely have a willful act here—"

And then, to his relief, the climbing Golvins passed his apartment without a second glance and kept going.

Whatever was happening, it apparently didn't involve Draycos.

"—a willful act which resulted in clear injury," he went on, bringing his full attention back to the Golvins standing in front of him. "However, I also find there to have been a certain amount of provocation in the incident. I therefore rule that Twnaontw will assist Siseni in his work until Siseni's leg is sufficiently healed for him to resume his duties by himself."

"This is outrageous," Siseni protested. "He has deliberately injured me. I deserve something more lasting than merely a few months of assistance."

"You mean like some of his land?" Jack suggested mildly.

Siseni brought his chin up. "Exactly."

"Which currently borders yours, I presume?"

Siseni glared at Twnaontw. "And the leaves from which fall onto *my* land."

"Sorry, but that's not the case at hand," Jack told him. So at its root the whole thing had been little more than an attempted land grab disguised as a cry for justice. Siseni had probably engineered the whole incident, in fact, attack and all. "Land disputes will be taken up at another time, if you'd care to file a complaint. In the meantime, I rule that for every hour you work your land, Twnaontw will work for a quarter hour."

Siseni's mouth dropped open. "A mere *quarter hour*?" he all but yelped. "That is an insult! I am a level Six of the Many—"

"In that case, perhaps we should make it a sixth of an hour

instead of a quarter hour," Jack cut him off. "Or perhaps even less."

Siseni's facial wrinkles were working overtime as his emotions surged like a spring flood. Jack waited patiently, and after a long moment the wrinkles faded away. "I will accept the judgment," he muttered.

"Good," Jack said. "You may both return to your work."

Drawing himself up, clearly trying to gather together as much dignity as he could, Siseni turned and stalked away, his limp rather ruining the effect. Twnaontw bowed his head briefly to Jack, then followed.

"A question, Jupa Jack," Thonsifi said quietly from beside him. "You say Twnaontw will assist until Siseni's leg is sufficiently healed. How will we know when that will be?"

"Was Siseni at the dinner party a few days ago that honored my arrival?" Jack asked her.

"He was."

"When did he leave?"

Thonsifi's lips worked with thought. "I believe at the thirteenth hour."

Barely an hour after the party had begun, and a full three hours before it finally closed down. "His leg was probably hurting him," Jack said.

"Yes, now that I think, I remember him saying exactly that," Thonsifi confirmed.

"I presume you have other dinners and festivals and such on a regular basis?"

"At least once a month," Thonsifi said. "More often if there are special events."

"Good," Jack said. "Then you keep an eye on him. The first

time he lasts at least three hours into one of these festivals, *that's* when his leg is sufficiently healed."

For a moment Thonsifi looked puzzled. Then, her expression cleared. "I understand, Jupa Jack. You are indeed wise beyond your seasons."

"Let's just say I know how people think," Jack said. "Next case—wait a minute," he interrupted himself. Across the Great Hall, the guard Thonsifi had sent out had reappeared and was coming toward them. "Let's hear what Sefiseni's found out."

The guard reached Thonsifi and conversed with her for a minute in their own language. Whatever was being said, Jack noticed uneasily, it was causing a quiet stir among the rest of the waiting Golvins. "It was the prisoner," Thonsifi said, turning back to Jack. "But it is all right. He has not escaped."

"What prisoner is this?" Jack asked, frowning.

"A loud noise alerted some of the young mothers who were resting in their apartments," Thonsifi continued. "The noise was investigated, and it has been learned that the prisoner was trying to escape."

"What prisoner?" Jack repeated. "Who is he?"

Thonsifi's face darkened. "He is a murderer, Jupa Jack," she said in a low voice. "He caused the deaths of four of the Many."

"When?" Jack asked. Could this prisoner be the human Draycos had smelled the night before? "What exactly happened?"

"It is no concern of yours, Jupa Jack," Thonsifi said. "The decision on his punishment has already been made."

"Maybe I'd like to rehear it," Jack said.

"It is no concern of yours," Thonsifi repeated. "May I bring the next case?"

Jack glowered across at his pillar, and the Golvins still standing guard around its base. In other words, foreigner, back off and butt out?

Fine. Jack would back off. For now.

But the One would hear about this . . . and Jack *would* find out what was going on.

In the meantime, there was work to do. "Very well," he said to Thonsifi. "Bring it on."

With questions about the mysterious prisoner swirling through his mind, he called an early lunch break. To his relief, and as Draycos had predicted, no one raised any objections to his decision to return to his apartment for a few minutes before rejoining the others for the midday meal.

Draycos was nowhere to be seen as he pushed aside the fringe and entered the apartment. "Draycos?" he called softly as he walked into the bedroom.

"Here," the K'da said, lifting his head into view from the far side of the bed.

"Catching a little nap, are we?" Jack asked, circling around the foot of the bed. "Wait'll you hear—*geez!*" He broke off as he came within sight of the black blood spread across the other's scales.

"I had to descend the shaft rather quickly," Draycos explained, getting gingerly to his feet. "It looked worse before."

"I'll just bet it did," Jack said, heading into the bathroom and grabbing one of the washcloths. "Get in here."

A few careful minutes later, he had wiped off most of the caked blood. "At least you look better now," he said as he rinsed out the cloth. "What's the rest of the damage?"

"It's not too bad," Draycos assured him. "A few bruised muscles and strained joints and lightly burned paws. A day or two of rest against your skin and I should be back to full health."

"I hope so," Jack said, laying out the cloth to dry and heading for the galley. "Because something new has just come up."

He related what little he knew about the prisoner as he got the K'da some meat and water. "At least now I know what the noise was that tipped them off," he concluded. "You falling down the shaft."

"Descending the shaft rather quickly," Draycos corrected as he wolfed down the meal. "Though I'm not sure whether to be pleased or regretful for my unplanned part of this incident."

"You don't think this guy's really a murderer?"

"I don't know," Draycos said. "But we've both seen the Golvin ability to shape and color the truth to say what they wish others to hear."

"Like in just about every case I've heard in the past six days," Jack said wryly. "Makes your ears itch after a while."

"In that they are not so different from other peoples," Draycos pointed out. "But it means we must be careful not to come to any conclusions until we know all the facts. I trust you'll be speaking to the One about that?"

"First chance I get," Jack said, clearing away the remains of the K'da's meal. "Meanwhile, I need to get back. Hop aboard, and let's go."

The chance arrived sooner than Jack had expected. When he returned to the Great Hall, he found the One waiting for him.

"Good midday to you, One Among Many," Jack greeted him. "This is a fortunate meeting."

"Perhaps not so fortunate," the One warned. "Thonsifi tells me you have asked for information on our prisoner."

"That's right," Jack said. "I was told he killed four of your people?"

"Yes," the One said, his voice darkening. "Four of the Many, none of whom was threatening him in any way." He eyed Jack. "Nor did they offer any provocation to him," he added pointedly.

So Thonsifi had also given him a rundown on the morning's decisions. "I'd still like to hear all the facts," he told the One. "I may decide that a rehearing of his case would be—"

"There will be no rehearing," the One snapped.

Jack took an involuntary step backward. The sudden blaze of fury was something he hadn't seen in these people before. "I understand your anger," he said, keeping his voice calm. "But there may be circumstances—"

"The circumstances are that he killed four of the Many, that he was found responsible for those deaths, and that he will remain a prisoner until his death."

"I understand," Jack said. "But as Judge-Paladin it's both my right and my duty to investigate these matters."

"And you have done so," the One said. "Your investigation is now ended."

For a long moment he and Jack gazed at each other. "Very well," Jack said. "With your permission, I have yet to eat my midday meal."

"Then eat and be filled," the One said. His surge of anger was gone, his voice that of the calm leader again. "More arguments and claims await you this afternoon." With a nod, he brushed past Jack and headed for the exit.

And with that, apparently, the conversation was over.

But that didn't mean the subject was closed, Jack promised himself. Not by a long shot.

CHAPTER 13

The click of the stateroom door being unlocked was their only warning. "Quick," Alison muttered, thrusting out her hand to Taneem.

Fortunately, they'd had a lot of practice in this lately. The K'da was up her sleeve and out of sight before the door even started to open. Alison even had time to flip her notebook back from the lock mechanism diagrams she'd been drawing to the pages with a far more innocent journal entry.

"Morning," Frost said as he strode into the stateroom. Dumbarton and the Brummga Mrishpaw were trailing behind him. "Enjoying your vacation?"

"Oh, it's great," Alison said. "Especially the sun deck. Are we going to be able to get another volleyball game going by the pool again before the formal dinner?"

"Cute," Frost growled. "I've got a job for you."

"If it involves scrubbing decks, the answer is no," Alison warned.

Frost's lip twitched. "It involves opening safes."

Alison raised her eyebrows. Taneem had told her Frost had suggested to Neverlin that she practice on the ship's safes. But it had sounded like Neverlin had scotched the idea.

Apparently, Frost had decided differently. This could be highly interesting. "What kind of safes are we talking about?" Alison asked.

"Let's find out," Frost invited, gesturing toward the door. "Grab your stuff."

The safe was a big walk-in vault with a keypad lock, unimaginatively hidden behind a panel at the back of a closet in one of the staterooms. It was, fortunately, a brand Alison had often worked with.

Even more fortunately, the closet's cramped space meant she could work without Frost or anyone else staring over her shoulder. That meant she could make a big show of the operation, dragging out the procedure and making the whole thing look more complicated than it really was.

She worked her sensors first, spending a couple of hours taking all the readings she could think of. After that, she took a few duplicates, just for show. Then, sitting down comfortably with her back pressed against the vault door, she sifted through the data while Taneem did her K'da over-the-wall magic.

She sat there until Taneem signaled by lightly touching her back with her claws. Then, declaring it to be lunchtime, she asked Frost to have some food delivered to her and returned to her stateroom.

There, after making sure no one had planted any new bugs in her absence, she and Taneem compared notes.

It was just as well that they had. Alison's own inspection had given her all she needed to get the vault open. But Neverlin had added an extra bonus to the vault that her sensors hadn't picked up.

There was a self-destruct mechanism on the inside of the

vault door, designed to incinerate everything inside the vault if not properly disabled. It probably wouldn't be very healthy for anyone standing just outside at that moment, either.

Fortunately, Taneem's scouting had also shown the key to disarming it. The bomb was wired through the keypad, which meant that some special code had to be entered before the actual unlocking code was used.

At that point, the rest was fairly easy. Alison had already assembled the MixStar deciphering computer packed into her belt and the soles of her shoes and was running her data through it. All she had to do to fix the self-destruct problem was make sure to wait until the computer had extracted two separate codes instead of stopping with just one.

She had the two codes and was halfway through her meal when Frost returned. "You ready?" he growled.

"These things take time, Colonel," Alison said. She took another look at his eyes—"Fortunately, I've had all the time I need," she added hastily.

"Good," Frost said coldly. "Let's go."

Alison braced herself. "I want something in return."

Frost stopped dead in his tracks. Slowly, deliberately, he turned back around. "What did you say?" he asked quietly.

"I want Morgan's papers back," Alison said, fighting to keep her voice steady. "I'll trade them for getting the vault open."

His forehead wrinkled. "Why? What are they worth to you?"

"I don't know yet," Alison said. "That's why I want them back."

For a moment Frost gazed hard at her. Then, to her relief, he gave a casual shrug. "Fine," he said. "Of course, my associate will probably want to see them when we get to Brum-a-dum."

"Then he can ask me nicely," Alison said, trying to imagine Arthur Neverlin asking nicely for anything. "Is it a deal?"

"Sure," Frost said. "You can have the papers as soon as you get the second safe open."

Alison froze halfway out of her chair. "The *second* safe?"

"Think of it as practice," he said blandly.

Alison grimaced. "Just exactly how many of these safes *are* there?"

"Four," Frost said. "But I don't know if I'll want you to open all of them. We'll see." He gestured. "You coming?"

Alison sighed. "Well, the volleyball game was probably off anyway," she said. "Sure, let's go."

The rest of the operation turned out to be something of an anticlimax. With all the careful prep work behind her, plus Taneem's scouting, all Alison had to do was punch in the two codes the computer had given her, twist the handle, and pull open the vault door.

"There you are," Alison said.

"Good work," Frost said, taking her arm and pulling her out of the closet and away from the vault. "You can take the rest of the day off."

"Thanks," Alison said dryly. As if she had any other pressing matters on her hands anyway. "Unless you'd like me to start on the other safe?"

"Tomorrow," Frost said, stepping into the vault. "Dumbarton, take her back to her room."

Neither Frost nor any of his men bothered her any more that day. Alison and Taneem spent the time working on Taneem's safecracking lessons, breaking only for dinner and a hot bath before bedtime.

And now that Taneem had actually seen the inside of a safe, she seemed to catch onto the theory even more quickly than she had before. In two days, when they reached Brum-a-dum, she should be ready.

At least, Alison hoped so.

The next day went pretty much the same as the previous one. After breakfast Frost collected Alison from her stateroom, and with Dumbarton and Mrishpaw in tow took her to another part of the ship. Her second project turned out to be a small safe inside a desk in a very luxurious office.

Like the vault, the safe was keypad-operated. Also like the vault, it again took her the entire morning to run her tests and scans. The safe's smaller size meant that Taneem didn't have as much room for her over-the-wall trick, but she was able to see enough to confirm that this time there were no booby traps. After lunch and the computer analysis, Alison opened the safe, and was dismissed again back to her room.

But unlike the previous day, this success came with an extra bonus. Frost himself delivered Alison her dinner tray . . . and with the food he brought her the shoulder bag full of papers she'd taken from Virgil Morgan's lockbox.

Privately, Alison had expected him to go back on his promise once he'd gotten his half of the deal. Perhaps he'd found enough of interest in the two safes that he felt Alison had earned herself a small reward.

Now she just had to make sure her work paid off.

The bag itself was the obvious target. But because it was so obvious, it would be the first thing Neverlin's people would check.

Fortunately for Alison, she had something a little more subtle.

It took her nearly half an hour, working slowly and carefully, to slide one of the needles from her sewing repair kit into concealment inside the edge of one of the larger pictures from Morgan's collection. The transmitter's range was fairly limited, but as long as she was within a few hundred yards she should be able to pick up the signal just fine.

Back on Rho Scorvi, Frost had bragged about having exotic technology that wasn't even on the market yet. Apparently, it hadn't occurred to him that two could play that game.

Just after noon the next day, ship's time, they reached Brum-a-dum.

The trip in was like the trip out from Semaline, only in reverse. The *Advocatus Diaboli*'s pilot found a nice, out-of-the-way orbit to park the ship in, someplace far outside the normal traffic patterns. Then Frost, Alison, and the rest of the inbound group climbed aboard a shuttle and headed in.

Once in atmosphere, they were routed to a regional-sized entrypoint that, if Alison was deciphering the Brummgan script correctly, was named Ponocce Spaceport.

They breezed through customs without even a token inspection. Outside, a half dozen cars were waiting, each equipped with a Brummgan driver and armed guard wearing close-fitting helmets and armored tunics done up in red, black, and white.

Frost led Alison to the first car, the rest of his mercenaries sorted themselves out into the others, and they were off.

"Can't say I'm very impressed by this friend of yours," Alison commented as the driver wove them in and out of the traffic. "Doesn't he even have a landing pad big enough for that shuttle?"

"He's got room for thirty of them," Frost assured her. "But there was a little problem with the defense transponder system a while back."

Alison nodded to herself. Jack, undoubtedly, and his little sneak escape a couple of months ago. "Not a big problem, I hope."

"Not really," Frost said. "But the simplest solution was to just shut down the transponders. That way, if anything tries to go over the wall—well, let's just say nothing will make it more than *halfway* over the wall."

Ahead and off to the right, between the other buildings, Alison could see glimpses of something tall and white. "Let me guess," she said. "Laser antiaircraft defenses?"

"And flame-jet antipersonnel ones," Frost said. "Don't worry your little head. We've got things covered."

Alison hid a grimace. So when it was time for her and Taneem to make their break, they were apparently not going to be going over the wall.

The bits of white Alison had seen turned out to be the outer boundary of their destination estate. But instead of being just a simple vertical slab, the wall was shaped like a breaking ocean wave, with the bottom section angling inward while the top section angled back out. The very tip of the top part curved over and downward, in fact, curving nearly back up beneath itself, again exactly like a breaking wave. The whole thing was about thirty feet high and appeared to be made of some sort of hardened ceramic.

Which meant she and Taneem wouldn't be going *through* the wall, either. They were, she noted uncomfortably, starting to run low on exit options.

The estate's main entrance gate was as impressive as the wall itself, and just as intimidating. It was made of more white ceramic, with gold-colored metal straps that were probably mostly there to impress visitors. Eight armed Brummgas were waiting in front of it, all of them dressed in the same red/black/white uniforms.

The car stopped by the guards and each passenger showed an ID card. One of the guards looked ominously at Alison after her failure to do likewise, but he nevertheless waved them through.

The gate opened and they continued on into the sort of elaborately designed and beautifully sculpted landscape Alison had expected. Half turning, she saw that each of the other cars in their convoy was undergoing the same ID check.

She also saw that the breaking-wave shape of the wall was duplicated on its inner side. An overall X shape, then, with an overhang on both sides to discourage trespassers and escapees alike.

Or maybe she was being unfair. Maybe the Brummgas just liked the look of a frozen white ocean on their property. Offhand, she wouldn't bet on it.

The house was also impressive, in a stone-faced mausoleum sort of way. The driver stopped at the front door, and with another group of Brummgan guards in attendance Alison and Frost went inside.

Standing in the middle of a huge foyer, glowering at their approach, was Arthur Neverlin.

Alison swallowed hard as they walked toward him, Frost's hand pressing against the small of her back to make sure she didn't dawdle. "So here she is," Neverlin said as they came up to him. His eyes flicked briefly to the bag over her shoulder, then back to her face. "The little girl who's going to solve all our problems."

"Kayna, this is my associate, Mr. Arthur," Frost introduced her. "Mr. Arthur, Alison Kayna."

"Really," Neverlin said. "How do you know?"

Frost's forehead wrinkled slightly. "What do you mean?"

"I mean this little girl apparently doesn't exist," Neverlin said coldly. "I've done a complete check of all official Internos systems. There's no record of her anywhere."

"And this surprises you?" Alison countered calmly. "I wouldn't be much use if anyone could just punch in my name and pull up my life story."

"Don't be a fool," Neverlin growled. "You think your *name* means anything? I also put in your age range, your full description, and those two scars on your left shoulder and lower rib cage."

Alison looked sharply at Frost in sudden understanding. "That's right," he confirmed. "You didn't think Dumbarton and Mrishpaw were just looking for cheap thrills when they made you take your clothes off, did you?"

"So who *are* you?" Neverlin asked.

"I'm Alison Kayna," Alison said, looking back at him. "As for the records, maybe you just didn't look hard enough."

"Or not in the right places," Frost said. "Let me guess. You were born and raised on an non-Internos world?"

Alison shrugged. "Could be."

"Perhaps Colonel Frost didn't make the situation clear, Kayna," Neverlin said, his voice quiet and very snakelike. "We aren't playing games here. *You* play games, and you don't live to see the sun go down. Do you understand?"

"Very well," Alison assured him, her mouth suddenly dry. "I also understand that you need my services." With a supreme effort, she forced herself to look Neverlin straight in the eye. "And if it comes to that, I doubt Mr. Arthur is *your* real name, either."

For a long minute no one spoke. Alison could feel Taneem sliding restlessly across her skin, and quietly put a hand against her ribs. Under the reassuring touch, the K'da settled back down. "You take chances, girl," Neverlin said at last, his voice dark. "Far too many of them."

"I wouldn't be in this business if I didn't like taking chances," Alison said. "So where's this safe you want me to open?"

Neverlin looked at Frost, a small smile twitching at the corners of his mouth. "You certainly picked yourself a wildcat here, Colonel."

"I think she can pull it off, sir," Frost said.

"We'll find out." Neverlin turned back to Alison. "*After* she has a proper field test."

Briefly, Alison wondered what would happen if she mentioned that Frost had already given her such a test. Two of them, in fact.

But she resisted the temptation. At the moment, Frost was at least a little on her side. The satisfaction of watching Neverlin's reaction to the news would hardly be worth making Frost want her dead.

"But that can come later," Neverlin continued. "First, we're going to the medical suite."

"What for?" Alison asked, tensing up again.

"What do you think?" Neverlin countered. "We're going to get your fingerprints, your retina pattern, your iris matrix, and your DNA profile." He raised his eyebrows. "As you said, maybe we just didn't look hard enough."

"Whatever makes you happy," Alison said, feeling her muscles relax a little. None of those tests would require her to undress far enough to reveal Taneem's presence. "In fact, since you're so keen on this, how about we make it a race?"

"What do you mean?" Neverlin asked.

"Your identity check against my safecracking skills," Alison said blandly. "We'll see which of us gets to the mother lode first."

Neverlin smiled thinly. "You're playing against my weakness, Kayna."

"You like long-shot bets?"

"Very much," Neverlin said. "And I always win them."

Except for that one long shot of trying to blackmail Jack Morgan into helping him murder Cornelius Braxton, Alison knew. But this was hardly the time to bring that up. "Then we're on?"

"Absolutely," Neverlin said. "You win, I pay you an extra twenty thousand for the job. I win, you open the safe for nothing."

Alison cocked her head as if thinking about it. "That seems fair," she said.

It wasn't, of course. With Neverlin's control over when Alison would be allowed to start working the safe—only after *he* decided she was ready—he could easily manipulate the timing of the contest to guarantee he would win. As usual, Neverlin's supposed long-shot bets included a stacking of the deck.

Still, a records search would help keep them busy. Maybe busy enough that neither would remember where he'd seen Alison's face before.

"Excellent," Neverlin said, beckoning to the group of Brummgas standing behind her. "As soon as the medical formalities are out of the way, Colonel Frost's men will get you settled in your room. Oh, and I'll take that." He pointed to the shoulder bag.

Silently, Frost reached over and pulled the strap off Alison's shoulder, warning her with his eyes to stay quiet. He crossed to Neverlin and handed him the bag. "And then tomorrow," Neverlin went on, fingering the bag thoughtfully, "you can start proving you're as good as you say you are."

He gave her a smile that didn't reach all the way to his eyes. "And," he added, "you'd better be right."

CHAPTER 14

The doctor—a Compfrin, Alison noted with interest, not a Brummga—was quick, efficient, and quiet. Fifteen minutes after arriving, Alison was on her way out again. A tall, wiry Wistawk wearing green and purple and a red cross-chest sash led the way, with Dumbarton and Mrishpaw plodding along beside her.

The room Neverlin had assigned her to was in the first basement level down, with an entrance off the main kitchen area. The slaves working in the kitchen seemed to not even notice them, but Alison caught enough sideways glances to know that everyone was indeed aware of the strangers passing through their midst.

After the luxury of the shipboard stateroom, her new room was a severe letdown. It was small and cramped, equipped with a bed, a rough wooden dresser, a chair and small table, an intercom that doubled as a clock, a single overhead light, and a small sink. "No shower?" she asked, looking around.

"The bathroom is at the end of the hall," the Wistawk said. "It is shared by all the slaves on this floor."

Alison looked at Dumbarton. *"Slaves?"* she demanded.

Dumbarton shrugged. "Had a problem a while back," he said. "The Patri Chookoock ordered that all visitors stay down here where it's more secure."

Jack, again. How many times, Alison wondered sourly, was she going to trip over him while she was here? "That mean all the rest of you are down here, too?"

Dumbarton gave her an indulgent smile. "We're not visitors, kiddo. We're allies."

"But you will not have to eat with the other slaves," the Wistawk offered helpfully. "Your meal will be served here in two hours."

"And I'm sure it'll be delicious," Dumbarton said as he and Mrishpaw left the room. "Enjoy."

The Wistawk left as well, closing the door behind him. Taneem stirred against Alison's skin, but Alison laid a warning hand on her shoulder. Once again, it was time to check for microphones.

To her mild surprise, there weren't any. Perhaps no one thought the slaves were worth the bother of monitoring.

Unfortunately, they were probably right. A lifetime of slavery usually left the victims in grave-sized mental and emotional ruts, with all the spark and fire and hope brutally crushed out of them.

The Chookoock family was especially good at that. Two months ago, when Jack had gone to the slaves and offered them freedom, only twenty-six had taken him up on it.

"Okay, it's safe," Alison told Taneem when she was finished. Sitting down on the bed, she held out her arm.

The K'da missed the cue, coming out instead from the back of Alison's collar. "I was so afraid in the hospital," she said, landing on the floor and turning her head back and forth as she looked around. "I thought they would discover me for certain. I thought we would have to fight."

"Not this time," Alison soothed her.

A shiver shook Taneem's body. "I wish we were not here."

"Pretty much everyone in a slave colony feels that way," Alison said, opening her makeup kit. "Let's see what kind of reception we can get down here."

She got out her mascara tube and unscrewed the end. A quick adjustment with her fingernail to shift its frequency and it was ready. "What are you doing?" Taneem asked.

"Usually this earphone works with the rest of the tube for listening to the inner workings of safes," Alison explained, inserting the end into her ear. "I've changed its frequency to pick up the bug I planted in the papers from Virgil Morgan's lockbox. Quiet now—let me listen."

But it was quickly clear that there was nothing to listen to. She could hear faint sounds, but they were distant and muffled. "Hasn't even opened the bag yet, I guess," Alison said, pulling the earpiece back out. "Probably busy debriefing Frost about the trip in."

"I wonder how much truth Frost will tell him."

"Not nearly as much truth as there actually is," Alison said, hiding a smile. Alison's grasp of English was remarkably good, especially given how little time she'd had to work on it. But some of her phrases and sentence constructions were still rather entertaining. "For starters, you can bet money that he won't say word one about me opening those safes."

"It's so very strange," Taneem murmured, her tail tip curving in an arch. "They are friends, like you and Jack. Yet they keep secrets from each other."

Alison felt a twinge of conscience. "That's because Frost and Neverlin aren't really friends," she said. "They're working together, but only because neither can get what he wants alone. But I doubt either trusts the other any farther than he can throw him."

"What do you mean?" Taneem asked, her tail curving into an even tighter arch. "They *throw* each other?"

"No, that's just a figure of speech," Alison said. "A sort of word picture. The point is that they don't trust each other, not like Jack and Draycos do."

"Or like you and Jack?"

"And that probably goes double for the Patri Chookoock or whoever's calling the shots for the Brummgas," Alison said, passing over the K'da's question. "Probably why we're here, in fact. After Draycos ran roughshod over the Patri's people, I'm guessing he insisted the safes be put under his control to make sure Neverlin and Frost didn't just throw him to the wolves. That's another word picture," she added.

"I understand," Taneem said, her glowing silver eyes steady on Alison's face. "You do not answer my question."

Alison sighed to herself. Taneem was definitely the persistent type. "What question?"

"The question about trust," Taneem said. "You *do* trust Jack, don't you?"

Alison thought about it. With the question going only that direction, she could actually give an honest answer. "Yes, I think I can trust him," she said. "Well, mostly trust him, anyway. We don't know each other well enough yet to *really* trust each other."

"And he trusts you, as well?"

"You'd have to ask him about that," Alison said evasively. Actually, she was pretty sure Jack *didn't* trust her. Not that she could blame him. "My point is that a group like Neverlin, Frost, and the Chookoocks is inherently unstable," she went on. "That means a fairly small push can make it fall apart."

"Because they don't trust each other?"

"And because they're in it purely for the profit," Alison explained. "The minute any of them sees an advantage to himself in betraying the others, he'll do it. Part of our job here is to play along and watch for a chance to give it that push."

Taneem seemed to ponder that. "Is that why you agreed to open the vault and safe aboard the ship?"

"Partially," Alison said. "Besides proving to Frost that I could do it."

Taneem seemed to straighten up. "I cannot help very much with your work," she said. Her voice was trembling a little, but there was a firmness of will beneath it. "But if the time for battle should come, I will be there for you. You may trust me, just as you would trust Jack and Draycos."

Something stirred deep within Alison. It had been a long time since she'd had someone close at hand who she could genuinely trust. So very long a time. "I know," she managed. "Thank you." She took a deep breath. "But first things first. Dinner, sleep, and then I need to prove to Neverlin that I can open his safes."

"Yes," Taneem said, her voice thoughtful. "I wonder why the K'da safes are so difficult."

"No idea," Alison said soberly. "I wish I'd asked Draycos about it when I'd had the chance. It never even occurred to me."

"You will figure it out," Taneem assured her. "I have faith in you."

"Thanks," Alison said. "In the meantime, I'm going to go see if this bathroom has a tub and some hot water. Will you be okay here alone for a few minutes?"

"There is room to hide beneath the bed if necessary," Taneem said. "Go and enjoy."

The bathroom had a tub, plenty of hot water, and—best of all—a little privacy. Alison enjoyed the bath as long as she dared, then dried and dressed. She returned to her room, to find that in her absence her dinner had been delivered.

And that the waiter was still there.

"You are the human Alison Kayna?" he asked politely. He was a Wistawk, tall and spindly and rather young.

"I am," Alison said, glancing around. There was no sign of Taneem. She must have made it under the bed in time. "Thank you for the dinner."

She sat down at the table and picked up the fork. The tray was military style, molded metal with five compartments for food. All five were filled with the proper nutritional range of meat, vegetables, bread, fruit, and even what appeared to be a sort of pudding.

The room itself might be insultingly simple, but at least Neverlin wasn't going to make her eat slaves' food, too.

She looked up, to find the Wistawk still standing there. "Was there something else?" she asked.

He hesitated. "My name is Shoofteelee," he said. "May I ask a question?"

"I suppose," Alison said cautiously.

Shoofteelee seemed to brace himself. "Are you a friend of Jack Morgan, who came to us as Jack McCoy?"

Alison stared at him. Was this some kind of trap? "What makes you think that?" she countered.

"Because they dislike and distrust you, as they did him," Shoofteelee said, the words coming out in a rush now that he'd committed himself to this line of conversation. "Yet they treat you specially, as they did him. You have the same air of nobility about you as he had." He looked furtively around the room and lowered his voice to a whisper. "As also did the dragon."

Out of the corner of her eye, Alison saw something gray twitch under the bed. "I'd be careful about trying to see nobility in people's faces," she warned. "It usually doesn't work."

"Then—?" He broke off, frowning. "What then are you saying?"

Alison hesitated. Still, if it was a trap, she was already in it. "I'm saying don't assume I'm a noble person," she said. "But as it happens, I *do* know Jack Morgan. *And* the dragon."

Shoofteelee's mouth curled open in a relieved smile. "I knew it," he breathed.

"The question is, what do *you* know about them?" Alison asked.

"I was here when—"

"And you might as well sit down," Alison said, waving him toward the bed.

"Thank you," Shoofteelee said, a little uncertainly. Stepping to the bed, he folded his lanky body onto it. "Thank you."

"You were telling me how you know Jack," Alison prompted.

"I was here when Jack Morgan came and offered us freedom," Shoofteelee said. "He and the black dragon defeated many of the Brummgas and led nearly thirty slaves to freedom, including six from the household itself."

"The bla—?" Alison caught herself just in time. Of course the story would be about a black dragon. K'da in combat mode turned black, no matter what their usual color. "But you weren't invited?"

Shoofteelee's eyes closed, waves of subtle color rippling

across his skin reflecting his deep emotional pain. "I was afraid," he said softly. "And I did not believe."

"Not really your fault," Alison said, feeling an obscure desire to soothe the other's ache. "If I hadn't seen some of the things the dragon can do, I wouldn't have believed him either."

"You seek to quiet my shame," Shoofteelee said. "But the shame is far distant to the agony of having been left behind."

"I understand," Alison said gently. "I'm sorry."

"Do not be sorry," the Wistawk said, the emotion clearing abruptly from his face. "For with you I have now a second chance. And this time I will *not* let it pass by."

"Whoa," Alison said, holding out her hands palm outward toward him. "Slow down a minute. I'm sorry, but that's not why I'm here."

Shoofteelee's face fell. "But we have waited for this chance. For Jack and the dragon." He lowered his eyes. "And we have hoped. We have hoped so much."

"I'm sorry," Alison said again. Under the edge of the bed she could see Taneem shifting restlessly, and it didn't take a genius to tell she was starting to feel all noble and guilty.

Shoofteelee took a deep breath and stood up. "But I keep you from your meal," he said, heading for the door. "My apologies."

"That's all right," Alison assured him, standing up as well. "Did the humans say anything else of interest?"

Shoofteelee eyed her a moment, perhaps wondering if she was even worth talking to anymore. "The older one—Mr. Arthur—told the other that he had heard that a Judge-Paladin had arrived at a place called Semaline. He seemed concerned about it."

"What did the other one say?" Alison asked.

Shoofteelee shrugged. "He seemed unconcerned," he said. "Perhaps even amused."

Alison nodded. Which implied whatever was going on with Semaline wasn't connected to their plot against the K'da and Shontine. Something from Neverlin's personal past, then?

She hoped so. At this stage, anything that distracted Neverlin worked to her advantage.

On the other hand, Semaline was where Jack and Draycos had disappeared. Having Neverlin's attention dragged that direction might not be such a good thing after all. "Thank you," she said. "I'd appreciate it if you'd let me know anything else you hear from them."

An ember of hope seemed to touch Shoofteelee's eyes. "I will do so, Alison Kayna, friend of Jack Morgan and the dragon," he said. "Farewell."

"Go in peace and merriment," Alison said.

The other frowned. "What?"

"I said go in peace and merriment," Alison said, suddenly feeling foolish. "It's a traditional Wistawk farewell."

There was another flicker of emotional coloring, a softer one this time. "I would not know of such things," he said. Turning again, he left the room.

With a sigh, Alison sat down again. "You hungry?" she asked Taneem.

One eye emerged from beneath the bed. "Not right now," she said, and then disappeared again.

Gone off for a private sulk, apparently. Shaking her head in mild disgust, Alison sliced off a corner of the meat with the edge of her fork. Sulking, because Alison wasn't ready to jump on a white horse and charge through an army of Brummgas she couldn't stop, toward a gate she couldn't open, for a bunch of slaves who probably wouldn't follow her anyway.

Fine. Let her sulk. Sooner or later, like it or not, she'd have no choice but admit there wasn't a thing the two of them could do for these people.

Until then, Alison would just enjoy the silence.

Carefully dividing the food in each of the tray's sections in half for when the K'da *did* decide she was hungry, Alison settled down to her meal.

CHAPTER 15

Draycos had hoped to be recovered from his injuries a day or two after falling down the shaft. But the damage was worse than he'd realized. It wasn't until the evening of the third day that he finally felt ready for a proper night's work.

"Remember, you're just supposed to find him," Jack warned as the K'da ran carefully through a final set of stretching exercises. "No questions, no comments, no interrogation."

"I understand," Draycos said.

Jack raised his eyebrows. "And no *singing,*" he added.

Draycos tilted his head questioningly to the side. "Are you still annoyed that I sang to Noy when he was ill?"

"No, not since it all worked out okay," Jack said. "I just don't want you making a habit of it."

"Not a single stanza or chorus," Draycos promised. "I'll be back as soon as I can."

Jack stepped to the door and eased the fringe aside a little. "Looks clear," he murmured. "Be careful."

A moment later Draycos was on the bridge, lying flat against the cold stone as he looked around. The Golvin community had indeed settled down for the night. Slipping down the side of the bridge, wedging the tips of his claws into the cracks, he made it to the ground.

At first glance, the task ahead of him seemed immense. There were thirty-eight stone pillars in the canyon, the tallest of them three hundred feet tall. With the apartment doors indicating approximately eight feet per level, and most levels with two separate apartments, there were nearly three thousand homes here. Theoretically, the prisoner could be in any one of them.

But Draycos was betting he wasn't. After all, they'd tried putting him in one of the apartments, halfway from ground to sky, with no way out. He'd responded by digging a hole into a ready-made tunnel. Draycos didn't know if all the pillars were built with light shafts to the lower apartments, but it didn't seem likely that the Golvins would risk being tricked the same way twice.

He also doubted they would have taken him outside the canyon. The westward distance across the desert, seventy miles, was daunting, but it might be possible for a determined man to cross, especially if there were oases along the way.

Which left exactly one other option.

The last time he'd scouted the eastern part of the canyon, three nights ago, the area had been deserted. Now, in contrast, there were two pairs of Golvins standing guard beneath the line of cliffside caves. Each of the guards carried a quiver of arrows and one of the compact bows Jack had told him about.

Draycos spent a few minutes studying the situation from behind a stand of tall plants. The two pairs of guards were about fifty feet apart, their positions bracketing one particular cave. They were standing amid the crumbled rock in a fifty-foot-wide corridor running between the line of fruit trees and the cliff face itself, with no cover anywhere for a stealthy approach from any direction.

Mentally, Draycos gave a warrior's nod to their setup. Even if the prisoner managed to get out of his cave, he wasn't going to get any farther than the canyon floor.

Which didn't mean, however, that someone else couldn't get in.

He had to travel about a quarter mile upstream before he found a good spot to climb the cliff. Keeping a wary eye on the guards below, he made his way up and then crossed over to the line of caves.

He was still a hundred feet short of his target cave when he picked up the prisoner's scent. Directly over the opening he paused for a moment, tasting the air and listening. He could hear no movement or other signs of wakefulness from inside. With one final look at the guards below, he slipped inside.

The cave was dark except for the moonlight slicing across the entrance. But there was enough light for Draycos to see the signs of the Golvins' hasty conversion of a storage cave into a prison. Several large bags were still stacked against the back wall, and there were a few scatterings of loose grain here and there against the side walls. In the center of the cave were a cot, a single chair, and a compact toilet/sink setup similar to the one in Jack's apartment. There was no galley, no shower, no battery-powered lights.

Lying on his side on the cot, the blankets wrapped tightly around him and pulled up to his ear against the night chill, was the prisoner.

Silently, Draycos padded across the cave for a closer look. The man, as near as he could tell from half a face and an angled lump beneath the blankets, was around thirty years old, though not much taller or heavier than Jack. He had long, tangled dark hair and a beard to match. Draycos leaned over him for a closer look.

And abruptly the man's breathing changed and his eyes snapped open.

Instantly Draycos dropped out of sight to the side of the bed. "Be quiet and don't move," he ordered in a low voice.

"Who is it?" the man asked tentatively, the cot shaking as he rolled over onto his back.

Draycos crouched lower. "I said don't move," he said again. "I merely wish to talk to you."

The movement stopped. "Who are you?" the man asked, a new wariness in his voice. "Is this some kind of stupid trick?"

"It's no trick," Draycos said. "I'm with the Judge-Paladin who arrived in the canyon nine days ago."

"Yeah, I saw him," the prisoner said. "What do you mean, you're with him?"

"I'm his associate," Draycos said. "He wishes some information about you."

"Then let's do it right," the other said. "I hereby formally request a hearing before Judge-Paladin—what's his name, anyway?"

"Jack McCoy," Draycos said, giving a name Jack had used before.

"I formally request a hearing before Judge-Paladin McCoy," the man said.

"I accept your request," Draycos said. "Unfortunately, it may not do any good. Judge-Paladin McCoy has already asked to see you and been refused."

The other grunted. "Not surprised," he said. "So what, he sent you instead to take my statement?"

"That's essentially correct," Draycos said. "Let's begin with your name."

"And the guards down there just decided to let you in?" the prisoner growled. "Come on—what kind of a fool do you think I am?"

"This is not an attempt to trick you," Draycos said, annoyance starting to stir within him. He'd come all this way and risked his life for *this?* "The Judge-Paladin was intrigued by the One's refusal and wished to investigate." His lashing tail slapped softly against one leg of the cot. "But if you don't wish to cooperate, I can leave."

"No—wait," the prisoner said. His own frustration had disappeared, replaced by puzzlement. "You're *not* Golvin, are you?"

"No, I'm not," Draycos confirmed.

"Because their voices go all funny when they get mad," the other continued, as if talking to himself. "But you're not human, either. Are you a Brummga?"

"I came here to ask questions, not answer them," Draycos said. "What's your name?"

"Well, the Golvins call me Naught-Naught-Naught Among Many," the prisoner said, a little bitterly. "But hey, you sound like you want to be my friend. Tell you what—you can call me Naught. Are you the one who made all that noise in the air shaft a couple of days ago, right before they stormed in and hauled me out of my nice high-rise?"

"Did you kill four Golvins?" Draycos asked.

Naught sighed. "Yes, I killed them. No, it wasn't on purpose."

"Self-defense?"

"Accident," Naught said. "The vehicle I was flying had a problem, and I crash-landed. Unfortunately, they were standing where I came down. Well, more crouching, actually. But you get the picture."

"When did this happen?" Draycos asked.

"About five years ago," Naught said.

Draycos felt his tail tip curve in a frown. Five *years?* "That seems far out of balance for a simple accident."

"I agree," Naught said. "So would your Judge-Paladin, I'd guess. But try telling that to the Golvins."

Draycos winced. Naught was right—the One's attitude had made it abundantly clear that he had no interest in hearing anything more about the case. "Where exactly did this crash happen?" he asked.

"Just outside the canyon, over on the east side," Naught said.

The side with the old mine Draycos had seen from the air. "Near the mine?"

"You mean that old entrance building sort of thing?" Naught asked. "A little north of it, actually. The four of them were poking around in the sand, doing God only knows what. By the time I saw them, it was too late. I had zero control left, and I just slammed into them. You *were* the one in the air shaft, weren't you?"

"The One didn't contact any of the Semaline authorities regarding you after the crash?"

"If he did, I never heard about it," Naught said. "And thanks to you and your noisemaker, it doesn't look like anyone's going to be talking to them anytime soon, either. You have any idea how close I was to getting out of there?"

"As a matter of fact, I do," Draycos said. "What sort of vehicle were you flying?"

"It was a long-range pursuit starfighter," Naught said. "A Djinn-90, to be exact. If that means anything to you."

Draycos felt his crest stiffen. That was the same type of pursuit fighter he and Jack had escaped from off Iota Klestis after the ambush of Draycos's advance team.

But no. This couldn't possibly be one of Colonel Frost's Malison Ring mercenaries.

Or could it? "What's your name?" he asked carefully. "Your *real* name?"

The other sighed. "Not that it seems to matter anymore, but I used to be called Langston."

"Langston?"

"Yes," Langston said. "StarForce Wing Sergeant Jonathan Langston." The cot creaked again as he waved an arm. "At your rather limited service."

For a half-dozen heartbeats Draycos was completely at a loss for words. For months he'd been hearing about StarForce, usually from Uncle Virge insisting Jack turn Draycos over to them. Jack had always insisted right back that Neverlin would surely have taken the precaution of bribing or neutralizing some of the men and women in key positions, and the subject had been dropped until the next time Uncle Virge brought it up.

And now here Draycos was, actually speaking with one of those warriors.

Maybe. "Can you prove that?" he asked.

"They left me my ID wallet," Langston said. "It's at the foot of the bed with the rest of my clothes."

Draycos swiveled his neck and located the neat stack. "Turn to face the back wall," he ordered. "Don't move."

There was another shifting of the cot as Langston obediently rolled over. Draycos went over to the clothing pile, located the wallet, and tucked it under his right foreleg. "I'll need to borrow it for a time," he said as he returned to the side of the cot. "The Judge-Paladin will want to examine it."

"Help yourself," Langston said. "I'm not likely to need it anytime soon."

"Possibly sooner than you think," Draycos said. "If the event is indeed as you described, you were wrongfully charged."

"And you and the Judge-Paladin will see that I'm released, I suppose?"

"We will," Draycos said.

"Well, good luck to you," Langston said. "Whoever you are."

Draycos hesitated. Then, somewhat even to his own surprise, he came to a decision. "Call me Draycos," he said. "I'll be back another time."

Getting up, he padded to the cave entrance. "Just watch yourself," Langston warned from the cot. "You *and* the Judge-Paladin. These Golvins may look silly and harmless, but they're not."

"Your presence here proves that," Draycos pointed out dryly. "Don't worry. The Judge-Paladin and I have a long history together of being careful." Gripping the stone at the side of the entrance, he slipped out into the night.

Jack, he knew, was going to love this.

"And you're sure he didn't see you?" Jack asked, squinting at the StarForce ID under the glow of the bedroom's light.

"I'm positive," Draycos assured him, pacing back and forth across the bedroom. "I was listening carefully to his breathing as

I left. I'm coming to realize that no human could spot me for the first time without some sort of reaction."

"You got that right, buddy." With a sigh, Jack flicked off the light. "Well, if it's not a real StarForce ID, it's a really good fake. And I mean a *really* good one."

"You've seen a genuine one?"

"I've seen a really good fake," Jack told him. "One of Uncle Virgil's associates made a living off things like that. But this doesn't make any sense."

"Why they should condemn him for a simple accident?"

"Why they should still have him here in the first place," Jack said. "I mean, they've been putting up a prisoner for five years. Feeding and clothing him—they *have* been feeding and clothing him, haven't they?"

"From what I could see, he appeared adequately fed," Draycos said. "Though I saw no clothing other than what he was wearing."

"Well, his own stuff probably hasn't worn out yet," Jack said. "My point is that the whole thing costs resources the Golvins could surely put to more productive use. They ought to be doing cartwheels at the chance to turn him over to a Judge-Paladin and be rid of him."

Draycos's tail tip was making slow circles in the air. "Unless there's a reason other than simple vengeance for keeping him here," the K'da suggested slowly. "He said the Golvins he'd killed were working not too far from the mine entrance."

"You think there's a connection?"

"It's an obvious direction to consider," Draycos pointed out. "Especially if the mine is also the reason your parents were murdered."

Jack felt his stomach tighten. He'd been living with that idea for over a week now, and it still sent shivers through him. "Draycos, we have *got* to get a look at that mine," he said.

"I agree," Draycos said. "Tomorrow night I'll attempt to scale the cliff and—"

"Listen to my words, symby," Jack interrupted. "*We* have got to get a look at it."

"I don't know," Draycos said doubtfully. "If there's something there the Golvins are hiding, I doubt the One will want you examining it."

"That may be what he thinks *now,*" Jack said. "But he's never seen me in full persuasion mode, as Uncle Virgil used to call it. Neither have you, for that matter."

"I'll look forward to the show," Draycos said dryly.

"And well you should," Jack said, pulling his feet into bed and under the blankets. "Better get some sleep. With a little luck, tomorrow could turn out to be a very interesting day."

CHAPTER 16

There were a dozen different techniques for getting a person to give you what you wanted, and Uncle Virgil had taught Jack every one of them. Even so, it took a full hour and almost the complete set before the One finally realized that he wanted to let Jack go look at the mine.

And even then he insisted that Thonsifi and the guard Sefiseni accompany their Jupa on his field trip. Jack thanked him, switched back into shirt and jeans before the other could change his mind, and together the group piled into the shuttle and headed up.

The shuttle's pilot turned out to be the same one who had flown Jack to the canyon after his kidnapping at the NorthCentral Spaceport. His name turned out to be Eight-Three-One Among Many. "I don't believe this is a wise idea, Jupa Jack," he warned as he once again threaded the shuttle through the system of arching bridges and guy wires up into the bright desert sunlight. "We were told there would be great danger if anyone went into the mine."

"I'll be careful," Jack assured him, studying the area as the shuttle moved toward it over the glistening sand.

The mine entrance was at the western edge of a long mound of sand surrounded by a confused tumble of gray and black rock formations cutting upward through the desert surface. Large plastic or ceramic beams framed the actual opening, which was under the partial protection of a thick rock overhang. Even from their distance it was obvious the entrance itself had filled with drifting sand.

There—to the left.

Jack winced as he turned his torso a little in that direction. What in the world did Draycos think he was doing, talking again in a crowded shuttle like that?

There—Langston's crash site.

Jack peered in that direction as he gave his upper chest a warning tap. He'd better set his partner straight about these slips, preferably before they set off on the return trip.

But the K'da was right. Even amid the random sand drifts and half-covered rock formations he could pick out the buried shape of Langston's starfighter. It was about a hundred yards from the mine entrance, in one of the few patches of sand that didn't have any large rocks in it. Probably why Langston had chosen that spot to ditch in.

It was also no more than twenty yards from the eastern edge of the canyon. The pilot was lucky, Jack reflected, that he hadn't missed the edge and gone straight to the ground below.

"Where do you wish me to land?" Eithon asked.

"Right out front," Jack said, shifting his attention back to the mine entrance. "Between those two big rock formations will do nicely."

A minute later Eithon set them down in the shade of the easternmost of the rocks Jack had pointed out. "Looks like we've got some digging ahead," Jack said as he climbed out. "I wish I'd thought to bring some shovels."

"I brought two," Thonsifi said, her voice reluctant. "They are in the storage area."

"Great," Jack said, stepping around the back of the shuttle and popping the hatch. The shovels were small gardening tools, but at least they'd work better than bare hands. "Let's get to it," he said, pulling them out.

The others joined him, all three Golvins with the same hesitation Jack had already heard in Thonsifi's voice.

But they tackled the job willingly enough. Thonsifi and Eithon handled the shovels, scooping away the sand, while Jack and Sefiseni moved larger stones and broken pieces of the entryway itself.

Within half an hour they had an opening big enough to get through. "Great work," Jack complimented them, wiping sweat from his forehead. "Let's go."

None of the Golvins moved. "It is not safe," Thonsifi said. "We were warned to stay away."

"Who said it wasn't safe?"

"Those who built the mine," Thonsifi said. "After we were told that the copper and iron were not ours."

At which point all the legal complications had set in. "No problem," Jack said. "You can all wait here. I don't mind going in by myself."

Thonsifi and Sefiseni exchanged looks. "The One Among Many told us to stay with you," Thonsifi said with a sigh. "If you go, so must we."

"You don't have to," Jack insisted. "I'm a Judge-Paladin. I can give orders, too."

"No, we will go," Thonsifi said in a slightly firmer voice.

"I was given no such instruction by the One Among Many," Eithon spoke up. "Do you also wish me to come with you?"

"No, thanks," Jack said. "We need someone to stay out here and watch the shuttle anyway." Though to watch it against what possible danger he couldn't imagine. "Load the shovels back into the shuttle, though, will you?"

"We do not have any carry lights," Thonsifi said.

"That's okay—I've got one," Jack told her, pulling out his flashlight. "Well, come on. If we're going, let's go." He turned and squeezed through the gap into the mine.

There was no immediate response from the others. Still, by the time he reached the edge of the daylight Thonsifi and Sefiseni were beside him. "Nice and easy," Jack said encouragingly, flicking on his light. "Stay close, and watch your footing."

The tunnel extended straight back for about fifty feet, then began a gradual slope downward. Jack's small light wasn't really up to the task of guiding three sets of feet, but fortunately it didn't have to. Midway down the slope they reached a section of tunnel where some dim backup lights were still working.

"They are still lit?" Thonsifi asked, looking at them in awe.

"They're long-term emergency lights," Jack told her. "Self-contained, with a twenty-year power source."

A minute later the tunnel came to an end at a large assembly/staging area. Two smaller tunnels extended out from opposite sides of the room, heading downward into darkness. "Those must lead to the actual mines," Jack said, shining his light around the staging area. The walls, floor, and ceiling were all made of the same white ceramic as the main entrance tunnel. The floor was covered with a thin layer of sand, all the surfaces stained with age and dust.

But even with all that, an explosion in here should have left behind some very visible evidence. At the very least there should be some powder burns, and probably some cracks and stress damage as well. Only there wasn't anything.

Which meant the explosion that had killed his parents must have been down in one of the lower tunnels.

He turned his light to shine into one of the entrances. The beam faded away, swallowed up by distance and darkness.

"Do we go back now?" Thonsifi asked hopefully.

"Not quite yet," Jack told her. The thought of going deep underground wasn't exactly filling him with bubbles, either. But this whole trip would be for nothing if he didn't at least find some clues as to what had happened to his parents. "Did the mine's owners ever say why they shut down the operation?"

"*We* are the mine's owners," Sefiseni bit out.

Jack looked at the guard in mild surprise. It was the first time the Golvin had ever spoken directly to him. "My error," he apologized.

"It was *our* copper and iron they were stealing," Sefiseni said accusingly, as if this was all somehow Jack's fault.

"I understand," Jack said soothingly. "The legal problems—"

"And Jupa Stuart and Jupa Ariel did nothing to stop them," Sefiseni cut him off.

Jack felt his stomach tighten. So he'd been right the first time. Sefiseni *did* consider this Jack's fault, or at least his fault by inheritance. "Well, *something* stopped them," he pointed out. "This place hasn't been touched in years."

"They said the tunnels were in danger of collapsing," Thonsifi said, looking nervously at the ceiling. "They also said the lower portions had become flooded."

In a desert? Jack frowned. Still, there was a river rolling along three hundred feet below them. Clearly, there was water around here *somewhere.*

He crossed the staging area to the left tunnel. Attached to the sides, at just about waist height, were identical five-inch-diameter open-ended pipes partially set into the walls and leading downward. Resting a hand on one of them, Jack turned an ear into the tunnel, though he wasn't quite sure what he was expecting to hear.

He heard nothing but his own breathing. On a hunch, he squatted down and listened at each of the pipes. Still nothing.

A whisper of weight came onto his chest, and he felt the front of his shirt move slightly as Draycos flicked out his tongue. The weight vanished again—*There is machinery down there.*

Jack sent a glare down at his shoulder. What in the world was making the K'da so blasted careless about talking in front of other people these days? Did he think the Golvins were deaf? "I'm going down a little ways," he called back to the others, pitching his voice a little louder than necessary in case Draycos decided to run some more commentary on the situation. "You two stay here—I'm just going to see if I can find any problems."

He headed off before they could object, shining his light on the rough floor of the tunnel in front of him. There was no white ceramic here, the whole tunnel had been carved out of brown and gray rock.

The floor was rougher than the entry tunnel had been. There was also a layer of rock dust over everything, with small to medium-big pools of dust and stone in practically every dip and depression. Combined with the shadows thrown by his light, it made for rather uncertain footing.

Fortunately, the two pipes running along the sides were just the right height for handrails. Keeping one hand running lightly over the nearest pipe, he continued down.

Another bit of weight came onto his chest and shoulder. "Native stone," Draycos murmured quietly. "We must be below the sand layer."

"Yeah, thanks for the tip," Jack muttered back, throwing a quick look over his shoulder. But neither of the Golvins had followed him in. "Is there something about tunneling machinery that really excites you?"

"Pardon?"

"Blurting it out in front of God and Thonsifi and everyone that way," Jack said. "I know these Golvins are kind of primitive—"

"What do you mean, blurting it out?" Draycos interrupted. "I haven't spoken since we left the apartment this morning."

"Oh, come *on*," Jack growled. *Gotcha!* he thought sourly. So much for the high and mighty K'da warrior ethic and the idea of always telling the truth. "It isn't the first time, either," he added. "When we were first coming in to the canyon—"

"I did *not* speak," Draycos insisted. "And what do you mean by *gotcha?*"

"I mean—" Jack stopped abruptly, a sudden icy shiver running up his back. "Did you hear me say *gotcha* just now?" he asked carefully.

"Very clearly," Draycos said, starting to sound a little huffy. "Furthermore, you said it in such a way that—"

"I didn't say anything, Draycos," Jack said. "I just *thought* it."

"I heard—" Draycos broke off abruptly.

For a moment neither of them spoke. "You never told me about *this* one," Jack said at last.

"This has never happened before, Jack," Draycos told him, his voice actually shaking. "Not with the Shontine. Not ever in the recorded history of my people."

Jack took a deep breath. "We're sure we're not just imagining things, right?"

For a moment there was silence. Then, as clear as if the K'da had actually spoken, Jack heard his voice whispering in his mind. *We stand before, we stand behind; we seek the truth with heart and mind.*

"My mother's poem," Jack said, his stomach tightening. "This is nuts, buddy. This is *really* nuts."

"It does take effort," Draycos said. "I had to concentrate on the words for you to hear them."

"Or else you had to be thinking really strongly about them," Jack said, thinking back. "Like on the shuttle on our way in, when you really wanted me to turn to the right so you could see better."

"I remember," Draycos said thoughtfully. "I wished very much that I could ask you to turn, but knew it would be unsafe in such close quarters. And then, to my relief, you did exactly that, allowing me to see and identify the mine."

"And I've been mad at you for a week and a half about it." Jack shook his head. "Sorry. You suppose it works when we're not together?"

"Let's find out." With a surge of weight, Draycos leaped out of Jack's shirt collar onto the tunnel floor.

"Ssst!" Jack hissed warningly, looking back up the tunnel. Fortunately, a gentle curve had put the entrance, and the two Golvins, out of view. "We don't want them to see you."

"They won't," Draycos assured him. "Did you hear anything just now?"

Jack shook his head. "Nope. Guess it only works when you're riding me. You're *sure* this has never happened before?"

"Trust me," Draycos said, a little dryly. "I would have heard."

"Another one for the record books," Jack said, forcing his mind back to business. "So where exactly is this machinery you're all excited about?"

"This way," Draycos said, flicking his tail at Jack as he headed again down the tunnel. "Perhaps you will find it interesting, as well."

Shortly ahead, the tunnel split into two branches, the pipelines along the walls splitting along with it. Draycos picked the left-hand one, continuing left when the branch split again about fifty feet ahead. "These must be some *really* impressive copper ores for them to have gone to all this work," Jack commented as they hit yet another branch and again turned left.

"From what I've read of your economy, this is far too much effort for copper or iron," Draycos said over his shoulder. "There—just ahead."

They reached the end of their branch of the tunnel, to find the machinery Draycos had predicted.

Six pieces of machinery, in fact. There were two self-propelled diggers on tanklike treads, a rock crusher, something that looked like a giant pump, and two machines with large vats that Jack couldn't identify. All of them were wrapped in clear plastic, the soft glint of lubricating oil visible on their treads and drive wheels and other moving parts.

"I could smell the lubricating oil," Draycos said as Jack gingerly ran a hand over one of the diggers. "I thought perhaps it was evidence someone was still working the mine."

"Not yet, but they're sure ready to," Jack said, peering into the empty vat on one of the unidentified machines.

"But why?" Draycos asked, sounding bewildered. "If the ores here are valuable, why wait to mine them?"

"Could be any of a dozen reasons," Jack said. "Maybe they're still fighting to get the mining rights away from the Golvins. Maybe they're waiting for the market value to go up."

He shined his light at the tunnel face, the beam sparkling against a glittering array of metal bits embedded in the gray rock. "Or maybe after murdering a couple of Judge-Paladins they thought it would be smart to shut down and lie low for a while."

"A wise move on their part," Draycos said grimly, looking around. "But I've still not seen any evidence of any explosion."

"Me, neither," Jack admitted. "Must be down one of the other tunnels." He peered back the way they'd come. "But we don't have time to go looking now. Thonsifi's probably tearing her ears off worrying about me."

"Or worrying about what the One will say about letting you come down here alone."

"That, too," Jack agreed. "By the way, while you were sniffing out lubricating oil, did you happen to smell any water?"

"None," Draycos said. "I suspect that part of the story was told merely to ensure the Golvins stayed out of the mine."

"Probably," Jack said. "Stupid lie to tell, though, here in the middle of the desert."

"Perhaps," Draycos said. "Still, there *is* a river not too far below us."

"Yeah." Jack frowned suddenly at him. "Hey, *I* was just thinking that a while back. You been eavesdropping on my mind?"

Draycos's tail curved in a frown. "Not consciously," he said slowly. "But perhaps we are beginning to share other thoughts on a subconscious level."

"Maybe," Jack said. The thought of someone poking around inside his skull made his skin crawl. Even if that someone was Draycos. "Or maybe we're just thinking the same direction. The river *is* a pretty obvious thought."

"True," Draycos said. To Jack's ears, he sounded a little relieved by that thought, as well. "But as you say, we should leave." Touching Jack's hand, he slid back up his sleeve. "I'll guide you out."

CHAPTER 17

With the marks of their footsteps easily visible in the dust, Draycos's guidance wasn't really necessary. A few minutes later, they rounded the last curve in the main tunnel to find Thonsifi and Sefiseni standing together in the entrance. Their faces, at least what Jack could see of them in the faint beam from his light, looked anxious. "It's all right," Jack called. "I'm here."

"We were worried about you," Thonsifi said as Jack emerged into the staging room, relief evident in her voice. "Eithon has been calling from outside. Another air transport has arrived in the canyon."

Jack felt the breath catch in his throat. The *Essenay*? "How big was—? Never mind," he interrupted himself. No point quizzing them when he could go look for himself. "Let's get back."

A minute later they were in the air again. Jack eyed the network of stone arches and guy wires as they approached the canyon, hope fading as he realized again that a ship the size of the *Essenay* could never make it in there.

Sure enough, as they flew over the edge and started down he could see, far below, a small two-man aircar squatting on the landing pit. "Any idea who that could be?" Jack asked.

"I do not know for certain," Thonsifi said, her voice trembling a bit.

Jack peered at her face. Jack was safe, and they were away from the mine. Yet her face was still anxious. "I didn't ask if you knew for sure," he said. "I asked if you had any idea. That means any thoughts or guesses."

She didn't answer. "Sefiseni?" Jack invited. "Eithon?"

"I saw a picture on the side of the transport," Eithon admitted reluctantly. "It is the same as the picture of those who stole the mine from us."

Sefiseni rumbled something in their own language. "Good," Jack said, trying to hide his own sudden uneasiness. Was this the response to Foeinatw's late-night InterWorld call ten days ago? "There are some questions I want to ask them."

As it had been the first time, the flight through the Golvins' aerial obstacle course was interesting to the point of occasional terror. But again they made it safely, and Eithon set them down more or less gently beside the visitor.

And now, up close, Jack could read the name beneath the stylized pick-and-shovel logo on the aircar's side.

Triost Mining Group.

A sudden memory flooded back on him: he and Draycos in the *Essenay's* dayroom, right after their first meeting and the mad escape from the Iota Klestis ambush.

We dealt with a people called the Chitac Nomads, Draycos had told him and Uncle Virge. *They assured us Iota Klestis was available for purchase.*

I don't know, Uncle Virge had answered doubtfully. *On paper, the place still belongs to the Triost Mining Group.*

Carefully, Jack focused his mind as he and the others climbed out of the shuttle. *Draycos?* he thought toward his shoulder.

Yes, I saw, the K'da's mental voice came back grimly. *Are these the same people?*

It's the same group, Jack confirmed. Near one of the apartment pillars he spotted a middle-aged man talking with the One and a couple of other Golvins. *Probably not the same specific people, though.*

Pardon?

I said it's the same group, but probably not the same exact people, Jack repeated. This telepathy stuff took more effort and focus than he'd realized. *Keep it down, now—I have to concentrate.*

The One's eyes shifted to Jack as he and the others approached. The man caught the subtle movement and turned. He was medium height and build, starting to widen out around the waist, with thinning hair and piercing blue eyes. "Ah," he said, giving Jack a friendly smile. "You must be the Judge-Paladin everyone's talking about."

"I'm Judge-Paladin Jack Melville," Jack confirmed, grabbing a new last name for himself at random. "You?"

"Genic Bolo, survey specialist for the Triost Mining Group," the other said, holding out his hand. His smile took on a slight frown. "I have to say, you look awfully young for your position."

"I've always looked young for my age," Jack explained, shaking Bolo's hand firmly but briefly, in the upper-class professional's style Uncle Virgil had taught him. "Even at twenty-four, a lot of people peg me as only seventeen or eighteen."

"I'd have made it even younger," Bolo admitted. "But don't worry about it. You'll appreciate the effect when you're fifty and still look thirty-five."

His smile turned a little rueful as he ran a hand through his thinning hair. "As you see, I've got the opposite problem."

"At least people take you seriously," Jack said. "What brings you here, Mr. Bolo?"

"Survey work, like the job title says," Bolo said. "We've got a petrometal station going in about a hundred miles east of here. I was told to see whether it would be cheaper for us to build a pipeline to the NorthCentral Spaceport for the stuff or to build our own tanker landing area next to the station."

Jack frowned. "I didn't know you could pump metals."

"Actually, we'd be pumping a slurry," Bolo said. "That's a lot of water or other liquid with metals or whatever suspended in it."

"Ah," Jack said. So that was what the tunnel pipes and vats were for that he and Draycos had seen. One pipe would bring water to the mine face, and the ore would be dumped into it in one of the vats. The resulting slurry would then be pumped back to the surface through the other pipe. "Interesting. I presume that in this case the liquid would be the oil part of the petrometal deposits?"

"Exactly," Bolo said. "You know much about mining?"

"Hardly anything," Jack said. "How long will you be in the area?"

"I'll be coming and going over the next few days," Bolo said, looking around. "Frankly, this canyon throws kind of a wrench into the whole pipeline idea. I think the head office must have forgotten it was even here."

Jack smiled tightly. Sure they had. "Well, I wish you luck," he said.

Bolo inclined his head. "Thank you. I must say, it's nice to see a human face out here in the middle of nowhere."

"Indeed," Jack agreed. "Perhaps after you're done for the day, you'd be able to join us for dinner." He caught the One's eye. "One Among Many? Would that be possible?"

"Yes, of course," the One said.

His voice and expression were polite enough. But Jack had lived with these people long enough to have picked up on all the smaller and more subtle touches of face and gesture.

The One was worried. He was badly worried.

"Sorry, but I can't," Bolo said. "I've got a ton of work to do, and not nearly enough time to do it all in." He paused, gazing at nothing as if thinking hard. "But I should be back here in two or three days," he continued. "Maybe we can find time then for a dinner or even just a lunch."

"Sounds good to me," Jack said. "I guess we'll see you when we see you."

"That you will," Bolo agreed, smiling as he nodded a farewell. He shifted his eyes to the One—"One Among Many," he said, nodding again. Then, brushing past Jack, he headed back to his aircar.

The One stepped to Jack's side. "You should not have invited him back," he said, his voice dark. "We do not want him here."

"*I* want him here," Jack told him. "I think he's the key to some questions that need answering."

"It will end in death," the One warned.

Jack felt his throat tighten. "It usually does," he said. He gestured to Thonsifi, who had come up silently behind him. "I'll start hearing cases in an hour," he told her. "Can you get the complainants lined up for then?"

She bowed her head. "I will," she said, and headed toward one of the apartment pillars.

"You need to rest after your visit to the mine?" the One asked.

"Actually, I need to walk," Jack said. Stepping around the other, he headed down the path toward the Great Hall.

"Where are we going?" Draycos asked quietly.

Jack took a deep breath. "To find the place where my parents were murdered."

He had reached the nearest end of the Great Hall before Draycos spoke again. "You don't believe anymore that they died in the mine?"

"No, they died right here in the canyon," Jack said, pausing at the base of one of the Great Hall's supporting pylons and looking around. It would most likely be on the far side, he decided, somewhere along the northern part of the river. The area up there was much more open than the part to the south.

And now that he was looking, he could see the hint of where the pathways had once been. Stepping around the river side of the pylon, being careful not to step into the water itself, he headed along the ground beneath the building. "In fact," he added to Draycos, "I'd lay money that it was right in the middle of arguments in the case."

Draycos stirred on his skin. "Apparently, I have missed something."

"No more than I did," Jack assured him, feeling slightly disgusted with himself. "This thing above us is the Great Assembly Hall, right?"

"Correct."

"Why *Great?*" Jack asked. "Why not just call it the Assembly Hall?"

He felt the K'da's sudden twitch of understanding. "Once there was also a Small Assembly Hall."

"Exactly," Jack said. "Only eleven years ago, it was blown to bits, or at least wrecked enough that it couldn't be fixed. So they tore it down."

"Or they didn't want evidence of what had happened to remain," Draycos said slowly. "Remember what the shuttle pilot, Eithon, said on the way?"

"That there was danger in the mine."

"Only the parts we visited seemed perfectly safe."

Jack shrugged. "Scare tactics."

"Or else the danger wasn't going to come from the mine itself," Draycos said.

The skin on the back of Jack's neck gave an unpleasant tingle. Trying to look casual about it, he glanced over his shoulder.

Bolo hadn't left. He was still standing by his aircar, fiddling with something in the rear storage compartment.

Only what he was really doing was watching Jack. "Oh, boy," Jack murmured.

"He's watching us?"

"Oh, yeah," Jack said, turning back around to face forward. "He's trying not to look like it, but he is."

"Perhaps we should abandon our search until later?" Draycos suggested.

Jack shook his head. "Too late. He already knows I was in the mine—he would have seen the Golvins' shuttle parked at the entrance on his way in. And there's no reason why I should be walking around under here unless I was looking for something that's not here anymore."

"Assuming he knows about that."

"Oh, he knows," Jack said. "I know his type, Draycos— Uncle Virgil hung around with far too many just like him.

They're all smooth and polite and professional on the surface, but underneath they're as vicious as anyone you've ever met. Their job is to fix other people's messes and loose ends. Usually by making a few messes of their own."

Draycos seemed to digest that. "I doubt he will take any action right now," he said slowly. "Though if he doesn't fear the Golvins as witnesses against him . . . ?"

"No, we're okay for the moment," Jack assured him. "Even if he doesn't mind shooting me in front of everyone, he still doesn't know how much I know or who I might have told it to. He has to worm all of that out of me before he makes his move."

"I suppose that's reasonable," Draycos said, a little doubtfully. "What then is our strategy?"

"Basically, we're going to play the game right back at him," Jack said. "See if we can figure out first who *he* is and what *he* knows."

"A dangerous game."

Jack sighed. "Yeah, but it's the only one in town."

They reached the other end of the Great Hall and emerged again into the sunlight. Jack continued along the river, peering into the water and the muddy bank.

A hundred yards from the Great Hall, he found it. "There," he said, squatting down and touching a small piece of blackened wood poking a couple of inches out of the mud at the edge of the river. "See it?"

Draycos shifted across Jack's skin to where he could look through the neck of his shirt. "A piece of wood?"

"A piece of *burned* wood," Jack corrected. "Very important difference." Carefully, he dug a finger into the mud beside the shard.

And winced as his fingertip ran into something sharp. "There's more under the surface," he said, feeling around. "Feels like more wood . . . yeah. Yeah, there's a whole—feels like a round column of it. Sunk pretty deep, too."

"A supporting pylon," Draycos said. "Like the Great Hall, only for the Small Hall they were able to use wood instead of stone."

"Treated somehow to keep from rotting," Jack agreed, rinsing his hand off in the river.

"Yet a bomb strong enough to destroy any structure this size would have caused serious damage to the entire canyon," Draycos said. "I believe your earlier conclusion was right: the Golvins themselves completed its destruction."

"And have been shaking in their vests ever since, wondering if someone would come looking for the missing Judge-Paladins," Jack said grimly.

"Not all of them, I think, have such guilty consciences," Draycos said slowly. "Otherwise, why would any of them have brought you here?"

"You're right," Jack said, nodding. "Only the One and maybe a few more know the whole truth."

"A truth which we need to learn."

"Oh, we will, buddy," Jack promised darkly. "Trust me. We will."

CHAPTER 18

The next morning, Alison had just finished dressing when Dumbarton and Mrishpaw arrived at her door. "They're ready for you," Dumbarton said.

"What, no breakfast?" Alison asked.

"They've got something there," Dumbarton said, jerking a thumb over his shoulder as the Brummga scooped up her bag of disguised burglar equipment. "Come on, come on—they're waiting."

They went back upstairs, across the main foyer, and up a wide staircase to a second-floor balcony. From there they walked down a nicely furnished corridor, then up another set of stairs, and finally to a domed chamber the size of a small conference room, only much more nicely furnished.

As Dumbarton had said, Neverlin and Frost were waiting for her. They were seated in comfortable chairs beside a line of five safes, looking rather like spectators at some sporting event. Along the side wall a small breakfast buffet had been laid out, with both hot and cold food. The aromas rising from it made Alison's stomach growl.

And over in the far corner, seated in a chair that looked rather like a throne, was an old, wrinkled, glowering Brummga.

"Morning, Kayna," Frost greeted her with a sort of gruff politeness. "Ready to start?"

"As soon as I've eaten something," Alison told him, nodding over at the old Brummga. "Who's your friend?"

An instant later, a hard blow across her shoulder blades sent her sprawling flat onto the thick carpet. "Hey!" she yelped, rolling back up into a sitting position and glaring up at the two mercenaries behind her. "What was that—?"

She broke off, throwing herself into a diving roll that barely managed to get her out of the way as Mrishpaw swiped at her again.

"Mrishpaw—stand down!" Frost snapped.

But the other ignored him. Taking a long step toward Alison, he raised his hand for another try. "Patri, call him off," Neverlin said quietly. "We need her alive *and* unharmed."

There was no order that Alison could hear. But to her relief, Mrishpaw jerked to a halt. For a moment he glowered down at her, then stepped back to Dumbarton's side. Breathing hard, Alison turned her head to look at the old Brummga.

He was gazing back at her from his throne, his face expressionless. "Does it have learned respect?" he rumbled.

Alison took a careful breath. "I humbly crave the pardon of the Patri Chookoock," she said.

Out of the corner of her eye she saw Frost stir a little at the subtle edge of sarcasm beneath the words. Fortunately, the Patri Chookoock didn't seem to hear it. "You may can stand," he said.

"Thank you." Keeping a wary eye on Mrishpaw, Alison got her feet under her and stood up. Jack had told her about his casual mistreatment here at the Chookoock estate. She should have been ready for some of the same.

"Now; shall we try it again?" Neverlin asked. "Are you ready to begin?"

Alison glanced sideways at the Patri. "I will begin at your pleasure," she said. "May I humbly suggest that I'll do better if I'm allowed to eat first?"

"You may indeed so suggest." Neverlin turned to the Patri. "Patri?"

"It were is better," the Patri rumbled. "Allow it to eat."

Neverlin gestured to the buffet. "Go ahead."

"Thank you," Alison said, bowing to each of the three in turn before crossing over to the food. It irritated her no end to have to play this kind of humility game, especially in front of a creature who made his money buying and selling living beings.

But the very first thing her father had taught her was not to let emotion get in the way of the job. If it took a little groveling to get what she wanted out of these people, she could handle that.

She ate a quick breakfast, making sure to thank the Patri twice more between bites, and then set to work.

The safes were tricky, though not quite as bad as the ones she'd opened aboard ship, and it took the entire day to get them open. But by the time the sun was sinking behind the white wall, even Neverlin was convinced. "Excellent," he said as he peered into the last of the empty safes and then closed the door again. "You were right, Colonel—she *does* seem to have some talent in this area."

"Or at least some very good equipment," Frost said.

"Either serves our purposes." Neverlin turned to the old Brummga. "Patri?"

For a long moment the Patri continued to stare at Alison, as he'd done pretty much nonstop the entire day. "It may try."

"Excellent," Neverlin said. "Colonel?"

Frost gestured, and Dumbarton and Mrishpaw detached themselves from a section of the wall near the door. "Escort her back to her room," he ordered them. "Instruct the slaves to give her whatever she wants for dinner." He shifted his attention to Alison. "You'll start first thing in the morning," he added. "I suggest you go to bed early and get yourself a good night's sleep."

His eyes narrowed in silent warning. "You'll need it."

With their entire day having been spent in the testing room, Taneem hadn't had a chance to eat anything since the previous evening. Alison made sure to order a large dinner, then left the K'da hiding under the bed while she had herself a quick bath to soothe away her tension.

She was dried and dressed by the time the meal arrived, brought in again by Shoofteelee. The young Wistawk was polite enough, but there was none of the simmering hope and enthusiasm he'd shown the previous evening. He accepted her thanks for the food, told her he'd overheard nothing new from Neverlin or Frost, and left.

After they'd eaten—with Taneem reluctantly but gratefully taking most of the food—Alison settled down for that good night's sleep Neverlin had recommended.

She'd been asleep just over two hours when a sudden hissing roar in her ear jerked her awake.

"What is it?" Taneem whispered anxiously.

"It's all right," Alison whispered back, forcing her muscles to relax. Ever since Neverlin had taken Virgil Morgan's shoulder bag from her she'd been waiting for him to open it. She'd therefore gone to bed each of the past two nights with the receiver from the bugged picture nestled in her ear.

Apparently, the moment had come.

The brief roar of paper rubbing against paper faded away, to be replaced by the sound of familiar human voices. "—know what you expect to find in there," Frost was saying. "Or why you even care about Morgan anymore. We've got the girl, and she's at least as good as he is."

"The question is whether *we* have her, or whether *she* has us," Neverlin said pointedly. "I don't like the fact that we can't pull up a single clue as to who she really is."

"Which argues that she's exactly what she claims to be," Frost countered. "Only an especially good professional thief would be able to keep her data and stats out of the system."

There was a tickling on Alison's neck as Taneem slid around her skin, angling for a spot where she could hear better. She ended up with her triangular dragon's head stretched partway across Alison's own face, her ear just below the receiver.

"Maybe," Neverlin said. "Well, well, well."

"What is it?" Frost asked.

"It seems our master safecracker Virgil Morgan has been thinking about changing specialties."

"To what?"

There was a faint crinkling of paper. "To blackmail."

"Yes, I saw those pictures," Frost said. "I couldn't quite make out what was happening."

"Obviously, neither could Morgan," Neverlin said. "Or else he was smart enough to know the police wouldn't be able to figure them out either. I wonder where he got them."

"What are they?" Frost asked.

"Pictures placing me at a little problem we had a few years back on—well, as a matter of fact, right there on Semaline," Neverlin said. There was another shuffling of papers. "All these other papers are from the same thing. Interesting."

"Just how little *was* this problem?" Frost asked. "Specifically, can Morgan call the cops down on us?"

"The cops would first have to find us," Neverlin said. "Assuming you hid the *Advocatus Diaboli* properly that's not likely to happen. Besides"—there was a rustling of papers—"we've got all his evidence."

"Unless he has more."

"Unlikely," Neverlin said. "It's clear that he's been adding to his collection over the years. No, I think everything's probably here in this one nice neat package."

Alison nodded to herself. So that was the reason for the *Essenay*'s occasional visits to Semaline. Jack's uncle hadn't been taking money *out* of the lockbox, as Jack had thought. He'd instead been putting new blackmail material *in*.

"And if he has copies?" Frost persisted.

"I suppose that's possible," Neverlin conceded, a hint of doubt creeping into his tone. "Though these are definitely the originals."

"You'd better hope so," Frost warned. "Because the fact that after eleven years a Judge Paladin has suddenly shown up and tripped your alarms ought to make you pause for thought."

"I suppose you're right," Neverlin said in a voice that sent a shiver up Alison's back. "There's no point in taking chances, especially not now. The next time Bolo checks in, I'll order him to wreck the mine."

"Will that be enough?" Frost asked.

"It'll bury any evidence of motive," Neverlin said. "That,

plus the fact that Morgan doesn't have his original documents anymore ought to do it."

"I meant do you think you should also do something about the Judge-Paladin," Frost said. "Braxton's making enough noise out there without the Judge-Paladins' Office letting itself in on the act."

"I suppose you're right there, too," Neverlin conceded. "And it's not like Bolo hasn't killed a Judge-Paladin before. He can handle the job."

There was another hiss of papers sliding over each other. "Meanwhile, we have a busy day tomorrow," Neverlin's voice continued, sounding more distant. Apparently, he'd put the papers back into the shoulder bag. "I think I'll check once more on the girl's record search, then get to bed."

"Good idea," Frost said, and there was a subtle double creaking of leather as both men stood up. "Because I've seen her before," he added, his voice fading away. "I *know* I have."

"You'd better figure out where," Neverlin warned, his voice fading the same way. "And fast."

There was the sound of a door closing, and then silence.

Alison waited another minute to make sure they weren't coming back. Then, grimacing, she pulled the receiver from her ear. "You get all that?" she whispered.

"Yes," Taneem said, sliding back to her usual place across Alison's back, legs, and arms. "This sounds very bad."

"It'll be all right," Alison said, forcing a confidence she didn't especially feel. So far Neverlin seemed to be concentrating his search on Internos and alien databases, official as well as criminal. If he stayed with those, she should be fine.

But if it occurred to Frost to dig into the Malison Ring's own database . . .

"What was that?" Taneem whispered suddenly.

Alison froze. Straining her ears, she could just make out a faint sound that might possibly be distant human speech. Someone coming down the hallway toward their room?

And then suddenly she understood. Mouthing a silent curse at her own stupidity, she jammed the receiver back into her ear.

It was indeed where the voice was coming from. To her dismay, though, while the sound became louder it didn't become any more understandable. Only random and disconnected syllables seemed to be getting through the soft but persistent hiss of background noise.

There wasn't even enough for her to identify the voice, though she was pretty sure it wasn't Frost or Neverlin. She turned her head back and forth, trying to adjust the receiver's position for better reception. But nothing seemed to help.

"It's Uncle Virge," Taneem said abruptly.

Alison frowned, straining her ears even harder. The K'da was right, she realized abruptly.

Which meant the *Essenay* was somewhere nearby, probably just outside the Chookoock family grounds. "Can you understand him?" she whispered.

"No," Taneem whispered back. "It's too faint. Too . . ."

"Too broken," Alison finished for her. Throwing off the blankets, she grabbed for her clothes. "Come on."

"Where are we going?" Taneem asked anxiously.

"We're two floors underground," Alison reminded her, pulling on her jeans and shirt. "We should get better reception outside."

"But are you allowed to leave the house?"

Alison stuffed her feet into her low-topped boots. "Let's find out."

CHAPTER 19

The hallway was deserted, as was the stairway leading up toward the foyer. Somewhere along the way the faint voice sputtering in her ear fell silent. She continued on anyway, crossing toward the archway leading into the grand entry foyer.

And stopped short as two armed Brummgas stepped into her path. "Stand," one of them ordered quietly.

"I'm not one of the slaves," Alison told him, trying to sound like she actually belonged here. "I'm Alison Kayna, working with the Patri Chookoock and Colonel Frost and Mr. Arthur. I just want to go outside for a few minutes to get some fresh air."

"Slaves are not allowed outside the slave quarters," the first Brummga insisted.

"I'm not a slave," Alison repeated. "I came with Colonel Frost. You can check with him if you don't believe me."

The two guards exchanged stares, their typically molasses Brummgan minds apparently working overtime on this one. "Not here," the first said at last, pointing to Alison's left, "Through the kitchen—door that way."

The kitchen was large and well stocked, though not as impressive as some Alison had seen. Threading her way between work stations, she made her way to the door at the far end.

It opened easily enough from the inside, but a quick check showed the outside handle was locked. Digging under the left cuff of her shirt sleeve, she pulled out one of the strips of tape hidden there. She pulled off its backing and carefully flattened the tape over the door latch to hold it open.

A moment later she was outside in the crisp night air, the door closed behind her. "Can you call him?" Taneem murmured as Alison headed toward one of the formal garden areas she'd spotted on the drive in.

"No, this is only a receiver," Alison murmured back. "I was hoping he might repeat whatever it was he was saying. I guess he's given up."

"But how would Jack know to come here to look for us?" Taneem asked.

"No idea," Alison said, looking around. "Let's try getting a little closer to the wall. No more talking—there might be patrols around."

The estate was deathly quiet at this hour of the night. The only sounds Alison could hear as she walked were the rustling of the wind through the bushes and her own softly crunching footsteps. She passed through the near edge of the garden area, its vibrant colors muted beneath the dim starlight, and continued on across a stretch of aromatic grass. Ahead and to the right she could see what seemed to be some kind of sports area.

"Freeze," a voice said quietly from her left.

Alison stopped in midstep. "I'm not a slave," she said. "My name's Alison—"

"I know who you are, little girl," the voice said.

With a soft rustling, a muscular man with wide shoulders stepped out from concealment between a pair of sculpted bushes fifteen feet away. In the moonlight Alison could see his short, military-style hair and a hint of deep lines in his face.

She had no trouble at all seeing the snub-nosed laser rifle pointed at her stomach.

"Oh, yes, I know who you are," the man repeated. "My name's Gazen."

Alison tensed, Jack's stories about Gazen flooding over her like a wave of arctic water. Gazen was the Chookoock family's slavemaster, a vicious, brutal man who had made Jack's brief time here a living hell. "I've heard of you," she managed.

"From Jack Morgan?"

"Who? No, from some of the other slaves," Alison said, feeling a cold sweat break out on her forehead. Too late, she realized she should instead have denied all knowledge of the man. If he bothered to check with the slaves, he could expose her lie within half an hour. "But I see you came out here for some solitude," she went on, taking a careful sideways step back toward the house. "Sorry to have bothered you."

"I didn't come here for solitude," Gazen corrected mildly. "I came here to kill people."

Alison's mouth felt dry. "Anyone in particular?"

"Yes." Gazen lifted the laser to his shoulder. "You."

For an eternity Alison just stood there, her knees locked, her feet rooted to the ground, her mind sorting desperately through her options.

But there weren't any. She was in the middle of open ground, with no access to weapons or cover or escape. Gazen's weapon was already up and aimed, and he was too far away for her to try jumping him.

Her luck had finally run out. She was going to die.

Or was she?

She frowned. There was something odd about Gazen as he stood there. Something in his eyes or stance that she couldn't quite put her finger on.

And then, against her skin, she felt Taneem preparing to leap.

"No," she muttered urgently, putting a hand on her shoulder. The gap was too wide even for a K'da to cover. Gazen would shoot Taneem, then he would shoot Alison—

And then, abruptly, Alison's conscious mind caught up to what her subconscious had already noticed.

Gazen wasn't looking at her. He was still facing her, and his laser was still pointed at her chest. But his eyes were darting around, probing the starlit yard and the darker shadows of bushes and trees and flower beds around them.

He was waiting for something to happen. In fact, from the expression on his face, he was *hoping* for something to happen.

But nothing did. Alison stood as still as she could, holding her hand against Taneem's head and praying that the K'da would stay put.

And then, finally, Gazen lowered the muzzle of his weapon. "So he really *isn't* here," he muttered, looking around openly now.

"Who isn't here?" Alison asked.

Reluctantly, it seemed, Gazen dragged his attention back to her. "Jack Morgan, of course," he said, his voice going even darker. "He's coming back to free the rest of the slaves. Didn't you know?"

Alison felt her lip twitch. Jack had never mentioned *that* part of his plan. "He is?"

Gazen nodded toward the north end of the grounds. "That's what they say out there," he told her. "They say Morgan's coming back someday. Him and that—" His voice cracked, and even in the faint light Alison could see the sudden intensity in his eyes. "Crampatch and the Patri Chookoock don't believe it," he said, dragging his voice back under control. "But I know better. Morgan *is* coming back. And when he does—" He hefted the laser. "Some of us, at least, will be ready."

Alison swallowed. "I'm sure you will," she said. "Well, then. If you don't mind—"

"Go back to the house, little girl," Gazen said. Backing up a step, he settled himself again on a low bench between the two bushes, laying his laser across his knees. "Go back to sleep."

"Yes, sir," Alison said. Keeping an eye on him as long as she could, she made her escape.

Neither she nor Taneem spoke again until they were safely back in bed. "Draycos told me stories about this Gazen human," Taneem said softly.

"So did Jack," Alison said, shivering. In some ways, she knew, Gazen was no more evil or vicious than men like Frost and Neverlin. Neverlin, after all, had ordered the destruction of Draycos's advance team. Gazen, as far as she knew, hadn't even been present during that attack.

But Frost and Neverlin were also smart and calculating. They were in this for profit and power. Men like that Alison could understand, and could deal with.

Gazen, in contrast, was just plain crazy. She could see it in his eyes, and hear it in his voice.

And she wasn't used to dealing with men like that. They scared her, right down to her core.

Distantly, she wished Draycos were here.

"Is there anything I can do?" Taneem asked anxiously, lifting her head a little from Alison's shoulder.

With a smile, Alison reached up to stroke her companion's smooth gray scales. No, Taneem was no poet-warrior of the K'da. But she was loyal, and she was willing, and she was doing the best she could. "No, that's all right," Alison assured her. "I'm fine."

She took a deep breath and tried to push Gazen from her mind. "Better get some sleep," she said, pulling the blankets a little tighter around her chin. "Tomorrow's going to be a busy day."

CHAPTER 20

Two days after his trip to the mine, Jack emerged from his apartment for the morning's schedule to find that Bolo had returned.

"Good morning, Judge-Paladin," the other said politely from the foot of the stone bridge. "I see you're an early riser."

"Comes with the job," Jack told him, looking over Bolo's shoulder to where Thonsifi and the two escorts were waiting. None of them looked very happy. "Speaking of jobs, how's yours going?"

"Almost finished," Bolo said. "A few more hours of actual surveying, and I'll be ready to start working up my report." He waved a hand, the gesture taking in the entire canyon. "So I thought I'd drop by and see if that dinner invitation was still open."

"I'm sure something can be arranged," Jack said as he reached the ground. "Is any of this last bit of work going to be in the area?"

"Actually, all of it is," Bolo said. "In fact—and you might find this interesting—the first thing I'm going to do is take a look in that abandoned mine out there."

Jack suppressed a grimace. Why, he wondered, wasn't he surprised?

Be careful, Jack, Draycos's warning whispered through his mind.

Bet on it, symby, Jack assured him. "You think there might still be something worthwhile in there?" he asked.

"No idea," Bolo said. "But according to the records, Triost still owns the rights to it."

"Really," Jack said. "I understood the ownership was still in dispute."

A flicker of something crossed Bolo's face, gone again almost too fast to see.

But Jack saw it. More to the point, he recognized it.

Jack had already known that Bolo wasn't who he pretended to be. Now, Bolo knew that Jack wasn't, either.

"Interesting," Bolo said, his voice under easy control. Definitely a professional. "Could be my information's out-of-date. Still, as long as I'm here anyway I might as well check it out."

He cocked an eyebrow. "I don't suppose you'd like to come with me? Just in case the rights *aren't* completely ours?"

"You mean to make sure you don't stuff your pockets with rocks on the way out?"

Bolo smiled faintly. "Something like that." He looked at Thonsifi. "You think you can spare your Judge-Paladin for a couple of hours?"

"Yes, they can spare me," Jack said before Thonsifi could answer. "Let me go back and change and I'll be right with you."

Bolo was sitting in his aircar when Jack emerged from the apartment again, this time in shirt and jeans. "I hope you know what you're doing," Draycos murmured from his shoulder.

"I don't like it, either," Jack conceded. Getting in a vehicle with a known enemy was not usually considered a smart thing to do. "But we need answers, and he's probably the best source we're going to find anywhere around here."

"And overconfident people tend to talk too much?"

"Exactly," Jack said as he headed toward the aircar.

A few minutes later they were rising through the chilly early-morning air. "This place is a real obstacle course, isn't it?" Bolo commented as he maneuvered them through the arches and guy wires. "No wonder most Judge-Paladins who come to Semaline never make it down there."

"No wonder," Jack agreed. "Though I understand there *were* two who made it in a few years back. Eleven years, to be exact."

Out of the corner of his eye, he caught the other's sideways glance. "I wouldn't know anything about that," Bolo said casually. "All I know is that the Judge-Paladin on this circuit usually just sets up shop near the NorthCentral Spaceport and invites people to come to him."

"Sounds rather lazy," Jack suggested. "You miss a lot if you don't look at the crime scene."

"Crime scenes can be messy," Bolo pointed out. "Even dangerous."

Jack shrugged. "Part of a Judge-Paladin's job."

"Some Judge-Paladins think so," Bolo agreed. "Others are maybe a little smarter."

Jack felt his throat tighten. Bolo was offering him one last chance to look the other way. "No one's ever accused me of being smart," he said. "So what exactly is the history of this mine?"

"Triost started work on it about fifteen years ago," Bolo said, his voice subtly changed. He'd offered Jack a chance and been refused. Now it was on to business. "They were making good progress when some lawyer got his claws into the Golvins and started making a fuss about it."

"It's on their land, isn't it?"

"That was one of the questions," Bolo said. They were free of the canyon now, and he turned the aircar toward the mine. "The other was whether the Golvins owned the mineral rights even if they *did* own the land."

"So the Golvins appealed to the Judge-Paladins?"

"Apparently," Bolo said as he set them down smoothly on the sand near the mine entrance. "I looked it up while you were getting changed, and you were right—some Judge-Paladin did look into it. But there's no record of him rendering any decision, either for or against us."

"Possibly because the Judge-Paladin died during the investigation."

"Really?" Bolo asked, sounding dutifully surprised. "There wasn't anything about that. Anyway, the case apparently was dropped, and after the standard seven years without activity the clearance court reverted the rights back to us. Hmm—looks pretty dark in there. I've got a couple of flashlights in the back."

He got them out, gave one to Jack, and they headed inside.

Stray wind currents around the opening had mostly erased the footsteps Jack and the two Golvins had made in the sand two days previously. Still, Jack could see the subtle furrows where those footsteps had been.

And *only* their footsteps. If Bolo had entered the mine recently, he hadn't gone in very far. That, Jack decided, could work to his advantage.

"Walls and ceiling look to be in good shape," Bolo commented as they headed down the entry tunnel. "Hasn't picked up much fill, either."

"Doesn't smell as musty as I'd expect, either," Jack added.

"Musty?"

"From all the water," Jack explained. "Triost claimed the lower levels were flooded."

They had reached the large assembly area before Bolo spoke again. "So what exactly were you expecting to find in here?" he asked as Jack turned toward the left-hand tunnel he and Draycos had visited on their last trip.

"I don't know," Jack said. "A little truth, maybe."

"Any particular truth you had in mind?"

Jack shrugged as he stepped into the tunnel. "Whatever the flavor of the day is, I suppose. Watch your step—the floor's a little rough here."

They started down, their feet making little shuffling sounds in the dust. Occasionally there was a clunk as one of them kicked one of the many rocks scattered around. "I gather you've been here before," Bolo said.

"What makes you say that?" Jack asked.

"The marks in the dust," Bolo said, shining his light past Jack's shoulder at the floor ahead. "The wind cleared out most of the tracks in the entryway, but it doesn't reach down here."

"Ah," Jack said, as if that was complete news to him. Somewhere along in here, he knew, Bolo would decide they were far enough down that Jack's body wouldn't be easily found. *He'll be pulling a knife or gun soon,* he thought toward Draycos. *Let me know when you hear him doing that, but stay hidden.*

Are you sure? Draycos's thought came back.

Not really, Jack admitted. *But making him think he's holding all the cards is the only way we'll get him to talk.*

They were within sight of the first branch point, where the tunnel split to right and left, when Jack felt the warning touch of K'da claws against his side. "Here's the really interesting part," Jack said. He dropped into a crouch as if trying to give Bolo a better look and pointed his flashlight down the right-hand branch.

And as he did so, he scooped up a handful of dust from one of the depressions in the tunnel floor and threw it over his shoulder into Bolo's face.

The other bellowed, his shout almost covering up the soft crack as a shot whistled past Jack's ear and shattered bits of rock from the tunnel floor. Jack was already on the move, sprinting forward and ducking down the left-hand tunnel, the one he and Draycos had taken on their last visit. Another shot smashed into the wall at the intersection as he passed, dusting him with rock powder.

Clenching his teeth, Jack kept going. The next intersection turn was only fifty feet away, and he got into the left-hand tunnel and out of Bolo's line of fire before any more shots came. *Now what?* Draycos's words came in his mind.

"We try to find a defensible spot where we can talk to him," Jack muttered back, his mind too busy with thoughts of tactics and survival to focus on this new telepathy thing. "Suggestions welcome."

There. Out of the corner of his eye Jack saw the K'da's tongue rise from his shoulder and point at a small curve in the tunnel just ahead. "Not much room back there," Jack warned

There is enough, Draycos promised. *I will hold the tunnel. Continue ahead and find me more rocks to throw.*

Jack ducked around the curve, and with a surge of weight Draycos leaped up through the back of his collar.

Jack slowed, shining his light on the floor. There were some rocks down there, but only a few big enough to make good weapons. He half turned, opening his mouth to point that out.

And flinched back as the K'da slashed his claws into the side wall, cutting out a shower of rocks and slivers and dust. "Go," he murmured to Jack as he picked up one of the larger rocks and curved his tail around it. Glancing out around the edge of the curve, he whipped his tail like a sling, hurling the rock back down the tunnel.

There was a thud, a snarled curse, and another shot blew a pit in the opposite wall. "I'll hold him here," Draycos murmured to Jack, scooping up another rock. "Go gather more ammunition."

Jack nodded and continued down the tunnel, hoping Bolo wouldn't hear his footsteps and wonder just who it was who was holding him off. Though between the shots and the thudding of the stones, that didn't seem likely.

He'd gone only twenty feet when he came upon a section where part of the tunnel wall had splintered beneath the slurry pipe. Along the floor by the break were a dozen of the kind of rocks Draycos needed. Pulling the front of his shirt out of his jeans, Jack held it like a basket and loaded in the stones.

The leisurely battle was still going on when he returned. "How's it going?" he whispered as he unloaded his prizes onto the floor where Draycos could reach them.

"He's taken shelter in the right-hand tunnel," Draycos murmured back as he whipped another rock around the corner. "At the moment, we're in something of a stalemate."

"At least we're not in a quick slaughter." Jack filled his lungs with dusty air. "Hey, Bolo," he called. "How's it going?"

"It's going okay," Bolo's voice came back. "You got a good arm there, boy."

"Thanks," Jack said. "You *do* realize, don't you, that killing a Judge-Paladin is a death-sentence offense?"

"What, *you?*" the other said contemptuously. "Don't make me laugh."

"I didn't mean *me,*" Jack corrected. "I was talking about my parents. You know—Stuart and Ariel?"

For a moment Bolo didn't speak. "I'll be frunged," he said at last, his tone oddly changed. "You're the *Palmers'* kid?"

"That's right," Jack said, a shiver running through him. Palmer. So that was his real last name. "I take it you're the one who murdered them?"

"Hey, I offered them a chance to be smart," Bolo said. The strangeness in his voice was gone, and he was all business again. "Just like I did for you a minute ago. They didn't take me up on it, either."

"I guess it runs in the family," Jack gritted out, forcing back a sudden flood of rage. He couldn't afford to let his emotions color his thinking. Not now. "Maybe you should have put it as a percentage of the mine. Is there really enough stuff in here to take that kind of risk?"

"I have no idea," Bolo said. "But it must have been worth it to *someone* in the Triost boardroom. Or maybe to one of the bidders. No one told me, and I didn't ask."

Jack frowned. "What bidders?"

"The companies trying to buy us up," Bolo said. "I suppose you want to know which one won?"

"Unless you want to let me out for a couple of hours to do my own research."

Bolo gave a low chuckle. "Sorry. Maybe you should just wait and ask your parents. You'll be joining them soon enough."

A painful knot formed in the pit of Jack's stomach. "Maybe; maybe not," he said as calmly as he could. "I figure you'll run out of bullets before I run out of rocks. And don't forget the Golvins know where I am."

Bolo snorted. "I wouldn't count on them if I were you."

"Why not?" Jack asked. "Do they understand bribes better than I do?"

"They understand fear," Bolo said darkly. "I made it very clear to them the last time what would happen if they told anyone what had happened, or came anywhere near this mine, or made any other sort of trouble."

"I take it I fit into that third category?" Jack suggested.

"You don't even rank that high," Bolo said. "You're just a little follow-up work I should have taken care of eleven years ago. If you don't mind my asking, how exactly did I miss you?"

"I had help," Jack said. "I suppose fear's a good enough motivator. But you really should have spread it around a little more instead of just threatening the leaders. And Foeinatw, too, of course."

"Who?"

"Four-Eight-Naught-Two," Jack said. "The one who called a couple of weeks ago and told you I was here."

"Oh, right," Bolo said. "Him."

"Yes, *him*," Jack said, feeling a trickle of contempt. The man couldn't even remember the names of the people he'd bribed or bullied or threatened into helping him. "Too bad he wasn't the one flying the day they ran into me at the spaceport."

"Yes, it was," Bolo agreed, his voice darkening. "Mostly too bad for you."

"We'll see," Jack said. "Who ended up buying up Triost?"

"We back to that again?" Bolo said. "You're awfully nosy—you know that?"

"What do you care?" Jack countered. "I'm already dead, right?"

"You're making a recording, aren't you?" Bolo asked. "Getting all this nice confession on perm. You don't really think anything like that's going to survive the morning, do you?"

"You'll find out at your trial," Jack said. "Who bought Triost?"

Bolo chuckled. "Good one, kid. At my trial. You've got spirit—gotta give you that."

"Thanks," Jack said. "Who bought up Triost?"

"The rich get richer, kid," Bolo said. "First law of the universe. Braxton Universis."

Jack caught his breath. Braxton Universis. The megacorporation owned and operated by Cornelius Braxton.

The man whose life Jack and Draycos had saved only four months ago. If he'd hired Bolo eleven years ago to murder Jack's parents . . .

"Well, it's been nice talking to you," Bolo went on. "But I've got places to go and things to do. You got two choices here: come out of hiding and make it quick and painless, or stay where you are and make it a lot harder on yourself."

Jack frowned, trying to wrench his mind away from Braxton and Braxton Universis. "Thanks, but I kind of like it here."

"That's good," Bolo said. " 'Cause this is where you're going to spend what's left of your life. So long, kid."

From around the corner came the sound of running footsteps. Draycos whipped his tail, hurling a stone blindly around the curve.

And suddenly the whole tunnel exploded in a flash of light and an earsplitting thunderclap.

CHAPTER 21

A massive shock wave caught Jack across the face and chest like a full-body slap, hurling him backward down the tunnel.

But even as he dropped toward the rocky floor, he sensed Draycos leaping past him. A fraction of a second later, he slammed into the K'da as they both hit the floor. They rolled over a couple of times and came to a halt.

"You all right?" Jack asked, wiping dust and grit off his face as he scrambled to his feet. For a second his knees wobbled, and he had to grab the slurry pipe for support.

The K'da said something, but Jack's ears were still ringing too hard from the explosion to hear it. "What?" he asked. "No—come here." Brushing at his shirt with one hand, he held out the other toward Draycos.

Draycos put a paw on his hand and slithered up his sleeve onto his back. *I am unhurt,* the K'da's reassurance came into Jack's mind, bypassing his dazed hearing. *You?*

"I'm okay," Jack said, blinking a few times. The tunnel was filled with dust that was only slowly starting to settle. "The guy's consistent, anyway. He used a bomb on my parents, and now he tried to use one on me."

Draycos's snout rose from Jack's shoulder and his tongue

flicked out twice. *I do not sense any airflow, Jack. We may be trapped in here.*

Jack smiled tightly. "I'll bet that's what Bolo thinks, too. Let's take a look."

His flashlight was a few feet farther down the tunnel, glowing faintly through the pile of rock chips that had partially buried it. Jack retrieved it, then backtracked to the site of the explosion.

Bolo had done a good job. The tunnel near the intersection was completely blocked by a pile of shattered rock. "Probably a shaped charge set against the ceiling," Draycos said as Jack played his light over the top of the pile.

"Had it all ready to go, too," Jack agreed. "I wonder what he would have done if I'd refused to come to the mine with him."

"Perhaps there would now be no Great Assembly Hall, either," Draycos said.

Jack grimaced. "Yeah." Taking a deep breath—and instantly regretting it as the floating dust set off a coughing fit—he turned around. "I guess we'd better get started."

"Will you need help?" Draycos asked.

"No, I can handle it," Jack assured him. "You stay here and keep an ear out for any other tricks Bolo might have up his sleeve."

It took a few minutes for Jack to reach the end of the tunnel. It took another minute for him to cut away the protective plastic from one of the two diggers with his multitool. His one fear, that the diggers' power cells would have drained over the past eleven years, proved unfounded. A minute of trial and error as he figured out the controls, and he and the machine were on their way back up the tunnel.

He arrived at the blockage to find Draycos digging carefully at one edge of the rock pile. Beside the K'da, the slurry pipe against the wall had been freshly sliced open. "All set," Jack announced. He pointed at the pipe. "Getting bored?"

"I was concerned the air might fail before we finish," Draycos explained. "Fortunately, the collapse doesn't seem to have damaged the pipe."

"Good," Jack said, holding out a hand. "Come on aboard—there's not enough room here for all of us."

A minute later Draycos was on his back, and Jack plowed his new toy into the rock pile.

The job went surprisingly quickly, though as Jack thought about it he realized that a machine designed to eat into a solid rock face would have little trouble with what were basically just very large chunks of gravel. The toothed roller on the front end dug into the pile, taking in the rocks and sending them back into a set of grinders where they were chewed up still further before being ejected out the machine's back end.

Every couple of minutes the pile would shift, scattering the rocks and sending more dust into the air. But the fresh breeze from the slurry pipe helped blow it clear. Fifteen minutes into the task, Jack could already see a gap at the top of the pile. Five minutes after that, the pile was low enough that he could see the huge dome Bolo's explosive had blasted in the ceiling.

And ten minutes after that, he was able to shut down the digger and crawl carefully over what was left of the pile to freedom.

"I suppose the next question is what we do next," Jack muttered to Draycos as he trudged back up the tunnel. "Bolo and his aircar will be long gone by now, and from here to anywhere is going to be a really long walk."

Why not go back to the canyon?

Jack rolled his eyes. With their ears recovered from the blast there was no longer any reason not to just talk to each other. Clearly, Draycos was delighted with this new parlor game he'd learned and was determined to practice it every chance he got.

Personally, Jack found it a lot harder and more distracting to focus his thoughts that way. But he supposed the K'da was right. *I have no problem with that,* he said, concentrating hard on forming each word in his mind. *The problem's going to be getting someone's attention from up on the rim. Unless you were thinking of climbing down with me hanging on to your tail.*

He had a quick mental image of the K'da giving one of his crack-jawed smiles. *I think that would be a bit more than the Golvins are ready for just now.*

Ahead, Jack could see a faint glow as the beam from his flashlight reflected off the white ceramic ceiling of the assembly area. They were almost home. *So again, what do we do?* he asked. *Wait for Thonsifi to start wondering what happened to me and get Eithon to fly her up here?*

That is certainly a possibility, Draycos said. *We may need to spend the day here, but surely she will not allow the sun to set without coming to see if you need assistance.*

I don't know, Jack replied doubtfully. *Now that we know why the One wasn't happy to see me in the first place, I don't think he'd be all that heartbroken if I never came back.*

They had reached the end of the tunnel now. With a sense of relief, Jack stepped into the big assembly room.

And without warning, a hand lanced out from just inside the room and grabbed his shirt collar. Before he could do more than gasp, he was yanked sideways off his feet, the arm shifting around to catch him around the throat.

"Cute, kid," Bolo's voice grated in his ear. The arm tightened around Jack's throat, and he felt the muzzle of a gun press up against the back of his head. "Just tell me everything, huh? I'm already dead, huh? Where was your friend hiding, the end of the tunnel?"

"I . . . don't know . . . what—" Jack tried to say, pulling at Bolo's arm as he fought desperately to get air into his lungs.

"Save it," Bolo snarled, squeezing his arm even tighter. "This slurry pipe here, the one you cut or broke open to get some fresh air? It's really good at conducting sound, too."

Lifting Jack half off his feet by his neck, Bolo dragged him around the corner to stand in front of the tunnel entrance. "You—down in the mine!" he shouted. "I've got your friend. Come out or I'll blow his head open."

There was no answer. Jack could feel Draycos moving around on his skin, and could sense that the K'da was trying to talk to him.

But he couldn't understand. He couldn't feel or hear or concentrate on anything except the arm choking the life out of him. White sparkles were starting to dance across his vision, and he could feel his knees starting to wobble as the strength drained out of his legs. His hands, clutching uselessly at Bolo's arm, were going numb.

"You hear me?" Bolo's voice came distantly in his ears. "Come out!"

The jabbing pressure on the back of Jack's head disappeared. Out of the corner of his eye he saw Bolo's other hand appear over his shoulder, pointing his gun down the tunnel.

And suddenly Jack was shoved violently forward against Bolo's arm as Draycos burst from the back of Jack's shirt between the two of them, breaking Bolo's grip on Jack's throat.

Someone screamed, but whether it was Draycos or Bolo Jack couldn't tell in his daze. He staggered forward away from the sudden clattering noises behind him, one hand clutching his aching throat. The side of the tunnel loomed ahead of him, and he barely got his other hand up in time to keep himself from running face-first into the rough stone.

From behind him came a sudden loud thud, and then an equally sudden silence. Still gasping in air, he turned himself around.

Draycos was crouched on the assembly room floor, his neck arched, his jaws partially open. His glowing green eyes were on Bolo, sprawled on the floor beneath him. Bolo's gun was also on the floor, lying in the dust a couple of feet from the man's limp hand. "Uh-oh," Jack murmured.

"I'm sorry," Draycos said, looking at Jack. "I was only trying to disable him."

"It's okay," Jack said. It hurt his throat to talk, and his voice was unexpectedly raspy in his ears. "Hard floor in here."

"Harder than I realized," Draycos said ruefully, looking Jack up and down. "What about you?"

Jack shook his head. "I'll be okay. You?"

"I'm unhurt," Draycos said. He looked back down at Bolo. "What do we do now?"

Jack gazed down at the dead man, a strange mixture of emotions swirling through him. Uncle Virgil, criminal though he was, had consistently hammered into Jack that he was never, *ever* to kill anyone.

Of course, that hadn't been so much from respect for life as it was the fact that killing during one of their jobs could bring huge penalties down on top of them. Still, the training was there, and it had taken firm hold over Jack's heart and soul. So much so, in fact, that when he and Draycos had first linked up he'd made a point of explaining to his new partner that K'da warrior rules about summary justice didn't apply here in the Orion Arm.

And yet, despite all that, Jack couldn't help but feel a dark satisfaction at Bolo's death. After eleven years, justice had finally been done for his parents.

Resolutely, he turned his eyes away. "What we do," he told Draycos, "is get in that aircar and get the blazes out of here."

"What about Jonathan Langston?" Draycos asked.

Jack grimaced. He'd forgotten all about the Golvins' secret prisoner. "What about him?"

Draycos cocked his head slightly to the side, and Jack grimaced again. "You're right," he conceded with a sigh. "Fine. We'll go back and get him out."

"We must at least try to determine whether or not his story is true," Draycos said, stepping away from Bolo and padding to Jack's side. "You must find a way to convince the One to allow a hearing."

"Not necessary," Jack assured him. "Langston's telling the truth."

Draycos's neck arched with surprise. "How do you know?"

"Simple logic," Jack said, rubbing at his throat. "Tell you later."

They went out to the aircar and Jack climbed into the pilot's seat. He glanced around, checking the controls—"Uh-oh," he muttered.

"What is it?" Draycos said, lifting his head from Jack's shoulder.

"That," Jack said, pointing at a small flat box half hidden beneath the instrument display panel. "It's a UniLink, a gadget for patching through to the nearest InterWorld transmitter and sending direct messages." He pulled it out on its attached cable and peered at the display. "And I'd say it's just been used."

"Do you think Bolo sent out word of your death?"

"Let's hope that's all the message said," Jack said, tucking it back away out of sight and turning on the main engines.

"Wait a moment," Draycos said. "Can we use that to contact the *Essenay*?"

Jack shook his head. "A UniLink's designed to send to only one specific location, which means it's got the target receiver preloaded," he explained. "They're also typically loaded to the gills with encryption and ping-testers. No, we'll have to grab Langston and head back to the spaceport InterWorld building and call Uncle Virge the old-fashioned way."

As a passenger, Jack had already seen that flying into the canyon took a great deal of concentration and skill. As a pilot, he quickly found out that it took all that and then some. Twice the shifting winds nearly blew the aircar sideways into one of the stone columns, and once he came within inches of ramming a guy wire he hadn't noticed.

But after what seemed like twice the time all his earlier trips had taken, he made it through and set the aircar down onto the landing pit.

A small crowd was waiting there, standing in a nervous-looking cluster at the northern end of the pit. A pace or two in front of the others were Thonsifi and the One.

"Good morning, One Among Many," Jack greeted the latter as he walked toward the group. "My apologies for the delay. I'm now ready to begin the day's judging."

"Where is he?" the One demanded, his eyes flicking past Jack's shoulder to the aircar's empty passenger seat.

"You mean Bolo?" Jack asked pointedly. "The man who wrecked your other Assembly Hall and murdered two Judge-Paladins?"

The One twitched violently, his face turning into a solid mass of wrinkles. "Disaster and death," he whispered. "I was right. You have brought disaster and death upon us."

"Relax—I'm not blaming you," Jack said. "Neither will the Judge-Paladins' Office when they—"

"No!" the One cut him off, his voice edging into panic. "You cannot tell them! You must not tell them!" He jabbed his right arm straight up into the air.

And suddenly, the entire front of the waiting crowd sprouted bows and arrows.

All of the arrows pointed straight at Jack.

CHAPTER 22

For a long moment no one moved or spoke. *Jack?* Draycos asked urgently into the taut silence.

Jack measured the distance with his eyes. Way too far, especially against multiple armed opponents. *Stay put,* he told the K'da. "You don't want to do this, One Among Many," he said quietly. "And there's also no need. You and your people were Bolo's victims in his crimes, not his accomplices. You have nothing to fear from me."

"Do you think it is *you* we fear, Jupa Jack?" the One demanded, his voice a mixture of bluster and anguish. "It is *his* people we fear. *His* people who will now unleash vengeance against us."

Jack felt his stomach tighten. He should have seen that one coming. "Not if I can get the Judge-Paladins' Office on this quickly enough," he said. "Let me go to the spaceport and get a message off to them."

The One's face wrinkled. "We cannot take the risk," he said, his voice regretful but firm.

A chill ran up Jack's skin. "You planned this from the beginning, didn't you?" he said quietly. "Once I was here, you never intended to let me go."

"I am sorry, Jupa Jack," the One said. "I should have sent you away when you first arrived. Now, it is too late." He slowly lowered his arm, and the arrows pointed at Jack dipped slightly to aim instead at the ground in front of him. "You will return now to your apartment."

"As you wish," Jack said, starting to breathe a little easier. He and Draycos were still in big trouble, but at least it didn't look like they were going to be shot. Yet. "But understand this. I said before that you weren't in trouble with the Judge-Paladins' Office. You still aren't. But if you continue to hold me a prisoner you *will* be."

"Your meals will be brought to you as usual," the One said, as if he hadn't heard a single word of the warning. "Your duties are . . . for the moment . . . suspended." He gestured, and two of the armed Golvins stepped over to Jack's pillar and took up positions on either side of the bridge. "You will go now," he said.

Jack looked at Thonsifi, but her eyes were avoiding his. Clearly, she was upset by all of this. Just as clearly, she wasn't going to interfere. "Very well," Jack said. With as much dignity as he could pull together, he strode between the two waiting Golvins and climbed the bridge into his apartment.

For a moment he paused just inside the doorway, peeking between the colorful streamers as he watched the crowd drift away. Thonsifi was the last to go, her eyes and expressionless face turned up toward his apartment. But finally she, too, lowered her head and walked away. The two Golvins at the foot of his bridge slung their bows over their shoulders within easy reach, and settled themselves as if for a long stay.

Draycos leaped out of the back of Jack's shirt and eased an eye between two of the streamers. "What do you think?" Jack asked.

For a moment the K'da was silent. Then, with a twitch of his tail, he stepped back from the doorway. "They have the look of determination," he said.

"Yeah, so did the One," Jack agreed grimly. "I don't think we're getting out of here anytime soon. Not without a fight, anyway."

Draycos twitched his tail again. "I don't wish to fight these people."

"You think I do?" Jack retorted. "I wasn't just spinning soap dust when I said they were victims. But we can't help them—or ourselves—if we're stuck in here."

"Agreed," Draycos said. "Still, despite their weapons, these are not a warrior people. A few uneventful days, I think, and their vigilance will fade into routine and boredom."

Jack glanced out the doorway at the landing pit. "Though they'll probably stash Bolo's aircar out of sight before then," he warned.

"We'll find it," Draycos assured him. "In a few days we should be able to make our move."

And while they sat here doing nothing, the K'da and Shontine refugees were moving ever closer to their destruction. "I'm sorry, Draycos," he said, dropping wearily onto the couch. "I should have gone straight to Langston's cave, picked him up, and headed straight out again."

"In hindsight, perhaps you should have," Draycos agreed. "But any blame must be shared between us. I also didn't expect such a strong reaction from the One."

"The real irony is that he's probably jumping at shadows," Jack said. "He thinks there's a whole army out there ready to come charging in to avenge Bolo's death."

"You don't believe that will happen?"

"I'm sure of it," Jack said. "You don't share a secret like a double Judge-Paladin murder with any more people than you absolutely have to. I'm guessing that with Bolo gone, the only one who knows anything about this is whoever it was who hired him in the first place."

"Who you believe may have been Cornelius Braxton?"

Jack made a face. "I thought you couldn't read my mind long distance."

"I can't," Draycos confirmed. "But your reaction in the tunnel when Bolo named Braxton Universis wasn't difficult to interpret. And I know that you've never fully trusted the man."

"Do *you* trust him?" Jack countered.

"I have no reason to distrust him," Draycos said. Which wasn't exactly the same thing, Jack noted privately. "I also see this as more likely the work of Neverlin. It certainly would close the last puzzling links in the chain."

"Which chain is that?"

"How Neverlin knew where our advance team would be arriving," Draycos said. "Our contact group had talked to the Chitac Nomads about buying Iota Klestis for our peoples. The Nomads apparently consulted with Triost, which Uncle Virge said still owned the planet. If Neverlin was in close contact with someone in Triost—"

"Like, say, someone he'd pulled off a double murder with?"

"Exactly," Draycos said. "It would then be reasonable for this person to pass the news about us on to him."

"I suppose," Jack conceded. "That still doesn't let Braxton entirely off the hook, though. In fact, maybe he and Neverlin planned this genocide thing together."

"Neverlin tried to kill him."

"Maybe they had a falling out."

For a moment Draycos didn't respond. "I don't believe Braxton is involved," he said at last. "But you're right, I have no proof. And as you suggest, until we have such proof, it would be prudent to assume all around us are enemies. Or at least potential enemies."

"Yeah," Jack said. "What still gets me is why they were murdered in the first place. If someone was worried Triost was going to lose control of the mine—"

He broke off as the truth suddenly slapped him across the face. "No," he breathed, sitting bolt upright. "They weren't worried about Triost *losing* the mine. They were worried about them *getting* it."

Draycos cocked his head in a frown. "I don't understand."

"That's because you're an honorable poet-warrior and not a sleazy-minded corporate thief," Jack said bitterly. "Look. Braxton Universis wants to buy Triost Mining. But they don't want to spend any more money on the deal than they absolutely have to."

He waved a hand upward in the direction of the mine. "But in the middle of their negotiations they find out there's this little mine out in the middle of nowhere that's tied up in a dispute with the locals. They also find out that a pair of Judge-Paladins have been called in to settle the issue."

Draycos's neck arched. "And if the Judge-Paladins ruled for Triost, the company's value would have gone up."

"And so would its price," Jack said, his stomach churning with anger and disgust. Was *this* all his parents had died for? "So someone decided to make sure there wouldn't be any ruling until after the deal had gone through."

Draycos lashed his tail. "But to commit *murder?* Weren't they afraid there would be an investigation?"

"Maybe they thought they could cover it up," Jack said. "Besides, even if there was, who would the investigators look at? Not Triost. You heard Bolo—the ruling eventually rolled over in their favor."

"I assumed he was lying about that."

"I assumed so, too, but maybe not," Jack said. "Triost got the mine, Braxton got Triost, and everyone's happy."

"Except your parents," Draycos said quietly. "And you."

Jack stared past the K'da at the colorful streamers rustling in the breeze. His whole body felt like it was on fire, his mind churning back and forth between the urge to scream and the urge to hammer his fists on the stone walls.

And the urge to kill.

"Jack?"

With an effort, Jack pulled his eyes and mind back to his companion. "Tell me, Draycos," he said. "What's the official K'da poet-warrior ethic on the subject of hatred?"

For a moment Draycos didn't answer. "Hatred is an emotion," he said at last. "An honest expression of your feelings of the moment, and therefore nothing to be ashamed of."

"But if I actually did what I want to do right now? I suppose you'd say that was wrong?"

"You cannot find satisfaction in revenge, Jack," Draycos said. "Revenge is a trap which promises something it cannot deliver."

Jack hissed a sigh. "Only justice works, huh?"

"That has been my experience." Draycos's tail twitched. "However, the end result of justice is often the same as the end desired by revenge."

Jack frowned. "Meaning?"

The K'da's tail arched slightly. "If you can prove Cornelius Braxton ordered your parents murdered, and if you wish me to do so, I will kill him."

A shiver ran up Jack's spine. To think it in the dark corners of his mind was one thing. To hear it stated aloud was somehow something else entirely. "I'll keep that in mind," he managed.

For a long moment they gazed at each other in silence. Then, with another twitch of his tail, Draycos turned toward the galley. "In the meantime, we can probably both use some extra healing time. Are you hungry?"

"No, thanks," Jack said. "But go ahead."

"Thank you," Draycos said, popping open the refrigerator and pulling out a plate of meat and fruit. "You said earlier you were convinced of Langston's innocence?"

"Well, his story fits the facts, anyway," Jack said, getting up and sitting down at the table. "We know now why those four Golvins he creamed with his Djinn-90 were poking around topside in the first place. Bolo had warned them not to go into the mine. But like an idiot, he'd also told them the lower parts were flooded."

Draycos's neck arched in sudden understanding. "They were attempting to dig a new tunnel to the water?"

"You got it," Jack said, vaguely pleased that he'd figured it out before the K'da. "I'll give you four to one odds that their families' land is all the way on that side of the canyon, probably as far away from the river as you can get without running into the trees. If they could tap into this supposed new water supply, they could pipe it over to the edge and voilà—instant rainfall."

"They were near the mine," Draycos murmured, his tail

lashing restlessly. "The One was afraid that if he let Langston leave, Bolo would find out."

"Exactly," Jack said, nodding. "He couldn't take the chance that they'd been close enough to the mine to make Bolo mad."

Draycos's tail tip was making the slow circles of deep thought. "Only it didn't," he said. "We know that because Bolo's informant Foeinatw would surely have sent a message to him about the incident."

"Which Bolo apparently ignored," Jack said grimly. "Which means that Langston's been rotting away out here for five years for nothing."

Draycos flicked his tongue out. "He will not be happy when he finds that out."

"I'm pretty sure I'm not planning to be the one to tell him," Jack said candidly. "Let's at least get him back to civilization before we mention that part."

"Agreed," Draycos said. "Now all we have to do is decide how best to do that."

Jack looked back at the doorway. "Like you said, we've got some time. We'll think of something."

CHAPTER 23

"Three days," Frost growled as he led Alison up the wide stairway. "Three *days.*"

Alison didn't answer. Frost and Neverlin had been getting more and more this way over the past two days, annoyed and impatient and positively twitchy.

But then, Alison was starting to feel a little annoyed herself.

Because despite their veiled accusations, she hadn't been idle all this time. In fact, she'd probably worked harder, and thought and sweated harder, than she ever had in her entire life.

None of it had done any good. She was stuck. Had been stuck, in fact, for the past day and a half.

"Well?" Frost prodded as they reached the heavily guarded corridor leading to the Patri's private suite. "*Say* something."

"Like what?" Alison retorted. "It's tricky. You all knew it was tricky. That's why you hired me."

"Which so far doesn't seem to be doing much good," Frost countered. Apparently, he was in the mood for an argument this morning.

"Relax, will you?" Alison said as soothingly as she could manage through her irritation. "When I blow the thing up, *then* you can complain about it."

Without warning, Frost came to a halt, his hand snaking out to grab Alison's upper arm and yank her around to face him. "Who told you about that?" he demanded.

"Told me about what?" Alison asked, shrinking back as his fingers dug into the skin beneath her thin shirt. Out of the corner of her eye she could see the Brummgan corridor guards reaching warily for their weapons.

For a long, tense moment they stood there, Frost staring hard into Alison's face. Then, slowly, his hand relaxed its grip. "The first two guys Mr. Arthur brought in blew up the safes they were supposed to open," he said at last. "Well, blew up the contents, anyway."

Alison swallowed hard. So *that* was what was in the mysterious packet Taneem had seen fastened to the safe's inside ceiling. Like Neverlin had done with his own vault aboard the *Advocatus Diaboli,* the K'da and Shontine advance team leaders had thoughtfully added a self-destruct mechanism to their safes. "What did— I mean—did it kill them?"

"In a way," Frost said. "The Patri had them both shot."

"I see," Alison said, forcing herself back on track. "And none of you were planning to mention this bit of recent history?"

"I think Mr. Arthur would probably have said something when you got ready to actually open it," Frost said. "Only so far, you haven't gotten that far, have you?"

Reaching up, Alison pushed at the hand still holding on to her arm. For a moment Frost resisted, probably just to show her that he could. Then, he let her push the hand away. "You just let me work my own way," she told him. "I'll get it open."

"You'd better." Turning, Frost started down the corridor again. Neverlin and the Patri were seated in their usual armchairs, well back from the safe resting on a transfer platform in the middle of the room. "Good morning, Alison," Neverlin greeted her, his voice neutral. He wasn't any happier about the delay than Frost, Alison knew. But at least he hid his impatience better. "Is this going to be the day?"

"I don't know," Alison said. "We'll see."

Neverlin inclined his head to her. "Then let's begin."

Alison nodded back, then nodded politely at the Patri. The old Brummga made no response, but remained slumped in his chair, his eyes half-closed as if he were about to fall asleep.

It was all an act, of course. Brummgas were hardly the most intelligent or insightful beings in the Orion Arm, and it was easy to dismiss them as mobile stacks of brainless muscle. But their personal survival instinct was as good as anyone else's. The Patri had entered into this scheme with every expectation of making a huge profit out of it.

But things were not going well. They were certainly not going the way Neverlin and Frost had originally intended. It was entirely possible that the Patri's glacier-speed thought processes were even now reexamining the whole situation.

In fact, as Alison turned and stepped over to the safe it occurred to her that perhaps *that* was the real reason for Frost's nervousness. Maybe this grand alliance was starting to show cracks.

In the meantime, Alison had a safe to open.

She laid out her tools, studying the safe as she did so. It was a big thing, about the size of a small desk, rectangular in shape, its single door equipped with a double-twist combination lock and a break bar for pulling open the door once it was unlocked. Along the safe's left-hand wall, midway between top and bottom, was a horizontal line of twenty indentations big enough and deep enough to fit the first joint of a Brummga's finger. The whole thing was made of an incredibly hard metal that the Patri's experts had apparently been unable to identify.

A hard metal that had impact and heat-stress marks over nearly a third of its surface, and that had been warped visibly from its original shape. Clearly, this was the safe that had been aboard the *Havenseeker,* the only one of the four advance team ships to crash.

Frost had now said two other safes had been destroyed. Neverlin had apparently decided, not unreasonably, to let her practice on the one whose contents might already have been ruined by the crash.

Which meant there was a fourth, undamaged safe somewhere. Possibly somewhere in this very house.

"You said yesterday it was a simple combination lock," Neverlin reminded her as she put together her audio sensor.

"I said it was straightforward," Alison corrected. "I didn't say it was simple."

"Then what's the delay?" Neverlin persisted.

"There are still a few problems to work out," Alison said. "Unless you want this one to blow up like the other two did."

She had the minor satisfaction of seeing Neverlin turn a dark glare on Frost. Setting the end of the sensor against the door above the lock, she pretended to be digging out yet more deep, mysterious clues.

And tried desperately to think.

Because the lock really *was* pretty simple. The problem was much farther in.

Taneem had spent over two hours over the past three days peering into the safe's interior as Alison sat with her back pressed against one or the other of the safe's side walls. Late at night on each of those days, after Alison had run the most recent data through her MixStar computer, the K'da had described what she'd seen, giving the girl a verbal map of the safe's interior. Alison had listened, and asked questions, and tried to make sense of it all.

But that sense refused to come.

For one thing, the safe was way too big, with enough room in there for two or three good-sized travel cases. Alison herself could probably fit inside, in fact, though it would be a tight squeeze. Yet the only contents were a handful of little plastic or ceramic diamonds the size of Alison's thumb.

There was also that packet fastened to the ceiling, which was connected to a wire grid that covered the entire inside of the safe. Now that Alison knew the packet was a self-destruct bomb, she realized that the grid itself was part of the whole defense system. Anyone trying to cut or blast their way through the walls would cut one or more of those wires, blowing the bomb and destroying the diamonds.

But the bomb wasn't just attached to the grid. There were also two other cables, longer and thicker, stretching from the bomb to the wall with the twenty indentations. In fact, from Taneem's description, Alison had concluded that the cables disappeared into the wall exactly opposite to the fourth and sixth of those indentations.

And at *that* point, she had found herself stuck with a whole stack of unanswered questions.

Had there been other cables connecting the bomb to the other indentations, cables that might have been knocked off in the crash? From Taneem's description it looked like the packet had places where such cables could have been attached.

But the K'da couldn't see anything lying loose inside the safe except the diamonds. Could the cables have somehow been destroyed?

A look at the last undamaged safe might provide some answers. But Alison didn't dare ask for such a thing. Especially since she wasn't supposed to know that a fourth safe even existed.

Leaving the sensor attached to the metal above the lock, she sat down with her back pressed against the safe door and pulled out her notebook and pen. She felt Taneem shift around on her back, once again using that ever-so-useful K'da trick for looking through walls.

"You know, we *can* get you a chair," Frost said.

"No, thanks," Alison said, making little marks in the notebook as if she was taking actual notes. Taneem's job today was to see if she could get a better look at the spots where the two cables and the wall connected.

For a few minutes Alison stayed as she was, pretending to listen to the sensor's output and making more little squiggles in her notebook. Then she felt Taneem shift again on her skin, and there was the touch of K'da claws on her right side. Alison half turned, moved the sensor to a new position, and then resettled herself against the door a few inches farther to her right.

The next three hours were spent mostly in silence. There was an occasional clink as she rearranged the components of her equipment, or a muted clunk as she attached or reattached the various sensors. Sometimes she would accidentally kick the safe as she moved around it. Twice during the morning a messenger slipped in to deliver a murmured message to the Patri.

But aside from that no one spoke. The three watchers, for that matter, hardly even moved in their seats. It was, Alison reflected grimly, rather like working in a tomb.

A little before noon, she finally called a halt. "I need to go back to my room for a while," she informed the others. "I need to do some thinking."

"You can't think here?" Frost asked.

"I want to lie down," Alison explained. "Humans do their fastest thinking standing up, but they do their best thinking lying down."

The Patri stirred in his seat. "It is stalling," he rumbled.

Alison turned to him, her mouth gone suddenly dry. There hadn't been a single scrap of doubt in that voice that she could hear. "I'm not stalling," she protested. "All I want to do is—"

"What do you mean, Patri Chookoock?" Neverlin cut her off, his eyes suddenly hard and cold.

"It makes the same moves over and over," the Patri said. He gestured toward the safe, his eyes never leaving Alison's face. "Today it does the same as it did two days ago."

"I'm checking my readings," Alison put in before Neverlin could say anything. "Some safes have floating codes and chron flippers."

"It is stalling," the Patri accused again. "It cannot solve the puzzle and thus seeks an opportunity to run away from it."

And out of the corner of her eye, Alison saw Frost stiffen.

She flicked her eyes toward him. But whatever it was she'd seen had instantly been buried behind an expressionless face. "With all due respect, I'm not going anywhere," Alison said. "I've got twenty thousand riding on this." She raised her eyebrows at Neverlin. "Forty if I can do it before Mr. Arthur finishes his Easter egg hunt."

Neverlin's eyes narrowed. "Look, Kayna—"

"Actually, I think we could all do with a break," Frost cut

him off smoothly. "In any event, it *is* almost lunchtime. Kayna can eat in her room and take whatever thinking time she needs. When she's ready, we can all meet again. Is that acceptable?"

Neverlin had switched his narrowed-eyed stare to Frost. But he merely nodded. "Fine with me. Patri Chookoock?"

"*If* it is ever ready," the Brummga growled.

"She will be," Frost promised. "Come on, Kayna. I'll take you back to your room."

Neither of them spoke until they reached Alison's slave-level room. Alison walked inside; without waiting for an invitation, Frost followed. "Isn't it interesting how the human mind works?" he commented conversationally as he closed the door behind him. "I've been watching you for two weeks without a clue. And then, a single offhand comment from a fat, ugly lump with stuffed cabbage for brains, and suddenly it comes clear."

Alison held her breath. If he'd gotten a clean look at her in the Rho Scorvi forest . . .

"Running away." Frost leveled a finger at her face, his casual manner abruptly gone. "You're a deserter from the Malison Ring."

Alison's breath went out in a huff. Bad enough, but not as bad as she'd feared.

But definitely bad enough. "The what?" she asked. It might still pay her to play stupid.

It didn't. "Don't waste my time," Frost bit out. "Your hair's different—shorter and darker—but I remember the face from the newslist. You joined up about eight months ago, went through basic, then disappeared the week you were sent to your first post."

"All right," Alison said as calmly as she could. "I admit it. I got scared and ran."

"Oh, you didn't get scared," Frost said. "And you didn't just run. Because I also remember that your training camp C.O. reported there might have been a breach in his computer system during the six weeks you were there."

Alison grimaced. So she'd left a trail behind her on that job. Between the Malison Ring and the Whinyard's Edge, she wasn't running up a very good record here. "I was just trying to clear out my record," she said, letting a little tremor drift into her voice. "I knew I couldn't handle the job, and thought—"

"Spare me," Frost snarled. "I've had about as much of you as I can stomach."

"Okay, fine," Alison said, dropping the tremor. "Game's over. I'm not exactly thrilled by the company, either, if you want to know the truth. But you still need me."

"Maybe not as badly as you think," Frost said. "Like you said, the game's over. So here's what's going to happen. You're going back to that room—today—and you're going to open that safe."

Alison stared at him, her throat tightening. "I can't," she said. "I don't know how to deactivate the self-destruct bomb."

"Then you'd better figure it out, hadn't you?" Frost advised coldly. "Because if it goes off, the Patri will have you shot." He shrugged. "Either way, I'll be happy."

Across her back, Alison felt Taneem shifting position. Quickly, she put a warning hand on her shoulder. "Can I at least have an hour to think?"

"Sure," Frost said, opening the door again. "Take all afternoon if you want." He leveled his finger again. "But sometime before midnight tonight, you're going to open that safe." Stepping out into the corridor, he closed the door behind him.

CHAPTER 24

For a long minute Alison just stood there, staring at the closed door, her mind skidding like an out-of-control bobsled.

One way or another, she was going to die tonight.

Taneem bounded out of her back collar. The sudden weight threw Alison off balance, and she barely caught herself before she could slam into the wall. "I'm sorry," Taneem apologized as she turned back around. "I came off too quickly."

"No, it's okay," Alison said, looking at the K'da with a surge of guilt. *Take care of Taneem,* Jack had told her just before he'd disappeared on Semaline.

Instead, Alison's failure was going to get her killed, too.

"Are you worried?" Taneem asked, stepping closer and peering into Alison's face.

"Yes, I'm worried," Alison told her honestly. "In fact, I'm terrified."

The dragon twitched her tail. "How may I help?"

Alison sighed as she sat down on the edge of the bed. "I don't think you can," she said.

"You *will* solve the problem," Taneem said firmly. "I know you will."

Alison looked away from that earnest dragon face. "I don't

think so," she said quietly. "I'm stuck, Taneem. I can't figure out what the people who designed the safe were trying to do."

She started as something settled onto her lap. She looked down to see Taneem's head resting there, those silver eyes gazing up at her. It was so exactly like the way her old Newfoundland used to do that it brought tears to her eyes. "You're very clever, Alison," Taneem said. "I've heard both Jack and Draycos say so."

Alison had to smile at that. "*Jack* actually paid me a compliment?"

Taneem's tail flicked. "I'm not sure he meant it as a compliment," she conceded. "I think he was being annoyed with you at the time."

"That sounds better," Alison said. Her smile faded. "But all that cleverness doesn't seem to be working. You were right—we should have tried to get away back on Semaline."

"No, it was *you* who was right," Taneem insisted. "The risk was worth taking. As you pointed out, if we'd attacked our captors we might well have died."

"Instead of dying now," Alison said, stroking Taneem's head. "At least you they won't have to worry about burying."

And was instantly ashamed of herself. It had been horribly insensitive to remind Taneem that she would go two-dimensional and simply disappear when she died. She opened her mouth to apologize—

The words frozen in her throat. *Would simply disappear . . .*

And suddenly she had it. "That's it," she murmured. "Taneem, I've *got* it."

"I knew you would," the K'da said, lifting her head from Alison's lap. "Tell me."

"They were smart," Alison said, her whole body feeling limp with relief. "They were *very* smart. You know anything about fingerprints and retina patterns? Well, no, probably you don't."

"Were those some of the tests the doctor performed when we first arrived?" Taneem asked.

"Yes—right," Alison confirmed. She'd forgotten Taneem had been there for that.

Which was a strange thought all by itself. Was she really getting so comfortable with Taneem's presence that she could actually forget the K'da was there against her skin?

"Anyway, fingerprints and those other things are sometimes used like keys to make sure the wrong people can't open a door or safe or something," she said, getting back to her explanation. "That's what those indentations on the side of the safe are for. One of the crew puts their fingers in the right holes, that triggers some sensors, and then you can open the safe without the bomb going off and destroying everything inside."

Taneem pondered that a moment. "So the reason the other two safes were destroyed was that the people didn't know which indentations to use?"

"Partly," Alison said. "But mostly, they didn't have the right fingers."

Taneem cocked her head. "I don't understand."

"See, the problem with this kind of lock is that sometimes they can be fooled," Alison told her. "All a bad person has to do is kill someone who has access and then take his fingers or his eyes."

Taneem's neck arched. "That's *barbaric!*"

"I agree," Alison said. "Though it's actually a little more complicated these days. The point is that the safe's designers didn't want that happening here." She smiled grimly. "So whose digits do you suppose they keyed the lock for?"

Taneem's jaws cracked open in a wide smile. "They keyed it for K'da toes."

"Exactly," Alison said, nodding. "Add in the fact that you need a K'da/Shontine combination in order to look over the wall and figure out which indentations to use, and you can see that Neverlin and the Valahgua pretty well shot themselves in the foot when they wiped out Draycos's team."

"Only they don't know it," Taneem said thoughtfully. "What then do we do?"

"We open their safe for them," Alison said, standing up and holding out her hand. "Come on, let's get some lunch. Then we'll show them how a *real* safecracker does things."

Frost had apparently expected Alison to stall as long as she could. As a result, he was the last to arrive when the group gathered again in the Patri's suite after lunch. "Good of you to join us, Colonel," Neverlin said with an edge of sarcasm as Frost slipped into the room. "Alison says she's ready."

"Does she," Frost said, giving Alison a long, hard look as he crossed to his usual seat.

"Yes, she does," Alison said. "Or were you expecting her to wait until a little closer to your deadline?"

Neverlin frowned. "Deadline?"

"Colonel Frost told me before lunch that I had until midnight tonight to get the safe open," Alison explained.

Neverlin turned an unreadable expression on Frost. "Or?" he prompted.

"The Patri Chookoock was right—she was stalling," Frost said before Alison could answer. "I thought she could use a little extra incentive."

"And as you see, it worked," Alison said, watching Neverlin closely. "You ought to let the colonel take charge more often."

"We'll certainly consider it," Neverlin said coolly as he turned back to Alison. "And we're waiting."

Alison nodded and turned back to the safe. That had been risky, she knew. But the more she could create or encourage strains between Neverlin and his allies, the better. Kneeling down in front of the safe, she stretched out her left arm along the line of indentations, resting her palm on top of numbers four and six. "I hope someone's got my money ready," she commented as she got a grip on the combination dial.

And as she did so, she felt a whisper of weight come onto her palm as Taneem lifted her forepaw from Alison's hand and slid two of her toes into the proper indentations.

Alison keyed the combination she had worked out. There was a soft snick from somewhere inside the safe. Praying that she'd gotten everything right, she took hold of the break bar and pulled.

Without any fuss or muss, or smoke or explosions, the door swung open.

Neverlin and Frost were there in an instant, Frost shoving Alison aside in his eagerness. Fortunately, Taneem was able to get her toes out of sight before Alison's hand was pushed away from the safe wall. "Hey!" Alison protested as she lost her balance and landed flat on her rear.

Both men ignored her. "Well?" the Patri rumbled from his chair.

"They're here," Neverlin said, his voice almost shaking with excitement. He pulled his cupped hands out of the safe, full of the little diamonds Taneem had described. "And *not* burned to ashes."

The Patri gestured to one of the Brummgas standing guard by the door. "Order that its money is to be prepared," he said. "Order, too, that a transport be made ready."

"Let's not be too hasty," Frost cautioned, peering down at the diamonds. "This *is* from the one that crashed, remember. I think we should make sure the data's intact before we turn her loose."

"He's right," Neverlin seconded. "I'm sure she won't mind hanging around another day or so." He sent Alison a cultured sort of smirk. "After all, she's the one who suggested we should listen to the colonel more often."

Carefully, Alison suppressed a smile. She'd been afraid she would have to find a way to make that suggestion herself. "Not a problem," she assured them. "Just remember that another job will cost another twenty thousand."

"Understood," Neverlin said. "Colonel, would you escort Ms. Kayna back to her room?"

"I'll have Dumbarton and Mrishpaw do it," Frost said. "I think I'd better stay and help you check this out."

For a long moment the two men gazed at each other. "Whatever you'd like," Neverlin said at last. "Ms. Kayna, we'll see you later."

The afternoon dragged by. Alison spent the entire time alone in her room, wondering each minute if someone was about to arrive, hand her twenty thousand, and escort her out through the gate.

Kicking her off the Chookoock estate before she and Taneem had a chance to find and open the other safe.

But no one came. Shoofteelee arrived with her dinner at the usual time, with his usual polite but somewhat distant attitude. Alison and Taneem ate, then settled in for an evening that promised to be as long and nerve-wracking as the afternoon had been.

Again, no one had arrived by the time the lights-out warning tone came over the room's intercom. Alison was already in bed by then, getting in a little pre-bedtime doze in anticipation of a sleepless night ahead. Once the house was quiet, she and Taneem would go in search of that final safe.

And they would succeed. Alison had no doubt about that. Not anymore. Taneem's quiet faith, plus the afternoon's triumph, had blown away her earlier crisis of confidence like mist in a windstorm.

It was an hour after lights-out, and the slave areas around her had gone silent, when she heard the sound of her door being quietly opened. "Kayna?" Dumbarton's voice called softly.

"Who is it?" Alison asked, slurring her words slightly as if she'd been startled out of her sleep.

"Dumbarton and Mrishpaw," Dumbarton said. "Come on—Mr. Arthur wants to see you."

Alison winced. They weren't going to throw her out *now*, were they? "What about?" she asked, throwing off her covers and pulling on her shoes.

"You always go to bed with all your clothes on?" Dumbarton asked suspiciously.

"Hardly ever," Alison said, standing up. "I was resting and fell asleep."

"Sure," Dumbarton said. "Quiet, now."

They headed up through the slave areas, crossed the deserted kitchen, and emerged into the starlight through the same door Alison had used on her own midnight trip a few nights previously.

But it wasn't Neverlin who was waiting for her in the darkness. It was Frost.

"There you are," he greeted her in a low voice. "Good news: the data diamonds gave us everything we needed to know."

"Glad to hear it," Alison said, the skin on the back of her neck starting to tingle. "Where's my money?"

"Where you'll never see it." Frost jerked his head toward an open-topped car waiting a few feet away. "Take her to the slave area," he ordered the two mercenaries. "And kill her."

CHAPTER 25

They had Alison to the car before she could untangle her tongue. "Wait!" she said, the word coming out more like a croak. "Wait! You can't—"

"Good-bye, deserter," Frost said. Turning with military precision, he disappeared back into the house.

"Just relax," Dumbarton advised as Mrishpaw picked her up and deposited her into one of the car's rear seats. "If you struggle, he'll just make it hurt more." He turned his back and started to climb into the driver's seat.

And in that instant, Taneem struck.

She exploded out of the back of Alison's shirt collar straight into Mrishpaw's face, slapping her forepaw against the Brummga's head with enough force to slam him bodily into the car's rear fender. The reaction from the blow sent Taneem herself flying in the opposite direction, dropping her nearly three yards away. She hit the ground and spun around, leaping at Dumbarton just as he turned his head to see what all the commotion was about.

His hand was diving for his gun when the K'da's second blow slammed into his head and dropped him like a limp puppet over the steering wheel.

"Are you all right?" Taneem asked Alison anxiously, her

whole body trembling like a leaf as she crouched on the grass beside the car.

"Yes, I'm fine," Alison said, shaking a little herself. This was the second time she'd seen Taneem attack, and there was still something about it that brought out all her deepest, darkest fears. The price of having read too many books of dragon legends when she was young, she supposed.

Meanwhile, she and Taneem had *real* problems to deal with. "We need to get them out of here before some patrol trips over them," she said, looking around. Mrishpaw had slipped off the back of the car where Taneem's slap had landed him and was now sprawled on the ground. "Give me a hand."

Together, she and Taneem managed to hoist the big Brummga up into the backseat. Pushing Dumbarton out of the way, Alison got into the driver's seat and started the car. Choosing a pathway heading northwest, aiming them midway between the main gate and the slave areas where Frost had been sending her, she drove off. "Where are we going?" Taneem asked, crouching low on Mrishpaw's body.

"I wish I knew," Alison said grimly. "There have to be places in an estate this size where we can hide for a while. Unfortunately, we don't know where any of them are."

"Can't we simply leave?"

Alison shook her head. "The gate is way too well defended," she said. "The wall's even worse."

"Yet Jack and Draycos were able to escape," Taneem reminded her.

Alison hissed a curse at herself. "What am I thinking?" she growled, reaching over to Dumbarton's collar and pulling off his comm clip. "Here—you drive."

"What?" Taneem asked, sounding startled.

"Just take the wheel—I'll handle the pedals," Alison said, leaning out of the way. "Come on, you can do it."

A pair of K'da paws reached over her shoulder and gingerly wrapped themselves around the wheel. Keeping half an eye on the road, Alison tuned Dumbarton's comm clip to the *Essenay's* frequency. "Thanks," she said to Taneem, taking back the wheel. "Cross your toes." Fastening the comm clip to her collar, she clicked it on. "Jack?"

"This is Uncle Virge," the computerized personality came back instantly. "Are you all right?"

"Not really, no," Alison told him. "We just had to clobber two of Frost's men and we're on the run."

"You don't know the half of it," Uncle Virge said grimly. "I've been monitoring their transmissions for the past half hour. Frost is organizing a group to go back to Semaline. They've figured out that Jack is there."

"He's still *there?*" Alison echoed, frowning. "Then what in blazes are *you* doing here?"

"I'm here because once those two goofs picked you up, I knew they *hadn't* gotten Jack, and I knew then where he had to be," Uncle Virge said. "I figured he'd be safe there for a while."

"Yes, but—"

"And he'd ordered me to watch out for you and Taneem," Uncle Virge snapped. "All *right?*"

"Sure," Alison said hastily. "Sure. Calm down."

"I *am* calm."

"I can tell," Alison said. She and Taneem were still in trouble, but with the *Essenay* here, at least she now had the beginnings of a plan. Maybe. "Okay—first things first," she said. "Do *they* know where Jack is?"

"Probably," Uncle Virge said.

"How?"

There was just the briefest pause. "I don't know."

"No more games," Alison said coldly. "Jack's in danger, *I'm* in danger, and if we don't do something about it real quick you're going to find yourself all alone in a very big universe. Understand?"

"Yes," Uncle Virge said, his voice subdued. "What do you want to know?"

"Let's start with Jack," Alison said. "Who is he?"

Uncle Virge sighed. "The son of the late Stuart and Ariel Palmer," he said. "Both of them Judge-Paladins."

Alison felt her mouth drop open a fraction of an inch. She'd already pegged the *Essenay* as some kind of diplomatic or governmental ship. She'd proved it, in fact, by activating the computer's built-in privacy lock system on the trip back from Rho Scorvi.

But she'd assumed Virgil Morgan had conned or stolen the ship from some minor official or else bought it on the black market from a corrupt diplomat. For it to have been stolen from a Judge-Paladin, let alone *two* of them—

"I know what you're thinking," Uncle Virge cut into her thoughts. "But it wasn't like that."

"Whatever it was like, it can wait," Alison said. "How do they know where Jack is right now?"

"Because he's probably at the scene of his parents' murder—"

"Their *murder?*" Alison cut him off. "I thought Jack said they were killed in an accident."

"Because he wasn't ready for the truth yet," Uncle Virge said.

"Besides, there was still the little matter of assembling evidence to identify their killers."

Alison felt cold all over. Was *that* the little problem on Semaline Neverlin had mentioned earlier?

And if so, did he know who Jack really was?

"Anyway, I think some of the residents of the area must have recognized him as the Palmers' son and taken him back there," Uncle Virge went on.

"Why?"

"Probably to judge their disputes for them," Uncle Virge said. "They're all alone out in the middle of nowhere—"

"Okay, okay—not important," Alison interrupted. "What's important is that we get Jack and Draycos out of there, and fast. How soon can you get back to Semaline?"

"I can do it in four days if I really run the fuel tanks," Uncle Virge said. "That'll get me there about the same time as Frost's ships. Maybe a couple of hours sooner."

"Sooner would be nice," Alison said.

"Tell me about it," Uncle Virge said with a grunt. "Problem is, pushing it that hard will drain our credit balance. We might end up stranded there."

"Don't worry about that," Alison assured him. "There are a bunch of fuel credits in my cabin. You and Jack can use those when you come back to pick me up."

"Wait a second," Uncle Virge warned. "If you're counting on Jack to get you out of there—"

"Don't worry, I'm not," Alison assured him. "But I'll need you to send an InterWorld message for me before you take off."

"Who to?"

"The nearest Malison Ring Class One base," Alison said. "I think the one on Tristram Four is the closest, but you can check."

There was a brief silence. "The Malison Ring," Uncle Virge said, his voice gone flat. "Frost's friends."

"Not exactly," Alison said. "You're going to send the message using the voice of General Aram Davi, the Malison Ring's commander in chief."

"*What?*" Uncle Virge demanded. "Who do you think I *am*, girl?"

"I think you're a computer," Alison said. "And the voiceprint and tonal patterns you'll need are already installed in one of the files Jack set up for me to use."

There was another brief pause as Uncle Virge accessed the file. "You must be out of your apple-buttered mind," he said, sounding as flabbergasted as Alison had ever heard him. "Where in space did you *get* all these?"

"My dad's a collector, okay?" Alison said briefly. "You never know when someone else's voice might come in handy. So can you do it, or can't you?"

"I can do it," Uncle Virge said, still sounding a little floored. "What's the message?"

Alison grinned in the darkness. Frost was going to love this. "Tell them that Colonel Frost is being held prisoner at the Chookoock family estate on Brum-a-dum," she said. "Order them to scramble a force to rescue him."

"I was right the first time," Uncle Virge said. "You *are* insane."

"Not at all," Alison said. "They won't question an order coming from General Davi. Especially since you'll also be giving them one of his authorization codes."

"Where am I—oh," Uncle Virge said. "I will be dipped in butter. You have his *security codes*, too?"

"I had access to a Malison Ring computer system a while back," Alison said. "I got in a little deeper than anyone thought."

"And then what?" Uncle Virge asked. "All Frost has to do is tell them he wasn't kidnapped and they'll go home."

"He can't, and that's the real beauty of this," Alison said, smiling again. "They won't accept any response while he's still inside the house—he could be talking with a gun to his head."

"Then he comes out and shows them he's all right."

"He can't do that, either," Alison said. "He's been using Malison Ring troops and equipment for his own private scheme, remember? For all he knows, this kidnapping story could be nothing but a ruse to lure him out into the open so that they can nab him."

"I like it," Uncle Virge said approvingly. "Anyone ever tell you you had the makings of a very devious person?"

"That's high praise, coming from you," Alison said dryly. "Send the message, do what you can to make sure they've bought it, then hightail it back to Semaline."

"All right," Uncle Virge said. "But look, even if they buy it, Tristram Four is a good three to four days away from here. Are you going to be all right that long?"

"If I say no, what are you going to do about it?" Alison countered. "Right; that's what I thought. Don't worry, I think I know a place where we can hide for a while. You just concentrate on Jack and Draycos."

"I'll get them out," Uncle Virge promised grimly. "You watch yourself, lass."

"I will," Alison promised. "Oh, one other thing. How did you even know I was here?"

"Through your comm clip, of course," Uncle Virge said. "Your kidnappers practically gave me the Chookoocks' address."

Alison thought back. "But the clip was off."

"Well . . . not exactly," Uncle Virge said, sounding a little embarrassed. "Jack rigged that clip to be permanently on. You know, as a precaution?"

Alison felt her lip twist. So much for Taneem's question about whether Jack trusted her. Just as well that he didn't. "Remind me to be mad about that later," she told Uncle Virge. "In the meantime, go get him out of there."

She clicked off the comm clip and slipped it into her pocket. "Do you really know a place where we can hide?" Taneem asked.

Alison shrugged. "Let's find out."

The landscape around them changed from grassy lawn to sculpted trees, and the path split three times before they reached Alison's objective.

The wall.

"I don't know," Taneem asked as they sat in the car looking up at the wall's wave-shaped overhang. "This seems very uncertain."

"In theory, it should work just fine," Alison said, studying the white ceramic gleaming in the starlight. The shadowed underside of the wave was much harder to see, but she was almost positive that the inward-curling edge of the wave curved upward a little right at the end. The big question was whether it curved up enough to form a trough where she and Taneem could lie hidden from view.

The even bigger question was whether they could get up there to find out.

"The entire wall's about thirty feet tall, which puts that wave trough between twenty and twenty-five," Alison went on. "First thing to do is see if you can jump that high."

"I'll try." Crouching down, Taneem gathered herself and leaped.

Alison held her breath. The K'da soared upward, and with a faint scrabbling of claw against ceramic she caught the edge of the wave. For a second she hung there, then stirred and pulled herself up and disappeared into the trough.

Alison looked around. There were no aircars or other ground vehicles visible. Apparently, her escape was still undiscovered.

Which wasn't surprising, actually. Frost was busy organizing the Semaline attack force, and Alison doubted that anyone else in the house knew about his order to kill her. Until the colonel started wondering why Dumbarton and Mrishpaw hadn't shown up to give him the good news about her death, she was unlikely to be missed.

There was a flicker of motion, and she looked over as Taneem dropped again to the ground. "I think there is enough room for us," she reported. "Though it is filthy with feathers and bird droppings."

"That's okay," Alison assured her. "Now the big question: can you carry me that high?"

"No," Taneem said, ducking her head apologetically. "I could lift you perhaps half that distance, but not the entire way."

Alison chewed at her lip. Desperate needs, the old saying whispered through her mind, called for desperate measures. "Halfway it is," she said. "Help me get Dumbarton and Mrishpaw out of the car."

It took some creative maneuvering, plus a lot of grunting,

but within a few minutes Alison and Taneem had the two mercenaries out and settled under one of the nearby shrubs. "Here's the plan," Alison said, doing a quick search of the unconscious bodies. Neither was carrying a gun, but Mrishpaw had a slapstick belted at his side. Pulling it from its holster, she held it up. "We're going to back the car up a ways and get in. I'm going to wedge the accelerator with this, and we'll charge full-bore toward the wall."

"*Toward* the wall?" Taneem asked, her neck arching.

"Straight toward it," Alison confirmed. "With the wall curved that way we should run up along it like a Great Galaxy Romp roller coaster heading into a crazyloop. You'll be holding on to me, and when the car's at its highest point, you'll jump us toward the lip. If we do it right, we should land nice and neat inside the trough."

Taneem's tail was lashing agitatedly at the air. "I can't do that," she said, her voice trembling. "No. I can't."

"We have to try," Alison said firmly. "We don't know the grounds. The Brummgas do. They'll know about any other place we might find to hide. This is the only spot they might not think of."

"But we could be killed." Taneem looked up at the frozen white wave above them. "Draycos could do it—he has the strength and skill. But I'm not like him. I can't."

"Taneem." Reaching over, Alison put her hand on the side of the K'da's snout and pulled her head gently around to face her. "Earlier today, I didn't think I could figure out the safe," she said. "But you had faith in me, and I did it. Well, I have faith in *you*. You can do this. I know you can."

Taneem's glowing silver eyes stared unblinkingly into hers.

Alison held her gaze, mentally crossing her fingers. Then, the K'da gave a little sigh. "What was it Uncle Virge said back there?"

" 'You're out of your apple-buttered mind'?"

"That was it." Taneem sighed again. "Very well. Live or die, we will try it."

CHAPTER 26

Alison ran the car fifty yards back and pointed it at the wall. "We'll aim to hit it at a slight angle," she told Taneem as she found a good spot to wedge the slapstick against the accelerator. "That way, it'll hopefully go flying a different direction than we do."

"That would probably be best," Taneem agreed from behind her, a hint of dark humor peeking through the tension in her voice.

Alison smiled to herself. Taneem was still young, and still very much unsure of herself. But she had spirit, and she had courage.

Actually, in many ways she reminded Alison of herself.

"Okay," Alison said, pulling her feet up into a crouch on the seat and reaching down with the slapstick. "Ready?"

Taneem wrapped her forelegs tightly around Alison's chest beneath her arms. "Ready."

Bracing herself, Alison jammed the slapstick against the accelerator.

The car leaped forward. Alison steered with one hand, holding herself steady against the dashboard with the other.

The wall rushed toward them. Letting go of the wheel, Alison grabbed tightly to Taneem's forelegs. If this didn't work . . .

And with a crunch of metal and plastic, they hit the wall.

The car leaped upward beneath them, the force throwing Alison off balance and nearly tossing her out of the vehicle. The wall and land and sky twisted dizzyingly, and she was yanked off her feet as Taneem leaped. For a frozen fraction of a second she seemed to be drifting through the air, feeling her body turning sideways. The pressure of the K'da forelegs around her torso abruptly vanished—

With a teeth-rattling thud against her back and legs and head, she slammed against something hard.

And as the stars cleared away from her vision, she found herself looking down at the ground far below.

"Taneem?" she croaked. The word came out with a grunt of pain; she hadn't realized just how hard she'd hit the ceramic.

"Here," Taneem's voice came from her shoulder. "I realized suddenly that we would not both fit side by side."

"Good thinking," Alison said. The words came out easier this time. Carefully shifting her throbbing shoulder blades, she took stock of her situation.

Taneem had been right about there being enough room up here. But only just barely. Instead of lying flat in the trough, as Alison had expected, she found herself lying mostly on her right side with her body angling backward against the upwardly curving part of the wall.

It wasn't nearly as stable a position as she'd hoped for. As it was, leaning just a little too far forward would move her center of mass over the edge, and she would be on her way to the ground twenty feet below and either a broken back or a full set of broken ribs.

Worse, lying half upright like this also meant she wasn't as well hidden as she'd hoped to be. Someone standing at the very base of the wall and looking up would have no trouble seeing that *something* was up here.

But with their stolen car now lying upside down at the base of the wall a dozen feet away it was too late to change plans. The noise of the crash had probably triggered alarms all the way back to the house, and within minutes hordes of ugly Brummgas would be converging on this spot.

Within minutes, hordes of ugly Brummgas were.

There was nothing subtle about their arrival, either. They swarmed in full force, with lights and noise and ground cars and the sounds of air support overhead. Most of them were Brummgas, but there was a scattering of humans among them.

Including Gazen, the slavemaster she'd had her run-in with a few nights ago. He wandered around the edge of the activity, his posture one of brooding watchfulness. He had his snub-nosed laser rifle slung in military ready position over his shoulder.

For perhaps ten minutes the guards wandered around the area, examining the car and the tire tracks on the wall, their big feet stomping over any of the more subtle clues Alison might have left behind. One of them spotted Dumbarton and Mrish-paw, and the center of activity shifted for a minute while they bundled the unconscious mercenaries into one of the cars and sent them back to the house.

Their attention returned to the wall and car for another few minutes. Then, at a command from one of the humans, they split into two groups, one heading north toward the slave area, the other heading south toward the gate.

One of the humans stayed where he was, standing by the overturned car. As the noise of Brummgan feet faded into the night, Alison could hear him talking softly on his comm clip.

"—thought she could ram it through the wall, I suppose," he said. "Pretty stupid. Or just desperate . . . No, I sent them out in both directions. Whichever way she went, she has to be on foot. Shouldn't be too hard to pick up . . . Yes, sir, I told them you wanted her alive if possible."

The man glanced to the side as another figure came into Alison's view beneath the overhang. It was Gazen, still wandering thoughtfully around. "No, sir, no sign of anyone else . . . Yes, sir, I'll keep you posted." He touched his comm clip, turning it off.

"You're wrong, you know," Gazen told him. "He's here."

"Who, Morgan?" The other man snorted. "That would be a neat trick."

"Morgan specializes in neat tricks," Gazen countered mildly.

"Well, if he's here, we'll get him," the other promised, his voice dark. "We'll get both of them."

"And the dragon?" Gazen asked.

"Him, too." The other gave an audible sniff. "Unless you'd rather we save him for you."

"Don't worry about it," Gazen said. His voice was still mild, but Alison could hear a grim anticipation lurking beneath it. "When he shows himself the next time, I'll be there."

"Yeah," the other man said. "Whatever." Brushing past Gazen, he disappeared out of Alison's sight. A moment later she heard the sound of a car heading north.

Gazen remained where he was, watching the other's departure. Then, slowly, he turned around in a complete circle. Once, he glanced up toward the wall's overhang, and Alison tensed. But he was looking above the spot where the car had crashed, and there was nothing there for him to see. "Come on out, dragon," he murmured aloud as he lowered his eyes again. "Come on out. Time to play."

Alison felt Taneem stirring against her skin. Gazen stood there a moment longer, then turned and headed north. He passed almost directly beneath Alison and disappeared, his footsteps fading into the night murmurs.

Alison silently counted out fifteen minutes. "Taneem?" she whispered at last.

A bit of weight came onto her shoulder, and a K'da tongue flicked past her cheek. "He's gone," Taneem confirmed. "All of them are gone."

Alison took a careful breath. "Well," she whispered. "It worked."

"It would seem so," Taneem agreed cautiously. "What now?"

Alison chewed at her lip. They certainly couldn't stay here forever. "Hang on," she said. "I'm going to try something."

Carefully, she started to lift her knees. The movement shifted her center of mass toward the edge, and for a second she thought she was going to fall. Hastily, she put her legs back down. She waited a moment for her heart to settle down again, then tried lifting just one knee.

Again, her center of mass shifted, but not nearly as far or as alarmingly. Drawing the knee toward her chest as far as she dared, she planted it against the inside of the lip and carefully pushed.

It worked. As she straightened her leg, the rest of her body moved a few inches down the trough. "There we go," she told Taneem, trying to keep her voice light. "It's not fast, but it'll get us there."

"Where will it get us?"

"To the slave areas," Alison said. "That's our best chance of finding food and shelter until the Malison Ring reinforcements Uncle Virge called get here."

"But won't the Brummgas search that area?"

"Trust me," Alison said grimly as she pushed herself another few inches north. "At the rate we're going, they'll have had time to search the whole place twice before we get there." She screwed up her nose as a small feather tickled her face. "I just hope we're not pushing out a trail of feathers even the Patri Chookoock could follow."

"They are surely used to seeing feathers below the wall," Taneem pointed out. "And there should be enough breeze to keep them spread out."

"If not, there's nothing we can do about it," Alison said. "And there's always the chance they won't even bother looking very hard for me. Now that Neverlin has what he wants, he and Frost could easily be gone by morning."

"With the information they need to destroy Draycos's people."

Alison winced. That was, unfortunately, the downside to this whole thing. "We've got over a month before they arrive," she reminded Taneem. "And there's still one safe that has all of that same information. We just have to figure out how to get to it."

"There are many parts of this that I don't understand," Taneem said. "But you have never lied to me before. I will trust you."

Alison gazed out into the night, her throat tight. "Thank you," she managed. "We'd better stop talking now. If we happen on any patrols, it would be nice if we know it before they do."

CHAPTER 27

Privately, Draycos had expected it to be at least a week before the Golvin guards relaxed their watchfulness enough for him to risk another midnight excursion. To his mild surprise—and to Jack's obvious relief—barely two nights later, the K'da judged the time was right.

Man, are these guys amateurs, Jack's scornful thought echoed through Draycos's mind as the boy peeked out between the doorway streamers.

Draycos lifted his head from Jack's shoulder, brushing aside the partially open shirt with his snout. The two Golvins were seated side by side at the foot of the bridge, clearly visible in the moonlight, paying no real attention to the area around them as they chatted casually together in low voices. Their small bows rested against the sides of the bridge, the quivers propped alongside them. *I told you these weren't a warrior people,* he reminded Jack.

I know, but this is just ridiculous. The stream of thoughts paused, and Draycos sensed the boy trying to hide his anxiety. *You sure you're going to be all right?*

They will never see a thing, Draycos assured him. With a casual leap, he came out of the back of Jack's shirt. "I'll be back for you soon," he added quietly.

"Be careful," Jack warned. He looked out the door again and gave Draycos a thumbs-up.

Nosing his way between the streamers, the K'da slipped onto the bridge. He gave the area a quick scan, then turned halfway around and stretched up to the stone above the doorway. Setting his claws into the cracks and crevices, he started to climb.

He went up just far enough for his hind claws to get a grip of their own before changing direction and working his way horizontally around the pillar. When he reached the far side he turned head downward and climbed back down to the ground.

For a minute he paused there, crouched against the stone, his eyes probing as his tongue flicked out to taste the air. But except for the two guards lazing around on the opposite side of the pillar, the area was deserted.

The first thing on Draycos's list of things to do was to locate their transport. Fortunately, there were a dozen scents unique to flying vehicles, scents he could smell drifting along on the nighttime breezes. Keeping alert, he set off across the fields.

He found the Golvins' shuttle and Bolo's aircar together in a cavernous machine shop that filled the entire ground floor of the pillar farthest from the river. As usual with Golvin construction, the shop had no door, but both vehicles had been anchored to the floor with metal chains.

That, at least, would present no problem. Slipping inside, Draycos extended his claws and began working on the chains tying down the aircar. Within ten minutes, he had it freed.

Now came the tricky part.

The Golvins stationed beneath Langston's cliffside prison turned out to be no more alert than the ones back at Jack's apartment. Apparently, the novelty of nighttime guard duty, and the watchfulness Draycos had seen on his first visit, had worn off quickly after Langston's move to his new quarters.

Still, this time it wouldn't be just a poet-warrior of the K'da slipping in and out. This time, he would be attempting to smuggle out a full-sized human. Sternly warning himself against overconfidence, he climbed across the cliff to the cave mouth and slipped inside.

Langston was lying on his side on his cot, his back to the entrance as Draycos padded over to him. He reached out a paw to touch the man's shoulder—

"Draycos?" Langston murmured.

Draycos felt his tail twitch in surprise. "Yes," he murmured back. "You're a very light sleeper."

"I've been expecting you ever since I saw them lock up your Judge-Paladin," Langston said. "What's the story there?"

"The same as yours," Draycos said. "You're both victims of the fear created by an eleven-year-old threat."

"So what do we do about it?"

"We end it," Draycos said. "Tonight."

"Sounds good to me." Langston started to roll over.

"Wait," Draycos said, putting a restraining paw on the man's shoulder. "Before you look at me, I have to warn you that my appearance may shock you."

"Hey, in this light you could be covered with scabs and I'd never notice," Langston said. "No problem."

"I'm serious," Draycos said. "The guards outside aren't very alert, but even they would wonder at a startled shout coming from up here."

"I said no problem," Langston said, a little impatiently. "What's the big shocker?"

"I am a dragon."

There was a brief silence. "A dragon," Langston repeated, his voice flat.

"Actually, I'm a poet-warrior of the K'da," Draycos said. "But my appearance is that of a small dragon."

"Interesting," Langston said. "Can you fly and breathe fire?"

"Regretfully, no," Draycos said. "Both abilities could be very useful."

"I've always thought so," Langston said. "Okay, I'm ready."

He rolled over. Even in the dim light Draycos could see his face suddenly tighten. "Floos on a frissle. You weren't joking, were you?"

"Did you think I was?"

"Yeah, mostly." Langston reached out a hand, paused. "May I?"

"Certainly."

Gingerly, Langston touched the side of Draycos's neck. The touch steadied a little, and he ran his fingertips down the scales to Draycos's shoulder. "Well, if you're robotic, you're the best floosing robot I've ever seen."

"What would convince you I'm a living being?"

"Actually, right now I don't care what you are," Langston said. He threw off his blanket, and Draycos saw that he was fully dressed in a dark green jumpsuit and low boots. "Not as long as you get me out of here."

"That *is* the plan," Draycos agreed. "Collect anything you wish to take with you."

"It's collected," Langston said, reaching to the floor and picking up a handkerchief tied into a bundle. "How do we do this?"

"I climb sideways away from the cave," Draycos said. "You hold on to my tail."

"Ah," Langston said, sounding suddenly doubtful. "Your—uh—?"

"It will work," Draycos assured him. "You're not much bigger than my symbiont, Jack, and I have successfully carried him that way."

"Your *symbiont*?"

"Yes," Draycos said. "A symbiont is one who shares—"

"I know what it is." Langston shook his head. "I can see we're going to be having a long talk when this is over." Taking a deep breath, he stuffed his handkerchief bundle into the front of his shirt. "Let's do it."

The first stage of the journey was the hardest. Draycos had to climb quietly, without knocking any bits of stone onto the lounging Golvins below. More than that, he had to do it with a hundred and forty pounds of dead weight hanging on to his tail.

Fortunately, he'd done the trip enough times that he knew a route that would work. A few tense minutes later, they were safely away from the guards and starting down. A few minutes more, and they'd made it to the canyon floor.

"That was interesting," Langston said, crouching behind a cluster of tall grain plants as he rubbed at the cramped muscles in his hands. "What's next?"

"We collect our transportation, pick up Jack, and leave," Draycos told him. "Though flying through the canyon's many obstacles may be difficult in the dark."

"Don't worry about that," Langston assured him grimly. "Just show me to the pilot's seat and get out of the way."

"The vehicles are across the river," Draycos said, pointing with his tongue. "The nearest bridge is this way."

They had made it across the cropland to the river and were

nearly across the bridge when the nighttime silence was suddenly pierced by a warbling shriek.

Draycos leaped the rest of the way across the bridge, landing in a crouch on the far side. Langston was right behind him. "What the floos was *that?*" the human demanded.

"I would guess someone has discovered my sabotage," Draycos said, turning his head to look behind them. Across the canyon, shadowy figures were climbing rapidly up the cliff face toward Langston's former prison. "They're about to discover your absence, as well."

"Terrific," Langston growled. "What's Plan B?"

"The same as Plan A, only noisier," Draycos told him, flicking out his tongue. So far there didn't seem to be any Golvins between them and Jack's apartment. "We free Jack from his guards, attempt to fight our way through to the aircar, and escape."

"Simple, but lunatic," Langston said. Probing briefly into the river mud, he came up with a pair of fist-sized rocks. "After you."

Draycos headed off, angling their course so as to approach the pillar from the rear. Somewhere along the way, the K'da combat pattern kicked in, pumping extra blood into his muscles and turning his scales from gold to black.

But it was growing more and more clear that all the camouflage in the world would be of limited value. As they traveled, he heard a half dozen more of the shrieks, some from the direction of the vehicle shop, others from Langston's now empty prison.

The alarm was out. By the time they reached the pillar the whole canyon was starting to come awake.

"How many guards?" Langston whispered as they sidled around the cold stone toward the front.

"Two when I left," Draycos whispered back, slowing down. They rounded the final curve and came within view of the bridge.

To find that the two guards had been joined by two more. All four were standing alertly at the bottom of the bridge, two of them looking up toward Jack's door, the others looking back and forth across the area around them. All four had arrows out and nocked at the ready in their bowstrings.

"Not good," Langston breathed in Draycos's ear. "Mostly open ground, too."

"But delay will only make the odds worse," Draycos pointed out. "I'll circle around the other side and try to draw their attention and fire. If I succeed, move in and try to take them from the rear."

"Got it."

"And don't forget that these aren't our enemies," Draycos added firmly. "They're as much the victims of evil as we are."

"I'll try to remember that," Langston said sourly. "Good luck."

Draycos backed up and retraced his steps around the pillar, swinging wide toward the river. A minute later, he once again came within sight of the four guards.

For the first few crucial seconds they didn't seem to notice him among the shadows as he turned inward. Then, one of them jerked in shock as he spotted the black creature racing toward them. Gurgling something incoherent, he snapped up his bow and fired.

The shot went wild, the arrow swishing into the plants two yards to Draycos's left. But the gurgle and shot were enough to alert the other three. They twisted around to face Draycos, and three more bows were lifted toward him. Draycos dug his claws into the ground and dodged to the side, switching to an evasive zigzag pattern.

And suddenly Langston was there among the Golvins, clubbing coolly and methodically with his rocks. By the time Draycos reached them, all four guards were sprawled on the ground. "Piece of cake," the pilot said, a note of grim satisfaction in his voice. "Man. If I'd known it was that easy, I'd have done it a long time ago."

"This was the easy part," Draycos reminded him, peering at the fallen Golvins as he trotted to a halt. He couldn't tell if they were still breathing, but Langston's blows hadn't seemed overly violent. "The next part will be—"

"*Draycos!*" Jack's voice shouted from overhead.

Reflexively, Draycos leaped to the side as he twisted his neck up to look.

But the move was too late. Even as his eyes registered the fact that there was a fifth Golvin just emerging from Jack's apartment, he heard the snap of a bowstring.

And a searing jolt of pain exploded into his side.

With a desperate lunge, Jack hurled himself through the streamers at the doorway, slamming his shoulder into the Golvin's back with everything he had.

But he was too late. Even as the Golvin gave a strangled little squeak and toppled off the bridge, Jack saw Draycos jerk violently as the arrow buried itself into his side.

"No!" he yelped. Throwing himself onto the bridge, he half ran, half slid down the rough rock to the ground.

Draycos was lying on his side when Jack reached him, panting with shallow breaths, the arrow sticking out of his rib cage. "It's okay," Jack breathed, his heart thudding violently as he dropped to his knees beside his wounded friend. "We'll get this out." Steeling himself, he reached for the arrow.

"No—leave it alone," someone said from behind him.

Jack turned as a heavily bearded man—Langston?—dropped to one knee beside him. "He's hurt," he snarled.

"I know," Langston said, his voice grim. "But pulling it out will just make it worse." He held up one of the other Golvin arrows. "See this wide arrowhead? You pull it out, and it'll just tear more of the flesh and muscle. Besides, it's helping stanch the blood right now."

Jack looked down at Draycos. His glowing green eyes were half-closed, the muscles in his neck working with pain. "What if it's poisoned?"

"I don't think it is," Langston said. "These look like hunting or fishing arrows. There's no reason to poison those."

He looked over his shoulder. "But if we don't get out of here, and fast, it's not going to matter much. They're on the move."

"So we need to get to the aircar." Reaching down, Jack took one of Draycos's paws in his hand. "Draycos? Can you get aboard?"

The K'da blinked, turning his head as if noticing Jack for the first time. "Jack?" he croaked.

"The aircar's a bust," Langston said tightly. "They're on to us. Our only chance is to go to ground for a while." He thrust two Golvin bows at Jack. "Take these. I'll get your friend."

Jack brushed the bows aside. "I'll do it," he said. "Draycos? Come on, symby. You can do it."

The green eyes blinked, and Jack could see the K'da struggling to focus his thoughts through the agony. His paw shifted in Jack's grip.

And to Jack's relief he slid up the sleeve onto Jack's arm.

Langston stuttered out a startled curse. "Holy—Where did he—?"

"He's gone two-dimensional and is riding on my skin," Jack said. "It's a symbiotic thing—I'll explain later." He started to get up.

And froze in horror. Lying on the ground in front of him was the arrow that had been in Draycos's side. The arrowhead and first inch of the shaft were black with K'da blood. "It's not stanching the blood now," he heard himself say. "Oh, no. No."

"Come on." Langston grabbed his arm and hauled him to his feet. "We've got to hide."

They were halfway up the bridge before Jack's mind cleared enough to realize where they were going. "Wait a minute—this is no good," he protested, trying to pull out of Langston's grip. "It's the first place they'll look for us."

"That's why we're not going to *be* here," Langston countered, pulling harder on Jack's arm. In his other hand, Jack saw, he still had the two Golvin bows. "We're going up the air shaft to my old prison."

"That won't work either," Jack insisted as they brushed through the streamers into the apartment. "I can't climb up there. Even if I could, they must have blocked that hole by now."

"I don't think so," Langston said, crossing to the light shaft and looking up. "I think all they found was my decoy."

"Your what?"

"A little hole I dug and then camouflaged about as badly as

I could without being too obvious about it," Langston explained. "In case you hadn't noticed, these people aren't the brightest stars in the galaxy. You have any food in here?"

"There's meat and fruit in the refrigerator."

"Get it," Langston ordered. "No telling how long we'll be up there."

Numbly, Jack obeyed, stuffing as much as he could into his Judge-Paladin hat. "Ready," he said, coming back to the light shaft as he tucked the hat inside his shirt.

"Get in," Langston said, pointing to the shaft. "Sitting up; back against the left side."

Jack did so. The shaft was a little too narrow for him to stretch all the way out, forcing him to bend his knees. Even through his shirt he could feel the roughness of the wall, and wondered uneasily how that was going to affect Draycos.

"Now take this." Langston thrust one of the bows into the opening. "Turn it with the bow part up and the bowstring down and wedge the ends against the walls to your right and left. You probably want it about a foot in front of you and a foot or two above your head."

The bow, like Jack himself, was a little large for the opening. Pulling on the bowstring to compress the wood, he was able to get it in position. "Okay."

"Here's what you're going to do," Langston said. "You're going to pull yourself up with the bow while you walk your feet up the other side. Then you'll brace your back against the wall, move the bow up a couple more feet, and repeat. It's basically a climber's rock chimney technique, only with the bow to help."

Jack tried it. The method was awkward, but it seemed simple

enough. "Be sure to hold the bow near the ends when you're pulling yourself up or it might flip over on you," Langston said, peering in at him. "Keep going—I'll be right behind you."

Clenching his teeth, Jack headed up.

They'd gone perhaps thirty feet, and Jack's arms were starting to tremble, when Langston whispered a quick warning.

Someone was moving around in the apartment below.

Jack froze, gripping the bow as he pressed his back and feet against the walls. His mind flashed back to that first encounter with the Golvins back at the spaceport, when they'd been able to sniff out his parentage. If one of them thought to stick his nose into the light shaft, it would be all over.

Or maybe not. The air was moving *up* the shaft from below, he noticed now, carrying his and Langston's scents upward with it. Probably something to do with the stone having absorbed sunlight all day and still giving some of that heat back to the air inside the apartments. A minute later, the footsteps fell silent, and he heard Golvin voices calling faintly from outside the apartment. "Go," Langston whispered.

Jack resumed climbing. His arms and legs were beginning to ache, his back feeling itchy and sore and cold where it pressed against the stone.

But none of that mattered. All he could think about was Draycos, stretched across his skin.

Maybe dying.

The word terrified him. But he couldn't put it out of his mind. Over and over as he climbed he mentally called the K'da's name. But there was no answer.

And he was lying so still against Jack's skin. So very, very still.

"Jack?" Langston called softly.

Jack started out of a haze of ache and fear and guilt. "What?" he whispered.

"We're here."

Jack blinked the tears out of his eyes. To his surprise, he saw that the stone wall to his right had opened up onto a rough-hewn hole. "How do I get in?"

"First, make sure it's really still open," Langston said. "Reach in and give the far side a push."

Jack shifted his grip on the bow and stretched a hand into the hole. His fingers touched something slightly stretchy and gave it a push.

It popped out, sending a rush of warm air into his face. "Bless their simple little minds," Langston murmured. "Now put your feet in and just slide yourself through."

A minute later Jack was sprawled on the apartment floor, his arms and legs trembling with released strain. He barely noticed as Langston came in and crossed to the door. The other stood there a moment, and then came back. "So far, so good," he said, squatting down beside Jack. "How's your friend?"

"I don't know," Jack said, brushing at his shoulder. Did the skin where Draycos was lying feel hot? "Draycos?"

There was no answer. "I don't know what the floos is going on with this," Langston said. "But however this works, that wound is probably bleeding like crazy. We've got to get a look at it."

Jack closed his eyes. *Draycos,* he thought urgently as he pushed up his sleeve. *We need to look at your wound. We need you to come off. Can you do that?*

Abruptly, the K'da was there, pouring off Jack's arm more like a thick liquid than a living being. He collapsed onto the stone floor and lay there in a broken heap, not moving.

His entire side was covered in black blood.

"Oh, no," Jack breathed, his heart seizing up as he bent over his friend's still form.

"Here," Langston said, thrusting a wad of cloth into Jack's hands. Jack looked up, realizing only then that the other had pulled his jumpsuit half off and given Jack his flight shirt. "Soak it in the sink over there," Langston told him as he knelt down beside Draycos. "We need to get some of the blood off and find out how bad it is."

A small part of Jack's mind wondered whether running water up here in an empty apartment would be noticed by the neighbors. The rest of his mind didn't even care. He got the shirt good and wet and brought it back.

"If this is all the blood he's lost, I don't think we're in too bad a shape," Langston said, taking the shirt and carefully daubing at the bloodstained scales. "At least, if he's got the same amount of blood as other animals his size."

"He's not an animal," Jack growled. "I can do that."

"Have you had any medical training?" Langston countered, holding the wet shirt out of Jack's reach. "No? Well, I have. Star-Force's basic first-aid course, anyway. You just watch for now. There'll be plenty of nursing later to go around."

Jack grimaced. But the other did seem to know what he was doing. Under his careful ministrations the dried blood was starting to come off. "The real question is how much internal damage he took," Langston went on. "You happen to know how his organs are arranged?"

Jack shook his head. "Not a clue."

Langston grunted. "I was afraid of that. Still, his breathing seems steady. We'll just have to tie up his wound as best we can and keep our fingers crossed."

"You can use my shirt," Jack offered, pulling it off.

"Thanks." Langston set the shirt aside and got back to his cleaning. "So what exactly is he? Is he the last of his kind?"

Jack snorted. "Hardly. Or rather, not yet."

He told Langston the whole story. All of it, including the information on his parents that he'd uncovered since coming to Semaline. Somehow, talking helped keep his mind off Draycos.

Langston listened in silence as he worked. By the time Jack was finished, so was the first aid. "It's up to him now," Langston said, wiping his hands on his jumpsuit. "You know the saying: the patient does the healing, and the doctor takes the credit. So you think Cornelius Braxton himself was behind your parents' murder?"

"I don't know what to think," Jack said with a sigh. Suddenly he was feeling utterly drained. "Draycos thinks it's more likely it was Neverlin. But I just don't know."

"Well, it's not something we have to figure out tonight," Langston assured him. "Get some sleep. I'll take the first watch." His lip quirked upward. "Sorry about the accommodations."

"They're fine," Jack assured him, glancing around the empty apartment. All the furniture had apparently been moved to Langston's cliffside prison when Langston himself was. "I'll just fluff up some of the floor and settle in."

"That's the spirit," Langston said. "I'll wake you in four hours."

"Make it three," Jack said. "Draycos has already been off me for one, and I don't want to push his limits."

"I don't know," Langston said doubtfully. "He'll probably drop that bandage when he goes back on your skin."

"I know," Jack said. "But it won't do any good to keep it on and let him die."

"Point," Langston admitted. "Three hours it is."

Jack's last memory as he lay down on the floor beside Draycos was of Langston sitting cross-legged near the door, one of the bows in his hand, gazing thoughtfully out into the night.

CHAPTER 28

It took Alison all the rest of the night and most of the next morning to work her way through the Brummgan areas of the Chookoock estate. During that time Taneem smelled or heard three guard patrols, each time warning Alison with a touch of her claws.

It was nearing noon when they finally passed over the thorn hedge into the slave areas of the estate. Beyond the hedge, the neatly manicured lawns and trees abruptly turned scraggly and untended. The Brummgas, Alison reflected grimly, had no interest in maintaining this part of their grounds. The slaves, for their part, had no spare time for the job.

"How far are we going?" Taneem asked.

"No farther than we have to," Alison said, wincing as she pushed them another six inches north. Her shirt had torn through in several places, and even through the material that remained her back had been rubbed raw. "We at least need to make it to the forest. If we can find one of the isolation huts Jack talked about, maybe we can hide there for a while."

"And enlist the aid of the slaves?" Taneem suggested.

"Not if we can help it," Alison said. "The Brummgas have spies mixed in with them, remember?"

"Oh. Yes." The K'da moved restlessly on Alison's skin. "I don't understand why any slaves would be willing to betray their friends that way."

"It's a power thing, I suppose," Alison said. "To have even a little power over the other slaves is probably very appealing to some of them."

"Draycos says that traitors deserve death."

Alison pursed her lips. "I imagine that's part of the K'da warrior code," she agreed. "Let's keep it quiet for a while, okay?"

They made their slow way for another hour before Alison finally called it quits. "This should be far enough," she said, studying as much of the landscape as she could see from her vantage point. It wasn't much. "Now the big question: how do I get down?"

In answer, Taneem bounded from her shoulder and dropped to the ground. She landed on all fours in a crouch and swiveled her long neck back and forth as she surveyed the area. Then, looking up, she moved directly beneath Alison and rose up on her hind legs, her forelegs stretched upward. "Drop down," she called softly. "I'll catch you."

It sounded pretty risky. Unfortunately, Alison didn't have any better ideas. Getting a grip on the white ceramic, she rolled herself over the edge of the curl. She hung there for a couple of seconds to stabilize herself, then let go.

Taneem's forelegs caught her around her torso, and she hit the ground no harder than if she'd jumped off a chair. "Thanks," she said, wincing as the K'da's paws brushed across her sore back. "Let's get moving."

She got two paces before she was suddenly pulled up short by Taneem's paw on her shoulder. "Alison!" the K'da gasped. "Your *back*."

"Lovely, isn't it?" Alison agreed, twisting her neck to try to see for herself. "Feels just like it looks, too."

"My fault," Taneem said, ducking her head guiltily. "I should have helped take some of the pressure and pain. But I never even thought to do that."

"It's okay," Alison assured her. "It's not really that bad. Anyway, before this is over we may need you in top fighting shape. Better get aboard—we don't want some roaming Brummga to spot you."

They were not, as it turned out, as close to the forest as Alison had thought. Fortunately, there were plenty of scattered trees and bushes along the way to use as cover as they worked their way farther north.

It took them nearly half an hour to reach the forest. Along the way Taneem's nose and tongue picked up two groups of Brummgas, but both were too far away to be any danger to the fugitives.

Finally, they were there. Heading into the permanent twilight beneath the branches, Alison finally felt herself relaxing a little.

Her relief was short-lived. They'd been traveling barely five minutes when she heard the sound of footsteps crunching through the dead leaves.

Instantly, she dropped into a crouch beside a tall bush. "Taneem?" she whispered, her eyes darting around as she tried to tell which direction the steps were coming from.

"They're all around us," Taneem whispered back, her tongue flicking out rapid-fire now. "But there are no Brummgas among them."

Slaves, then. Apparently, the universe wasn't going to let Alison avoid them as she'd hoped.

And if she couldn't avoid them, there was nothing to be gained by letting them find her skulking under bushes like a criminal. It was even possible she could persuade them she was just another slave who'd strayed out of her usual territory.

She caught a glimpse of movement straight ahead. Taking a deep breath, she stood up.

A pair of Compfrins came around the trees, bundles of sticks in their hands. They caught sight of Alison and stopped short. "Hello," Alison said. "I seem to be lost."

The aliens exchanged looks. Then, one of them gave a soft whistle.

Abruptly the other footsteps Alison had heard fell silent. Then, they started up again, more quickly this time, and growing nearer. A Parprin appeared through the trees to Alison's right, followed by a pair of Jantris to her left, then an Eytra beside the two Compfrins. "I seem to be lost," Alison tried again.

One of the Compfrins stepped forward, coming to within three feet of Alison before he stopped. He paused there, his eyes laboriously tracing every line of her face. Then, he seemed to straighten up. "You are she," he declared.

"I am she what?" Alison asked carefully.

"You are the human Alison Kayna," he said. "The friend of Jack Morgan, who came to us as Jack McCoy." Before Alison could decide whether to confirm or deny it, the Compfrin took her arm. "Come," he said softly, steering her toward her left. "We have a hiding place prepared for you."

Alison eyed him suspiciously. Still, if it was a trap it was too late to run now. "Thank you," she said.

The hut they led her to was small, run-down, and very much

in the middle of nowhere. Definitely one of Jack's isolation huts, Alison decided. "Wait here," the Compfrin said as he opened the door for her.

"For how long?" Alison asked, stepping in and looking around. The hut included a small cot, enough extra space to turn around in, and not much more. Even her slave quarters back at the main house had been better than this.

"The Penitent will wish to see you," the Compfrin said. "He will come to you when he can."

"The Penitent?" Alison echoed, frowning.

"Our leader," the Compfrin said. "Wait, and do not fear. Someone will bring food and water for you soon."

"Just make sure he's not caught," Alison warned. "I'd rather go without than have him lead the Brummgas here."

"Do not fear," the Compfrin said again. He closed the door, and the footsteps again faded away.

"There's no place like home, eh?" Alison commented, sitting down on the bed. "What did you think of them?"

"I don't know," Taneem said. She peered cautiously out of Alison's shirt, then rather gingerly slid out into the other half of the cot. "They seem remarkably organized for people Draycos said would not even take freedom when it was offered."

"I was thinking the same thing," Alison said. "Which means this could be a trap."

"Should we not then escape?" Taneem asked.

"In theory, we can always do that," Alison reminded her. "After all, they still don't know about you." Carefully, she lay down on her side on the cot. The mattress was hard and stiff, but after spending the night sliding across rough ceramic, it felt as gloriously luxurious as her bed back home. "Besides, in theory, we also don't have anywhere better to go just now," she added.

"So we rest?"

"We rest," Alison confirmed, closing her eyes. "Maybe we eat and drink, too, if their courier makes it through."

She propped one eye open. "Mostly, *you* stay out of sight," she said.

"Until I'm needed?"

Alison closed both eyes again. "Don't worry," she said. "I'll let you know when that is."

They spent the rest of the afternoon sleeping. At least Alison did—she wasn't sure what exactly Taneem did with the idle time. As long as the K'da was quiet, she didn't really care.

The promised food and water arrived about midafternoon, delivered by the Parprin who'd been in the group that had escorted Alison to the hut. The food wasn't very good, but it was filling and Alison was ravenous. She and Taneem split the meal, and Alison went back to sleep.

It was dark outside by the time she awoke. "Any news?" she asked, stretching her arms carefully. Her back felt a hundred percent better, but the muscles and skin were still tender.

"No one has come close," Taneem reported. She was curled up on the floor beside a small crack in the wall, periodically flicking her tongue out to taste the air.

"I wonder if this Penitent got caught," Alison said, getting stiffly off the bed and taking a sip of the water they'd saved. "Or whether he just got cold feet."

"Jack used that expression once," Taneem said thoughtfully. "I'm still not sure—" She broke off, her tongue flicking twice through the crack. "They are coming," she hissed. "Many of them. No Brummgas."

"Great—a committee," Alison growled, glancing around. Aside from the single door, there was no way out of the hut.

At least, not any way the slaves could possibly anticipate. "Time to play backstop," she said, holding out her hand. "Hop on."

A second later Taneem was back on her skin. Five seconds after that, Alison had worked her fingers through another crack in the rear of the hut and Taneem had leaped off into the darkness. Taking a few deep breaths to calm herself, Alison turned to the door and waited.

A minute later she heard soft footsteps approaching. There was a quiet knock, and she pushed the door open.

It was the Compfrin who'd first identified her as Jack Morgan's friend. Arrayed behind him was the committee Taneem had smelled: two Parprins, three Jantris, three more Eytras, and four other Compfrins. All of them were armed, either with kitchen implements or else with tree-branch clubs.

One of the Eytras was standing a little in front of the rest. It was, Alison knew, the position a leader would normally take. "Good evening," she said, nodding to all of them and then focusing her attention on the Eytra. "Do I have the honor of addressing the Penitent?"

A ripple of surprise ran through the group. The Eytra himself gave no visible reaction. "I am," he said. "Stronlo is my name. Yours is Alison Kayna?"

"Yes," Alison confirmed. "Why the name Penitent?"

A flicker of pain crossed Stronlo's face. "I was there when Jack Morgan offered us freedom. I failed to grasp that offer, and have spent two months repenting my foolishness."

He straightened up. "But now I have been given a second chance," he said firmly. "Now that you have come to free us."

Alison felt her throat go dry. Shoofteelee, back at the house, had had the same attitude. And the same assumptions. "That's not exactly the case," she said carefully. "I came on a mission of my own." She had a quick flash of inspiration—"At the request of Jack Morgan and the black dragon."

"She lies," one of the Jantris murmured. "She doesn't know the dragon. She's a spy."

"Be calm," Stronlo advised him coolly. "If she is a spy, she will not leave here alive. Tell me what this mission was that the black dragon sent you to perform."

"I'm not permitted to talk about that," Alison said, thinking fast. If Uncle Virge had been properly persuasive, a Malison Ring strike force should be here sometime in the next two or three days. "But I may still be able to get some help for you. Tell me what exactly you have in mind."

"Prove first that you're a friend of Jack Morgan," the suspicious Jantri countered.

This was getting sticky. "How do you suggest I do that?" Alison asked.

"Tell us something about him," Stronlo said.

Alison lifted her hands helplessly. "Like what? Most of what I know about him you won't know and can't confirm. Anything you *do* know, the Brummgas back at the big house probably know, too. That means nothing I can say will really prove anything."

"Then repeat for us the poem he spoke to the human Noy," the Jantri said.

"You must be joking," Alison protested. "That dragon has hundreds of poems swimming around his brain. I have no idea which one he hauled out for Noy."

"Then perhaps you do not know him after all," the Jantri growled.

"The poem begins this way," the Compfrin beside her offered helpfully.

> "The night was calm, the battle near,
>   The enemy was set with fear.
>   Their eyes had hearkened,
>   The sky had darkened
>   Memories we held so dear."

"No," came a quiet voice from behind them.

The entire group spun around, their weapons snapping reflexively up into ready positions.

And there they froze as a muffled gasp rippled through their ranks.

Taneem was crouched above them on a large tree limb, her silver eyes shining like tiny moons in the darkness. "That was incorrect," she said into the taut silence. "*This* is the correct poem:

> "The night was calm, the battle near,
>   The enemy was wet with fear.
>   Their ears were hearkened;
>   They had darkened
>   Memories we held so dear."

She twitched her tail, her eyes shifting to the Jantri. "I am not the black dragon," she said. "But perhaps I will do."

"You will, indeed," Stronlo said, and Alison could hear a trembling of excitement flowing into his voice. He turned back to Alison. "The dragons have returned. The time is right."

"Right for what?" Alison asked.

"For hope," Stronlo said. "For freedom." He glanced back at Taneem. "For rebellion."

Alison felt a chill run up her back. "Rebellion?" she repeated carefully.

"It has all been planned," Stronlo said. "We are many, and we are ready."

"And the Chookoock family has all the weapons," Alison countered.

Stronlo gave a wide Eytran smile. "We have you and the dragon."

Alison hissed between her teeth. Two months ago, Draycos had single-handedly cleared out an entire layered Brummgan defense across these grounds. Clearly, Stronlo and his fellow rebels were hoping for a repeat of that victory.

But Draycos was a trained poet-warrior. Taneem was a child in an adult's body.

Even worse, the element of surprise had been lost. The Brummgas had seen Draycos in action once. They would know how to deal with those tactics this time.

But Alison could see that none of that mattered. Stronlo and his people were so hungry for the freedom they'd missed out on once that they would brush aside any risk to avoid missing it again. Even if it meant their deaths.

"All right," she said with a sigh. "But not yet. There are people coming who can help us."

"More friends of the dragons?" one of the Eytras asked hopefully.

"Not exactly," Alison hedged. "But they'll be good allies just the same. They should be here in two to three days."

"That is a long time to keep her hidden," one of the Parprins said uncertainly.

"We can do it," Stronlo said firmly. "We *will* do it."

"Great," Alison said. "Then we'll stay here, and hidden, and you'll get everything ready from your end."

"How will we know when these allies are here?" one of the Compfrins asked.

"Don't worry," Alison said grimly. "If it works out the way I expect, everyone for ten miles will know they're here."

They talked together for another half hour, mostly about the slave compound and the Brummgas' patrol routine. By the time they were finished, Alison had a pretty good idea of what she was up against.

After that, the slaves made their farewells and slipped away into the night, leaving a fresh supply of food and water behind.

"A rebellion," Alison commented grimly as she and Taneem went back into the hut. "Sticks and kitchen knives against lasers, slapsticks, and machine guns. What have we gotten ourselves into this time?"

"You don't approve," Taneem asked, her voice oddly cool.

"I don't approve of people getting themselves killed for

nothing, no," Alison countered, sitting down on the bed. "Because that's what's going to happen."

"You said the Malison Ring would help them."

Alison snorted. "I said that to try to stall Stronlo off for a couple of days," she said. "The strike force isn't going to care if a bunch of slaves get themselves slaughtered."

"The Malison Ring approves of slavery?" Taneem asked, her tail lashing.

"The Malison Ring has its own agenda, and that doesn't include playing white knight to every downtrodden group of people they run across," Alison said. "That's more Jack's and Draycos's style."

The tail lashed a little harder. "But not yours?"

Alison gazed into those silver eyes, her stomach tightening. What was she supposed to say? "We can't fix the whole universe, Taneem," she said. "No one can. Right now, we're in way over our heads. We're going to be lucky if we get out of here with our skins intact."

"I understand," Taneem said. "Like the Malison Ring, we have our own agenda."

Alison winced at the K'da's tone. "If it makes you feel any better, remember that part of that agenda includes protecting Draycos and his people."

Taneem's eyes glittered. "Draycos and *my* people," she corrected quietly.

"Right," Alison said, searching for a way to get off this topic. "Speaking of which, how in space did you know that poem of Draycos's? It wasn't something the Phookas sang together, was it?"

"Of course not," Taneem said, an odd mixture of pity and

revulsion in her voice. "They weren't . . . that is, *we* weren't able to create such songs. Draycos taught it to me afterward."

"And happened to mention that it was the one he'd sung to Noy?"

Taneem turned her head away. "I asked him to sing that particular one to me," she said. "He had said it was a song of encouragement, and I was . . ." She trailed off.

With a sigh, Alison reached out and stroked the gray-scaled neck. For a moment Taneem seemed to resist the touch, then relaxed beneath it. "We all get discouraged sometimes," Alison said. "It's not a crime."

Taneem flicked her tail. "Draycos doesn't get discouraged."

"I'd bet you my left arm he does," Alison countered. "The trick is to get out of that pity pit as fast as you can."

She exhaled tiredly. "And speaking of getting out of things, we've got no more than three days before Stronlo and his people do a full-bore Light Brigade charge to their deaths," she said. "Let's have a little snack, maybe get a little more sleep, and then put our heads together and figure out how we're going to keep that from happening."

CHAPTER 29

The search for the two humans lasted most of the night, with Golvins and lights moving erratically across the canyon floor. By morning, though, the searchers seemed to have given up and gone back to their normal daily lives.

Which wasn't to say there was no danger. For over an hour around sunrise that first morning Jack huddled in the back of the apartment with Langston, hardly daring to breathe, as the Golvins with apartments above theirs climbed down the pillar's ivy coating on their way to their fields and other jobs.

Fortunately, Langston had lived there long enough to have left plenty of residual scent behind. Apparently, it was enough to mask the fresher scents of the fugitives.

Late that evening, for the same hour, Jack and Langston again had to retreat to the rear of the apartment as the Golvins reversed direction and headed back home.

The next three days passed slowly. Though the morning and evening rush hours were the most dangerous, a scattering of Golvins moved up or down at other times during the day, making casual conversation dangerous.

Besides which, after the first day of the limited food rationing Langston worked out, Jack's stomach was rumbling so loudly and so constantly that it was a wonder none of the passing Golvins heard it.

But of more concern to Jack than his stomach, or even his safety, was Draycos.

His biggest fear on that long first night was that the K'da would be so deeply unconscious that he wouldn't be able to return to Jack's skin when it became necessary. Jack and Langston had solved that problem by having Jack strip off his clothing and stretch out on the cold stone floor with Draycos lying full length on top of him. As the time limit approached, the K'da simply melted back onto Jack's skin.

But as Langston had predicted, the bandage came off when Draycos went two-dimensional. Every time after that, whenever he came back off Jack's skin, they found that a little more fresh blood had oozed from the wound.

And while the K'da soon came back to a sort of dreamy consciousness, he remained weak and unable to do much except eat and sleep.

"I just hope he didn't take any damage he can't heal by himself," Langston commented midmorning on the third day as he carefully wiped off the latest bit of blood. "If your numbers are right, the rest of his people are still over a month away."

"He's going to get well," Jack growled. "He *is*."

"I know, I know," Langston said quickly. "I'm just saying, that's all."

But he was right, Jack knew as he gazed down at his sleeping friend. Draycos was recovering, but slowly. Much more slowly than he'd bounced back from other injuries. He needed medical attention, and medical treatment.

And he wasn't going to get either trapped in the Golvin

canyon. "You're right," Jack said with a sigh. "We need to get him out of here." He looked up at Langston. "Tonight."

"Let's not go off half-charged," Langston warned. "If he's got internal injuries or bleeding it might actually be more dangerous to move him than to let him just lie here quietly and heal."

"And starve to death?" Jack countered.

Langston grimaced. "Point," he conceded. "Okay: compromise. At current rations, we've got about three days left. Let's give him one more day to rest and heal. Tomorrow night, win, lose, or draw, you and I will sneak down the rabbit hole and see about grabbing that aircar."

"Deal," Jack said with a twinge of dread. If they moved Draycos too soon—or moved him too late—they could end up killing him.

He was just wondering if he should suggest they wait two days instead of one when he heard the sound of a distant explosion.

Draycos's eyes came halfway open. "Jack?" he murmured.

"I know," Jack said, getting to his feet and heading to the door.

One look at the rising pillar of smoke and sand above the eastern canyon rim was all he needed. "I don't believe it," he said. "They blew up the mine."

"*Someone* did," Langston said grimly from beside him. "But it wasn't the Golvins. You hear that?"

Jack strained his ears. "No."

"I do," Langston said. "It's the lifter subthrob from a Djinn-90 pursuit fighter."

Jack felt his heart seize up. "Oh, no," he breathed.

"Yeah," Langston said. "Offhand, I'm guessing your Malison Ring buddies have tracked you down."

And right on cue, three large starfighters shot into view over the canyon rim.

"That tears it," Langston bit out, stepping back from the door. "Come on."

"Where are we going?" Jack asked, following him to where Draycos lay.

"Into the rabbit hole," Langston said, scooping the rest of their food back together into Jack's Judge-Paladin hat. "They'll be firing up their sensors any minute now, looking for human heat signatures. Inside a pile of stone is our best bet."

"We're already *in* one," Jack objected. His muscles still ached from his earlier climb up the light shaft, and he wasn't at all sure he could handle a repeat performance. "Besides, those Djinn-90s are way too big to get down here."

His last word was punctuated by the rippling crack of laser fire. There was a second salvo, and the air was suddenly shattered by the sound of crumbling stone. "Not for long," Langston said grimly, stuffing the hat into his jumpsuit. "That was one of the stabilizing arches getting blown to gravel. A couple more of those, plus a few guy wires, and they'll be able to bring in any floosing ship they want."

Jack swallowed hard. And when that happened, he and Draycos would be caught like trapped mice. "You've sold me," he said, getting a grip on Draycos's paw. "Let's get that aircar and get out of here."

"No," Draycos said.

"It's the only way," Jack told him. "Come on, get aboard."

"We don't go down," Draycos insisted, his voice strained. "We go *up.*"

Jack looked at Langston, saw his same puzzlement mirrored there. "Draycos, Frost and his men are up there," he explained, searching Draycos's face for signs of fever or delirium. If the K'da was starting to drift off on them . . .

"But soon they will be down here," Draycos said. "Wing Sergeant Langston is correct. Once they have a path through the obstructions, all their ships will come down to join in the search. We can then cross the guy wires and arches to the edge of the canyon."

"Great, except that it's all desert out there," Langston said in a tone of strained patience. "There's nowhere to hide."

"Not even in the mine," Jack added. "They blew up the entrance."

"I know," Draycos said. "But we can hide in the sergeant's wrecked starfighter."

Jack opened his mouth. Closed it again. "Can we?" he asked, looking at Langston.

"I think maybe we can," Langston said, his forehead wrinkled in thought, a cautious excitement starting to creep into his voice. "I'll be floosed. The hatch should be—yes. A little digging and we can—and the whole thing's pretty well sensor-shielded. They'd have to specifically target it to pick us up."

"Assuming we can get to it," Jack warned. "But at least we've got a plan. Come on, Draycos."

This time the K'da obeyed. A minute later, Jack and Langston were once again in the light shaft, and once again starting to climb.

As all around them came the echoing sounds of destruction.

. . .

The sky had begun to go dark, and Alison was settling in for her fourth night in the isolation hut, when she heard the sounds of distant gunfire.

"What's that?" Taneem asked, her ears stiffening.

"Sounds like Stronlo and his friends got tired of waiting," Alison said grimly as she pulled on her shoes. "Great."

"What are we going to do?" Taneem asked anxiously.

"Try first to figure out what's happening," Alison said, cautiously pushing open the door. No one was visible among the deepening shadows. "After that, I don't have a clue." She held out her hand. "Come on."

She'd made it no more than fifty yards when Taneem whispered a warning in her ear. Alison dodged sideways behind a tree, and was pressed against it when a female Parprin shot past, heading for the hut. "Looking for me?" Alison called softly.

The Parprin jerked to a halt. "They have come," she gasped, hurrying back to Alison. "The Brummgas have entered the compound with weapons and restraints."

Another burst of gunfire echoed in the distance, and Alison winced in sympathetic pain. "So the spies figured it out."

"The Penitent has had no choice but to lead us to the attack," the Parprin said. "He asks for your aid."

And Taneem, Alison suspected, was more than ready to render that aid. And possibly get herself killed in the process

The question was how much Alison herself was willing to do for this lost cause.

"Alison Kayna?" the Parprin prompted as she hesitated.

Alison came to a decision. "Go back to the Penitent," she ordered the Parprin. "Tell him we'll do what we can."

For a moment the alien searched Alison's face, as if not sure whether to believe her. Then, with a curt nod, she took off again through the forest.

"We are going to fight?" Taneem asked, her voice wary.

"Do you want to?" Alison countered. "We don't have to, you know. This isn't our war."

"It was our arrival that created this danger," Taneem said. "We can't simply turn our backs on them."

"Even if it means Draycos's people—*your* people—will die?"

Taneem seemed to brace herself. "The K'da warrior ethic requires that we do what is right," she said quietly, the words almost swallowed up by another burst of distant gunfire. "No matter what the advantage or cost to ourselves."

Alison grimaced. She'd called it, all right. Death and glory, and honor and pride. Draycos had indoctrinated the young K'da, but good. "Lucky for us, we're not K'da warriors," she reminded Taneem. Putting the sound of gunfire to her left, she headed off southward through the forest.

Taneem's head rose from her shoulder. "Then we are going to abandon them?"

"Well, we're certainly not going to charge straight into the Brummgas' guns," Alison said. "If we're going to do anything, we're going to try to be clever about it."

"Then you *do* have a plan."

"I said *if* we do anything," Alison cautioned. "Let's first figure out the lay of the land."

"But the fire is coming from the slave compound," Taneem said, flicking her tongue past Alison's chin toward her left.

"One more good reason not to go there," Alison said.

"But—"

"But mostly we're not going there because that's not where

the Brummgas have their main attack line," Alison interrupted her. "The ones making all the noise in the compound are just there for show. Their job is to drive any potential rebels or escapees through gaps in the hedge into the *real* trap."

"Which is where we are going?"

"Which is what we're going to take a look at, anyway," Alison said. "Here we are. Everybody off."

Ahead, the hedge loomed over them, ten feet of densely tangled branches and long thorns. "You wish to go over it?" Taneem asked doubtfully as she leaped off Alison's skin.

"Not *over*," Alison corrected her. "*Through.* Get those K'da claws working."

Taneem gave a little hiss of malicious satisfaction. Lifting her forepaws and extending her claws, she set to work.

Two minutes later, she had carved out a hole big enough to sidle through. "Great," Alison said. "Now, we're going to head southeast—*quietly*—toward where the Brummgas should have set up their lines."

Taneem nodded and headed off at a brisk trot, her ears cocked, her tongue flicking out with every other step. Trying to suppress her own misgivings, Alison followed.

They didn't have far to go. Flickers of laser fire were coming from a line of bushes and small fountains scattered around the north end of the slaveowners' section of the grounds. The nearest firing position was no more than thirty yards away, with the entire combat line stretched across nearly four hundred yards. In the dim light, Alison could make out the hulking forms of some of the nearer Brummgas hunched over their weapons.

They weren't firing at random, either. To the north, at the base of the hedge, Alison could see the shadowy figures of

Stronlo's would-be escapees. Some were still coming, zigzagging in an effort not to be shot. But most were flat on their faces, pressed helplessly against the grass. From the slave compound behind them, in mocking counterpoint to the silent lasers, came more loud volleys of gunfire.

Alison felt her throat tighten, a sinking feeling in the pit of her stomach. So the trick had worked. The roving Brummgas in the compound had forced Stronlo's slaves to make their move, and now they were trapped.

With a sigh, she trotted to a halt. "So that's it," she murmured. "I'm sorry, Taneem—"

But Taneem hadn't stopped. In fact, she had picked up speed. "Taneem!" Alison snapped. "Come back!"

The K'da ignored her. To Alison's horrified disbelief, she gave a shrill warbling scream and aimed herself at the nearest Brummgan firing post.

And charged.

Jack had made it perhaps fifty feet up the light shaft when he heard the sound of rapid footsteps far below. "Langston?"

"Quiet," the other whispered urgently.

But it was too late. Even as Jack craned his neck to look, he saw the outline of a Golvin head appear in the opening in his former apartment far below.

The Golvins had found them.

And with that, Jack knew with a wave of utter weariness, it was all over. The Golvin would run and tell the One, and the One would tell Frost's men, and they would come and get him.

They would possibly kill Jack. They would certainly kill Draycos.

"Port side near the nose," Langston murmured. "Hatch opens outward."

Jack frowned as he blinked back sudden tears. "What?"

"The hatch," Langston said. His hand appeared from below, dropping the Judge-Paladin hat and food onto Jack's chest. "Good luck."

And before Jack could even form a coherent question, Langston flipped his bow over. With the bow tips clattering along the stones and his feet running backward along the far wall, he dropped rapidly down the shaft.

"Langston!" Clenching his teeth, Jack flipped his bow over as well. If Langston was going to die, he wasn't going to die alone.

But even as he started to slide down the shaft, a pair of K'da forelegs folded themselves off his arms to catch firmly against the side walls. *No,* Draycos's thought whispered in his mind.

"We have to help him," Jack insisted.

He is a true warrior, Jack, Draycos said, his tone firm yet somehow gentle. *He has made the decision to sacrifice himself for us, and for the K'da and Shontine people who stand at risk. Our job now is to make certain his gift was not in vain.*

Tears flooded into Jack's eyes, tears of guilt and anger and hopelessness. Draycos was right, of course. But that didn't make it any easier.

Come, Draycos said, shifting his grip on the side walls. *I will help you.*

That's all right, Jack said, turning his bow back right side up again. *I can do it.*

Shaking away the tears, his ears burning with the sounds of destruction still going on around him, he resumed his climb.

The first group of Brummgas never had a chance. There were three of them, and before their pea-sized brains could register what was happening, Taneem had leaped like a gray Fury into their midst.

The attack was probably nowhere near the level of Draycos's own warrior skill. But in the white-hot fury of Taneem's righteous anger, skill and training didn't seem to matter that much. Even as Alison broke out of her paralysis and ran to her aid, the K'da's claws and tail and jaws lashed out, sending Brummgas reeling backward or laying them flat out onto the ground.

In bare seconds, it was all over. Taneem shook herself once as she stood over her defeated enemies, then found the next group with her eyes and again charged.

But this time it would be different, Alison knew with a sinking heart. Taneem's first attack had succeeded largely through the element of surprise.

But that surprise was gone now. The rest of the battle line had been alerted, and Alison could see shadowy Brummgan forms turning as they recognized the new threat coming in along their flank.

The next nearest enemy firing position was over fifty yards away over open ground. Long before Taneem reached it, Alison knew, the combined laser fire would cut her to smoking ribbons.

Unless the K'da had help.

Taneem was perhaps halfway to her next target when Alison reached the remains of her first. So far none of the Brummgas had opened fire, but any second now that would change. Ignoring the scattered bodies, Alison scooped up one of the laser rifles and snapped it up to her shoulder.

And stopped, her mouth dropping open in astonishment.

The Brummgas were running. All of them, along the entire line, were abandoning their weapons and their posts and lumbering south toward the main house as fast as their tree-trunk legs would carry them.

What in blazes . . . ?

Alison looked toward the hedge, wondering if the slaves had brought up some unexpected and impossible superweapon. But the ones still on their feet were clearly unarmed, and the ones on the ground were only now warily starting to get up again.

She looked south, wondering if some silent retreat order had been given. But there was no one there, and no indication of any reason for such an order. There was nothing, in fact.

Nothing but Taneem.

And then, finally, Alison understood. The Brummgas remembered Draycos's last visit here, all right. And they'd certainly learned from that experience.

But they hadn't learned how to fight a K'da poet-warrior. They'd learned to run from him.

Alison filled her lungs. "Don't kill them!" she shouted to Taneem as she again started after the K'da. Surrendering and fleeing enemies, she knew, were always to be rewarded with their lives. It encouraged others to do the same.

She needn't have worried. Taneem passed the first running group of Brummgas without a glance, continuing on toward the next. Like a good hunting dog, the K'da was making sure to flush all the birds from their nests.

And then, from one of the groups of bushes, a lone figure stepped out of concealment. A human figure, Alison saw, with a shoulder-slung laser rifle at the ready. "Come on, dragon," he shouted, turning the rifle toward Taneem. "Come and get me."

It was Gazen.

Alison caught her breath. But Taneem didn't even flinch. Breaking from her straight-on charge, she turned sharply south, heading in a big circle across Gazen's line of fire.

"Come on, dragon," Gazen shouted again as he swiveled to keep facing her. He fired twice, his shots scorching the air in front of and behind the running K'da. "Come and face me like a warrior."

Alison braked to a halt and dropped to one knee, bringing her borrowed laser to her shoulder. With Gazen's silhouette partially obscured by the bushes beside him, she knew this would be a very tricky shot.

And she would get only one. As soon as that laser light flashed, he would turn his own weapon on her . . . and unlike Gazen, Alison had no cover nearby to protect her.

But Taneem couldn't circle forever. Sooner or later, Gazen would get tired of trying to taunt her into a direct attack, and he would kill her.

Clenching her teeth, Alison held her breath and squinted down the barrel at Gazen's profile.

And snapped the weapon up and off target as a handful of racing figures abruptly appeared from her left and slammed into Gazen's back. His laser fired once, blasting into the ground in front of him, before he disappeared beneath a mass of bodies.

Stronlo's rebels had arrived.

By the time Alison reached them, it was all over. "I heard you say not to kill them," Stronlo said, his voice grim as he panted for air. "But this one was special."

"I agree," Alison said, looking down at the body that lay motionless on the grass. She was just as glad that the lack of light hid the details. "As far as I'm concerned, you're welcome to him."

"Thanks to you and the dragon," Stronlo said

Taneem came up to them. "Is he stopped?" she asked.

"Permanently," Alison said. "Nice move, by the way. Did you actually see Stronlo coming up behind him, or were you just hoping?"

"Of course I saw them," Taneem said, flipping her tail. "A K'da warrior strives always to do what is right. But that doesn't mean a K'da warrior is stupid."

Alison nodded. "I'll remember that."

"What do we do now?" Stronlo asked.

"We wait." Half turning, Alison gestured toward the wall behind them.

Toward the wall, and the lights of the half-dozen Djinn-90 fighters hovering just beyond its built-in defenses. "The Malison Ring strike force has arrived," she said. "Let's sit back and see what happens."

By the time Jack reached the top of the pillar the sounds of crashing stone and shattered guy wires had ceased. The angled skylight opening was covered with a clear dome to keep out the rain, but Draycos's claws made quick work of the fasteners. A minute later, Jack eased his way to the edge of the pillar and looked down.

To a horrifying sight.

In a dozen places the cropland had been littered by rubble from the destroyed stone arches. The three Djinn-90 starfighters were moving slowly along through the air, their lasers blasting methodically away at the ground ahead of them. Golvins were everywhere, running toward the edges of the canyon like panicked ants.

There were bodies, too. At least twenty of them that Jack could see, either beneath sections of the crushed stone or lying in patches of burning crops.

And at the focus of the starfighters' attack was Langston.

He was sprinting across the ground, zigzagging between stands of plants and leaping over the irrigation canals, dodging the laser blasts as Frost's men herded him toward the nearest canyon wall. Behind the Djinn-90s, a much larger deep-space transport was drifting along, watching the scene like an approving mother wolf.

Jack shivered. "They're going to kill him," he said, the words twisting in his stomach. "As soon as they find out he's not me, they'll kill him."

"Then let us make sure his sacrifice is not in vain," Draycos said from his shoulder. "There—across that bridge."

With an effort, Jack lifted his eyes from the carnage below. His pillar was attached to the next by a stone arch, with another arch leading to the next pillar in line. Beyond that, a set of intact guy wires led the rest of the way to the edge of the canyon.

It would be a tricky climb. Tricky and dangerous both, especially with his muscle fatigue and Draycos's injuries.

But Draycos was right. It had to be done. Setting his foot on the arch, Jack looked over toward his goal, the distant bulge in the sand that hid Langston's wrecked starfighter.

He paused, frowning. There wasn't just one bulge there, he saw now. There were two, one much larger than the other.

He was still staring in confusion when the larger bulge stirred, the sand seeming to melt away from it.

And with a sudden gunning of its lifters the *Essenay* shot over the canyon rim straight toward him.

The ship was hovering above Jack's pillar, its hatch open, before the transport and starfighters below seemed to catch on to the fact that their quarry was slipping from their grasp. But by then, it was too late. The pillar itself blocked most of their frantic laser fire, and the gap they'd cut for themselves in the aerial obstacles was clear down at the other end of the canyon.

Five minutes later, with the Djinn-90s still trying desperately to close the gap, Jack keyed in the stardrive.

Eight men in Malison Ring uniforms were standing guard at the main gate as Alison led her party across the neatly trimmed lawn toward them. "That's close enough," the sergeant in charge warned, taking a step toward her. His shoulder-slung machine gun, she noted, wasn't quite pointed in her direction. "What do you want?"

"I have a group of slaves here," Alison said, taking another step and then likewise stopping. Behind her, she sensed Stronlo and the others doing the same. "All they want is to leave."

The sergeant shook his head. "Sorry. The Patri Chookoock was kind enough to open his gates and his estate for us. I don't think letting his slaves walk out the front door would be a proper way to repay his courtesy."

"Was it courtesy, or was it bowing to the inevitable?" Alison countered. "I saw the force you brought with you. You could have knocked your own hole in his wall if you'd had to."

In the light from the driveway markers she saw his eyes narrow. "You're not a slave," he said. "Who are you?"

"My name's Alison Kayna," Alison told him. "I'm sort of a negotiator."

"For slaves?"

Alison shrugged. "Slaves need someone to speak for them as much as anyone else. Probably more so."

"Probably," the sergeant conceded, his eyes flicking to the mixed group of aliens standing silently behind her. "Sorry, Kayna, but my orders are to keep the place bottled up until the major finishes his search. That means nobody leaves."

"But these aren't anybody," Alison reminded him. "By Brum-a-dum law, they're property."

Behind the sergeant, one of his men stirred. The other mercenaries didn't look all that comfortable, either. "Yeah, I know," the sergeant said, his voice darkening with contempt. "But we didn't come here to free a bunch of slaves."

"You're not here to keep them in, either," Alison countered. "Or did the Patri Chookoock hire you to do that?"

"Hardly," the sergeant said sourly. "In fact, he may be looking down the barrel of some real trouble right now, depending on what the major finds."

"Then you don't owe him anything. Right?"

The sergeant's face pinched uncertainly. "Well . . ."

"Sergeant?" the soldier who had reacted called. "Do we need to keep this gate closed? It's feeling kind of stuffy over here."

For a long minute the sergeant studied Alison's face. Then, his lip quirked. "Go ahead and open it," he ordered.

"The gate squad might object," one of the other mercenaries warned.

"Make sure they don't," the sergeant said flatly. "Janus formation—we don't want anyone sneaking in behind us."

He motioned Alison forward. "You wouldn't mind marching your livestock past my men, would you?" he asked. "Just to make sure the guy we're looking for isn't tucked away in the crowd."

"No problem," Alison assured him, gesturing in turn to Stronlo. The Eytra lined up his people and led them toward the waiting soldiers.

Shoofteelee, the house slave, was the last in line. His face was rippling with Wistawk emotion, his eyes already gleaming dreamily with the glow of freedom.

Alison waited until they had all cleared the gate before stepping forward herself. "Thank you," she said quietly.

"Like you said, they're property," the sergeant reminded her. "You have someplace to take them?"

Alison nodded. "I understand the Daughters of Harriet Tubman have a station nearby."

The sergeant nodded back. "Good luck."

And a minute later, for the first time in nearly a month, Alison found herself breathing free air again.

She'd almost forgotten how good that felt.

Stronlo was standing nearby, waiting silently with his newly freed compatriots. "Well, come on," Alison said briskly, heading down the entry drive toward the public street and the city beyond. "Your future's waiting."

CHAPTER 30

"There were forty-five in all," Alison commented as she sat down across the dayroom table from Jack. "And did I mention they got Gazen along the way?"

"Yes, you mentioned it," Jack said, his eyes on Draycos and Taneem lying side by side on the dayroom floor, talking together in low voices. "I'm glad for you," he added.

"Thank you." Alison gestured. "You always make sandwiches just so you can ignore them?"

Jack looked down at his plate. There was a sandwich there, all right, with two bites missing. He'd forgotten all about it. "I guess I'm not hungry."

Alison sighed. "Look, Jack. This self-condemnation isn't doing you any good. It's tearing you up inside, not to mention making Taneem, Draycos, and me walk on eggs whenever you're around. You've got to snap out of it."

"That's easy for *you* to say," Jack bit out, his dark depression abruptly turning into anger. "*You* freed a bunch of slaves. *I* got a bunch of Golvins killed. *And* Langston."

To his extreme annoyance, Alison didn't even flinch at his outburst. "You didn't get anyone killed," she said calmly. "Except this Bolo character, and it sounds like he deserved it. Frost's men are the ones who killed Langston and the Golvins and blew up their crops. Not you."

"They wouldn't have done it if I hadn't been there," Jack shot back. "And I wouldn't have been there if I hadn't decided to play detective."

"You weren't *playing* anything," Alison said sternly. "You were *being* a Judge-Paladin." She paused. "Like your parents before you."

Jack closed his eyes, tears welling up as the anger subsided again. "At least they only got themselves killed," he murmured. "I did it to a bunch of innocent people."

"Innocent people are usually the ones who get the short end of the stick," Alison agreed. "That's why it's so important to go after the ones at the top. People like Neverlin, Frost, and the Patri Chookoock."

"And maybe Braxton."

"I already told you Neverlin basically confessed to your parents' deaths," Alison said. "Don't worry—if Braxton's involved, too, we'll get him. But right now it's Neverlin we need to concentrate on."

"We?" Jack echoed. "There's no *we* here, Alison. There's just Draycos and me. Next decent planet we hit, you're gone."

Across the room, Taneem's head lifted, her eyes glittering toward Jack. "What about me?" she asked.

"You go with her."

Taneem's tail twitched. "I would rather stay with you and Draycos."

"Tough," Jack snapped. "You're both gone."

"No," Alison said firmly. "Not if you want to save Draycos's people."

"And who is it who put them at risk in the first place?" Jack lashed out. Abruptly he stood up, his hand snapping up almost of its own accord and slashing toward her face. "You rotten—"

The blow never reached her. In a single, smooth motion Draycos leaped up from the deck and bounded to Jack's side, his paw catching Jack's hand in a solid grip. "She's not to blame, Jack," the K'da said firmly. "Her life was at stake."

"Is that the kind of excuse a K'da poet-warrior would use?" Jack demanded, struggling to get his hand free.

"No, a K'da warrior would have skipped the excuses and used his time to best advantage," Alison said. Again, she hadn't even twitched. "He would have tried to sow dissension among his enemies." She raised her eyebrows. "And he would have figured out what Neverlin's new plan is."

Jack paused in his struggling, his anger foundering against fresh uncertainty. "What do you mean?"

"Remember earlier, when we discussed their plan and decided that Neverlin couldn't get at the Braxton Universis security ships he originally wanted?" Alison reminded him. "I know where he's planning to get his replacements."

"Where?"

"First a deal," Alison said. "I'm in for the duration. So is Taneem."

"This isn't your fight," Jack insisted.

"It is now," Alison said. "Frost tried to kill me." She considered. "And come to think of it, Neverlin still owes me twenty thousand for opening that safe."

Jack ground his teeth. "Why, you—"

"We're in, or you figure it out yourself," Alison said flatly. "Take it or leave it."

Jack looked helplessly at Draycos. But there was no help for him there. "Fine," he growled. "We take it. Let's hear the big secret."

"Uncle Virge, give me a star map," Alison called, taking both her plate and Jack's off the table. "Make sure the scale includes both Semaline and Rho Scorvi."

The table's surface changed, and a star chart appeared. "Now, when Neverlin had me kidnapped on Semaline, he told me the *Advocatus Diaboli* was four hours away," Alison said as Taneem padded to her side and peered over her shoulder. "Add that to the map."

A small bubble of space appeared around Semaline, marking the farthest distance a ship with the *Advocatus Diaboli*'s speed could get in four hours. "We also know that the ship was coming from Rho Scorvi, where it had picked up Frost and the rest of his crew," Alison said. "Mark that."

A cone appeared on the map, its tip on Rho Scorvi, its edges passing through the bubble around Semaline. "So," Alison said. "Inside that cone are all the places Frost might have been heading when Neverlin diverted him to Semaline to pick me up."

"Big help," Jack growled. "There must be two hundred systems in that area."

"At least," Alison agreed. "One last thing, Uncle Virge: add in the list of systems I gave you earlier."

A dozen spots of blue appeared on the map. One, and only one, was within the cone. "The blue spots are places where the Malison Ring is embroiled in major military actions," Alison said. "Where they've deployed large numbers of troops and vehicles." She paused expectantly.

Jack caught his breath as he suddenly understood. "*And* warships."

"Bingo," Alison confirmed, sounding very pleased with herself. "Do I need to spell it out any more?"

"He intends to steal Malison Ring ships," Draycos said thoughtfully, finally releasing Jack's hand.

"Or else to fake orders to bring in the ones he needs," Alison said. "Either way, it seriously narrows down his jump-off point. *And* it gives us something to look for in the data stream."

"That will help considerably," Draycos agreed.

"Thank you," Alison said. "And on top of that, there's still the last advance team safe."

"Which is on Brum-a-dum," Jack reminded her.

"Not for long," Alison said. "After the Malison Ring raid, Neverlin's not going to think that's a very smart place to keep it anymore. If we can figure out when he plans to move it, and if we can get to it, we now know how to open it."

"At which point we can get the rendezvous point directly," Draycos said, a note of cautious excitement coloring his voice.

"Maybe," Jack said, his stomach twisting. So again, Alison had won. He hoped she was properly proud of herself. "Congratulations."

He started to turn away. To his surprise, Alison reached across the table and caught his hand. "You lost one, Jack," she said. "It hurts. I know that."

"Everyone know what it feels like to lose," Jack retorted. "Do you know what it feels like to have people *die* because of you?"

To his surprise, he saw Alison's throat tighten. "Yes, I do," she said quietly. "You lost this one. We won't lose the next one."

"*If* we make sure not to focus on the wrong things," Taneem murmured.

Alison frowned at her. "What?"

"I was thinking of Gazen," Taneem said. "He died because he was focused only on me, and couldn't see those behind him."

"He never was much of a warrior," Jack said.

"Jack and Draycos are focused on saving Draycos's people." Taneem cocked her head. "What are *you* focused on, Alison?"

It was, Jack thought, a blasted good question. "Well?" he prompted.

"Don't worry about me," Alison assured him. "I have all the focus I need."

Jack snorted gently. "That's not an answer."

"No," Alison said, her eyes going strangely distant. "But it's all you're going to get."

"Ah—Wing Sergeant Langston," Frost said as two of the mercenaries brought Langston into the office and sat him down in the chair across from the colonel's desk. "You'll be pleased to know we've finally confirmed your identity."

"Certainly took you long enough," Langston commented, glancing around the room. It was far too nice a place for a simple mercenary colonel. Probably Arthur Neverlin's place, then. Or possibly Cornelius Braxton's.

Frost shrugged. "We had to dig through the missing-in-action files to find you." He smiled tightly. "Fortunately, you were there, and not in the AWOL files. It would have taken at least another day or two to crack into those."

"Don't worry about it," Langston assured him. "The food here is a lot better than the stuff the Golvins fed me for five years. I appreciate your getting me out of there, by the way."

Frost's eyes hardened. "And I appreciate *your* fine decoy

work in helping Jack Morgan slip out of our hands," he said. "That's a professional appreciation only, you understand, not a personal one."

"Yeah, and I'm sorry about that," Langston apologized. "If I'd understood how much you wanted him, I'd never have let him talk me into that. I can probably kiss away the money he promised me, too."

"He promised you money?"

Langston snorted. "Oh, yeah. Some nice soap-bubble sky-mansion about setting me up for life once he took out you and Neverlin."

"Yes, Morgan excels at such promises," Frost agreed. "It runs in the family. Unfortunately for you, even if he meant it, he's on the losing side."

"I'm starting to get that impression," Langston said sourly. "Though frankly, it'll almost be worth the money he's stiffing me to watch him go down in flames. Him and that nasty little pet dragon of his."

"You don't like our noble K'da poet-warrior?"

"He could have helped me," Langston said. "He could have come down the rabbit hole with me, silenced those Golvins, then helped me get back up. But he didn't. I don't know what kind of military he claims to belong to, but it's not one *I'd* ever want to serve in."

Frost leaned back thoughtfully in his chair. "Then perhaps you might be interested in having a front-row seat at their demise?"

Langston smiled. Finally: the invitation he'd been waiting for. About time, too. "Absolutely," he said grimly. "Just show me where I sign."

Timothy Zahn is the author of more than thirty original science fiction novels, including the very popular *Cobra* and *Blackcollar* series. His recent novels include *Night Train to Rigel, The Green and the Gray, Manta's Gift, Angelmass,* and *Blackcollar: The Judas Solution.* His first novel of the Dragonback series, *Dragon and Thief,* was named "A Best Book for Young Adults," an award given by the A.L.A. Jack Morgan's adventures continued in *Dragon and Soldier, Dragon and Slave,* and *Dragon and Herdsman.* He has had many short works published in the major SF magazines, including "Cascade Point," which won the Hugo Award for best novella of 1983. He is also the author of many bestselling *Star Wars* novels, including *Heir to the Empire, The Hand of Thrawn* duology, and the recent *Allegiance.* He currently resides in Oregon.